'*The Bones* is a great read – packed with humour, energy and loveable characters and full of good old-fashioned heart. Shelley Conway is adorable.'
  ~ Jacinta Halloran, author of *Dissection*, *Pilgrimage*, *The Science of Appearances* and *Resistance*.

'Lovingly evocative of its time and place, Katrina Watson's impressive debut novel is an empowering account of a young woman's journey of self-discovery through a vividly etched, adventure-filled landscape.'
  ~ Paul Strangio, author of *Keeper of the Faith*, a biography of Jim Cairns.

'Helen Garner meets Jed Mercurio. Katrina Watson's The Bones is a triumphant debut.'
  ~ M.J. Hyland, author of the *How the Light Gets In*, *Carry Me Down* and *This is How*. M.J. Hyland has been shortlisted for the Man-Booker prize and listed for many other prizes including the Orange Prize, and the Commonwealth Writer's Prize.

The BONES

To Maria & Trev
with love & thanks

Katrina x

**Katrina
Watson**

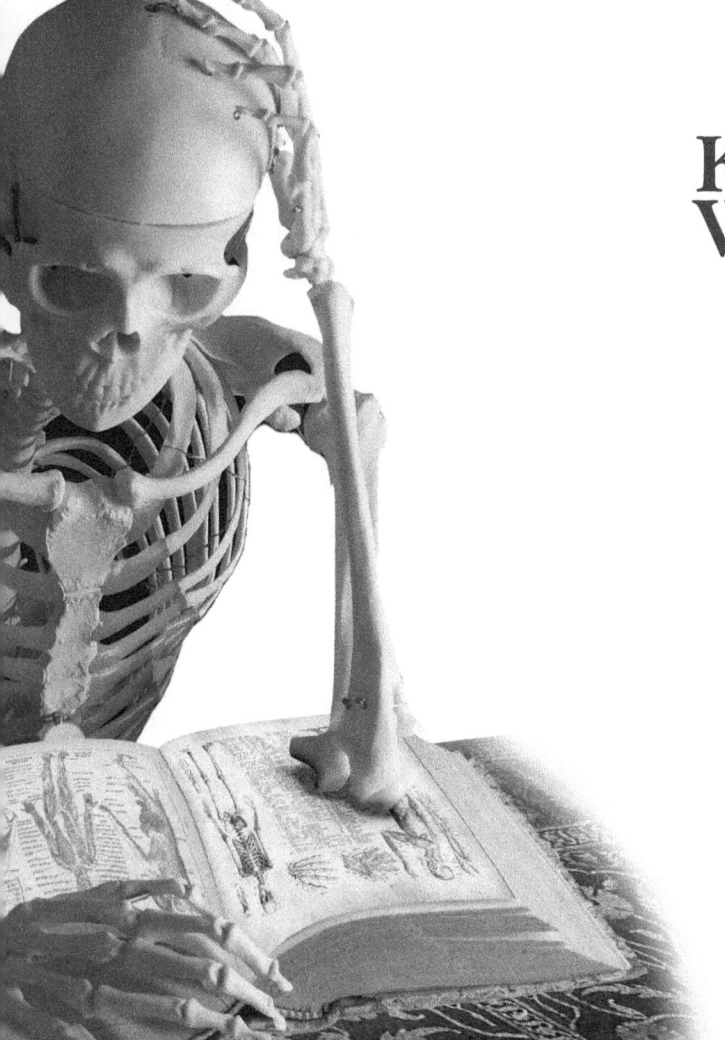

First published by Busybird Publishing 2023

Cover design: Busybird Publishing

Layout and typesetting: Busybird Publishing

Busybird Publishing

2/118 Para Road

Montmorency, Victoria

Australia 3094

*I acknowledge the Traditional Custodians of the land
on which we live and pay my respects to all Elders past,
present and emerging.*
~ Katrina Watson

For my four courageous children.

Calcutta

'Madame? Would you like your bones varnished or unvarnished?'

Shelley was starting to feel hot. Hot and a bit faint.

'Excuse me, Madame, but would you prefer the bones varnished or unvarnished?'

She must take slow breaths. Deep, slow breaths.

'Do you mind if I sit down?' Shelley was feeling those early symptoms of a panic attack.

She was in the showroom, the showroom of Trivedi Bros Anatomical and Scientific Supplies, Calcutta – the shop she'd been imagining for so many months. She was finally here and was being asked how many human skeletons she would like to buy, and whether she'd prefer varnished or unvarnished.

'Are you not well?' Amit had realised something was wrong and had come over. He was now kneeling down beside her, and his eyes were anxious.

'Amit, I'm sorry I just felt a bit faint. It's quite emotional for me here. Do you think we could step outside for a few minutes?'

Amit spoke to the manager who hurried to Shelley's side and helped her back up the little ramp that led to the outside world. Amit spoke to him in Hindi.

'I've told him you just need some fresh air for a few minutes. Let's sit over here, on that bench, next to the fishpond.'

Shelley tried to explain. 'You see I've been dreaming of proving the origin of the bones for so long but also at the same time hoping I wouldn't, because I knew it would be just terrible, and now it is terrible, and I cannot believe it.'

'Cannot believe what?'

'That someone is asking me whether I want my skeletons varnished or unvarnished. I think I'm in a nightmare.'

'Shelley, not many medical students would care as much as you do, care about the people who have ended up in those boxes of bones.'

'Amit, do you think I am weak because I care?'

'No, you are strong. But you will need even more strength, Shelley, a lot more strength to withstand what is to come. That is, if you really want to discover the truth.'

Melbourne

September 1970

Shelley had been dreading the bones table in the Anatomy exam.

But now here she was, waiting for Professor Smiling Death to look up. He was arranging his bones.

She studied the Professor's scalp, with its few white hairs combed over so precisely. The scalp was pink with brown spots. Lay people would call them freckles, but Shelley liked to use medical terms, of course. *Café au lait* spots. In Smiling Death's case there was also cappuccino, espresso, International Roast – the full menu.

'Name?' Smiling Death still had not looked at her.

'Shelley Conway.'

The Professor ran his finger down his sheet of paper.

She could read the typing upside-down: 'University of Australia, First Year Anatomy, Practice Examination, 1970'. Followed by a long list of names and initials.

Smiling Death put a tick against 'Conway, Miss S.' and then pointed to a chair. She sat down.

Everything on the table was white – the tablecloth, the trays, the bones – white as chalk. Smiling Death's lab coat was a dazzling white too. Those starched sleeves would have made such a ripping sound when he pushed his arms through.

They were surrounded by glass cases with prize exhibits bathed in fluorescent light – a beautifully dissected shoulder here, some perfectly displayed tendons of the foot there.

Smiler picked up a steel knitting needle and tapped it on a bone. 'What's that?' His smile was cool and efficient. Not a muscle wasted. Looked like it had been stitched in.

'The radius,' she said. Straight up, confident. He wasn't going to bully her.

The smile didn't change.

Keep calm, Shelley. She gave a friendly smile herself. 'I like the radius. It's my favourite bone.' There, he won't know how to handle that.

'Oh, is it now? Your favourite bone?' The Professor looked incredulous, just for a moment, and his smile split his face a little further, like a crack in a crevasse.

'Yes, it is, really, because—'

But before Shelley could tell him why she liked the radius, Smiling Death said, 'Well, you'll be able to tell me which radius it is, won't you?'

She'd studied the radius in Gray's *Anatomy* – drawn it, memorised the head, the neck, the styloid process, the insertions and articulations. But this radius looked strange – it was shimmering. Making moiré patterns like fly wire did sometimes. This was a warning sign – panic attack. Come on Shelley, stick to the plan. Don't let the bastard intimidate you.

She held the bone over her own left forearm. Upended it. Twisted it one way, then the other. Then held it over her right forearm. She couldn't gain control of the bone or the situation. She had no idea which side it was. Ridiculous, something so easy.

Sweat was forming on her top lip. She could hear roarings – noises like industrial turbines. Bugger it, anxiety was winning, and she was losing.

She had to say something.

'Left.'

'I see.' The smile tightened.

Smiling Death picked up the knitting needle again and tapped a depression at the end of the bone. 'And what happens here?' His voice was stretching out, slowing down and he seemed to be shouting at her. She must take deep breaths. It was a panic attack all right.

'Um – that's the wrist joint.'

'The wrist joint? Could you be a little more specific, Miss, er—' He checked his list. '—Miss Conway?'

Was he shouting at her, or was it her anxiety?

'What is the articulation here? It's an important one, isn't it?'

'Yes, of course. It's the scaphoid I think and the, the—'

Calm down, Shelley. One of those carpal bones. You know them. There are only eight. Stop panicking.

'The triquetrum?' After a second, 'I think?'

Smiling Death got up, walked to the window and smiled at the street three storeys below. Shelley could see the branches of the plane trees outside with their smudges of green. Springtime in Melbourne. Exam time.

Smiling Death drummed his fingers on the sill. He allowed just enough time for her sweat to drip onto the bone and tears to trickle down her cheeks, and then he turned around. His eyes were crystalline.

'Miss Conway, in Anatomy we don't think, we know.' He flapped his hand slowly up and down. 'That's what the articulation does, doesn't it, Miss Conway? It waves goodbye.'

The Professor returned to the table and turned over to the next sheet of paper on his pile. He spoke to his papers. 'You had better get yourself a set of bones, hadn't you, Miss Conway? And you'd better learn them. Or we'll be saying goodbye to you, won't we?'

The bastard.

But it was true. She didn't know her bones.

According to little white plastic letters on the black signboard outside the lifts, H. Jones, Anatomy Assistant, could be found in room 407. Shelley walked down the corridor through an avenue of steel filing cabinets, until she came to room 407. The door was half-open, and she could see a man with his feet on a desk, listening to a transistor radio.

He had on a grey dust coat and there was the bulge of a small convex bottle in the pocket.

She knocked, stood back. 'Excuse me.' And then a fraction louder, 'Excuse me. I'm sorry to trouble you, but would this be where they sell the bones?'

'It might,' said the man, without turning around. 'Depends who's asking.' He had a northern English accent. Sounded like someone in a BBC sitcom.

'My name's Shelley. I'm a first-year med student.'

The man swivelled his chair slightly and looked at her over one shoulder. 'Left it a bit late in the year for bones, haven't you?'

'I'm a lateral entry. Started the course after everyone else.'

H. Jones turned around further. Shelley recognised him as the Grey Ghost who cleaned up after dissection classes.

'Hmm, unusual. They don't usually do that. But I suppose you have come to the right place.'

She'd never heard the Grey Ghost speak before – at the end of dissection class he would just glide out of the filing cabinets at the back of the room to tuck the cadavers in for the night. He expected med students to scurry out of his way. Complete nuisances, med students.

H. Grey Ghost Jones looked Shelley up and down, and then rested his gaze on her chest. Unnerving. 'Ah yes, I've noticed you in dissection.' He stood up. 'The one with the hair. Now let me guess – you didn't do too well on the bones table last week, and the Prof has sent you up. That correct?'

He started to fetch a chair from the corridor. Mr Jones had a ring of steel-grey hair, with a bald patch in the middle. The longer hairs had wound themselves into curls over his ears, and as he walked the spirals bounced up and down. He was about the same height and width as a filing cabinet himself, and much the same colour, in his grey dust coat. But the resemblance ended there, because his face was very red. Must have a skin disease. Also, his two eyes looked in different directions, but both directions seemed to end up at her boobs.

He set the chair down behind the door. 'There's always plenty of bones, don't you worry about that. But you'll need to sit there for a bit. I don't want to miss this race.'

Shelley heard the race call starting off and then the tone and volume rising to a peak of excitement. But Silverlocks did not look at all pleased. His face had become a deeper red and his nose was now blotching into purple. Perhaps this was one of those heliotrope rashes. What condition was it that gave you a heliotrope rash? She'd have to look it up. In fact, what was heliotrope anyway?

Silverlocks pulled a newspaper from his pocket, slashed a diagonal line across it with a pen, and tossed it on the desk. The curls rebounded. 'Supposed to be a sure thing.'

'Hope you didn't lose too much money.'

Her words hung in the air, and she had the feeling she had breached etiquette. Maybe you shouldn't ever mention to a gambler, even in sympathy, the words 'lose' or 'money'. Not in the same sentence and not in the second person, anyway. Maybe.

'My only vice, the gee-gees. Almost.' He looked at her chest again, and then patted his pocket. Felt some keys. 'Now, bones. Leave your knapsack here, and you can come to the storeroom with me.' He gave her a smile of small grey teeth.

She didn't really fancy going to the storeroom with the Grey Ghost but she did need these bones. Shelley put her backpack down and the shells jingled as they hit the floor.

Mr Jones directed both his gazes towards the shells for a moment, raised his eyebrows, and then put his hand on the middle of her back. Ran it up and down a little.

'This way.'

He kept his hand at the level of her bra strap, and they walked down the corridor. Room 420 was at the end. Mr Jones removed his hand at last in order to retrieve his keys and unlock the door. Inside it was dark and smelt like a grain store. There were footprints from work boots in the white dust near the door, and a box of rat bait.

Through the gloom Shelley could see stacks of something black – was it timber?

Mr Jones pressed a switch and fluorescent lights flickered. Now it became clearer: those tall stacks were piles of wooden boxes painted black. Each box was about one-third the size of a coffin. Hundreds of boxes of bones.

'There we are. As you can see, we've got plenty. Now they're ninety-five dollars. Cash only. You get one side plus the skull.'

Mr Jones began to reach for the uppermost box on one of the stacks, but then stopped and pointed to a box sitting on the floor on its own. 'Actually, there's one here that we've put aside. Reduced. That one. Young male. Substandard bones, but still all right for Anatomy. And they're nice and white – I checked.'

'Aren't all bones white?'

'No, lass. They can be yellow, brown – you name it. But those are a good white. You can have them for seventy-five.'

'Um, okay. I'll take them. Should I open the box?'

'No, I'll do that.'

Mr Jones picked up the box and put it on a dusty wooden bench, then undid the metal clasp and opened the lid. Shelley caught a glimpse of straw, and some creamy coloured ribs and a skull. Mr Jones put his hands in and rummaged a bit. He lifted a few bones up, and checked down the sides and underneath, making certain of what, Shelley couldn't imagine.

He closed up the box and passed it to her so she could carry it by the little wooden handle.

Shelley followed Mr Jones back to his office and the bones shifted around as she walked. It sounded as if a pile of rocks was inside, but the box wasn't heavy. In fact, half a body of bones was lighter than she'd imagined.

'You can put the box down there.' Mr Jones pulled a docket book out of the top drawer of his desk, found a new page and slid the carbon paper in.

'Yes, you take a seat. Now have you got the correct money? Good girl.' He took the seventy-five, put most of the notes in one of his pockets and a couple in another. He started to write the receipt. 'Name?'

'Shelley Conway.'

'Ah, Shelley, that's right,' he said, looking at her backpack. 'Shelley of the shells. That's easy to remember. With silver bells and cockle shells, right?'

'Afraid so.'

'Well, you do look a bit like a mermaid with the shells and all that hair. Like that woman standing on the shell – you know that painting? Same colour hair, you and her. Only yours is curly.'

'Oh?'

'And she's naked.'

He was staring at her. His eyes going round. 'Yes, naked. And your hair, so curly.'

Change the topic, quick. Be crisp, Shelley, business-like. 'So where do the bones come from, Mr Jones?'

'We don't discuss that, Prof's orders.'

'Can't you give me a hint?'

'Orders is orders,' said Mr Jones. He looked at her breasts, no attempt to disguise it. 'But if you'd like to help me tidy up one night after dissection—'

'It's all right, but thanks anyway. I'm a bit busy. Part-time job and all that.'

Mr Jones held out the receipt. 'Well, you just let me know. Welcome any time.' He gave the little grey smile again. 'Any time. I'd be happy to help you with your Anatomy, any time.'

'Thank you, Mr Jones.' As if. His eyes skewwhiff, his face technicolour. She couldn't imagine anything worse.

'Call me Horrie.'

'Thank you, Mr Horrie.'

He patted her on the back as she left. Quite low down. More like her bum in fact.

Shelley headed to the foyer for the lift. She was trying to work out why the receipt would say 'Fifty dollars'.

Two second-year students with droopy moustaches and flares had pressed the 'up' button.

They looked at her as if she was a metastatic cancer that needed to be excised immediately.

'Just got your bones? You've left it a bit late,' said the taller one.

'Hey, aren't you the one in trouble?' said the shorter one. 'The chick who took on Prof Redlich?'

'I might be.'

'And aren't you the do-gooder, too?' asked the taller one. 'Always writing on the blackboards? Give blood, buy a raffle ticket and all that. That's you, isn't it?'

'Florence Nightingale,' laughed the short one.

'Mother Theresa, you mean,' said the other one.

'Vietnam war's finishing up, you know.' The short one was cacking himself. 'And guess what, we're gonna win.' He nudged the other one, 'Hope so, otherwise we might be called up.' Still kept laughing, amazing. How could med students have no idea what was going on in the real world? Privileged idiots.

'You just had your last moratorium, what a shame,' said the taller one. 'You might have to do a bit of study for a change.'

Sticking the boots in and loving every minute of it.

Short one asked, 'So what did you do to poor old Redlich, Miss Radical?'

'I didn't do anything to him.'

'You must have done something.'

'He told a disgusting joke and I left the lecture. That's all.'

'What did you say?'

'Just the truth – that he was sexist and disgusting. Sexist and disgusting and that I was leaving his lecture.'

'Was it the one about the Venetian prostitutes? He loves that joke.'

'Might have been.'

'Ah hah.' The students didn't try to hide their delight. 'So, what did he say?'

'He told the class that I was leaving because I couldn't wait to get to Venice.'

There was an explosion of sound – they were hawing with laughter, teeth all over their faces.

'I don't know why you're laughing.' How juvenile med students were. First years, second years, sixth years. Made no difference.

''Cos it's fucking funny. Bloody Redlich! He's so quick,' said one.

'He was just waiting for you to take the bait,' said the other.

'He's a sexist clown,' Shelley said brightly, but then did wonder whether she might indeed have fallen for a classic Redlich set-up.

The lift arrived, going down, and she got in – by herself, thank goodness.

There was her reflection in the steel lift doors. She did have a lot of hair, and it probably was the same colour as the hair of the lady in the painting. Red, undeniably red.

Horrie Jones, what a lech. He had made her squirm. And as for those two dickheads could they be right? Had she really just taken the bait, and had everyone laughed while Redlich reeled her in? How humiliating.

Creeps, all of them.

Shelley secured the box to her bike with three octopus straps. It was normally only a short ride to her little room in the residential College, where she had the privilege of being a live-in maid, but this ride was going to take longer – maybe fifteen minutes instead of five. She didn't want the box to fall off and explode all over College Parade. Bones everywhere. No way. No crashing over kerbs, Shelley.

She got herself, her bike and her bones safely into the bike shed and carried the box up the stairs to her broom cupboard of a room. The bones were fortunate – this was a broom cupboard in an exclusive College at Australia's top University. Clocktowers, cloisters and privileged young men. All that.

The maids' rooms were tucked behind turrets and squeezed under stairs. Shelley was one of the luckier ones who had a narrow window, or perhaps it was a slot for an archer – a little reminder of the old country for colonial Australians who felt homesick for things like bows and arrows.

Shelley pushed open her bedroom door with care, so it didn't crash into the chair. If she stood on the bed, she could close the door. If she moved the bed and the desk, and put the chair up on the bed, she could do her push-ups and sit-ups in the mornings.

Accommodation on the University campus in return for just a few hours of work per week, like about twenty – how lucky she was. Insults from the male students came free of charge.

She fetched a towel to put on her bed, and then placed the box on top. A miniature coffin it was – would anyone ever expect there to be half a human being in there? All those cars in College Parade – wouldn't they be amazed if they knew what was inside the black box on her pack rack? That the bumping noise made when she thumped over the holes in the asphalt was not due to rocks, but to bones from a dead person?

Better get a move-on. It wasn't long before her dinner shift – she had just on an hour.

She undid the catch. The hinges creaked. She could smell timber shavings. Shelley pulled the lid right open.

There were the bones, looking like they were gift-boxed, shredded straw and all. The skull was nestled in the middle like the big egg in one of those expensive Easter egg sets, with the other bones peeping around the edges. There were a good number of teeth, large and white. Someone must have brushed the teeth. Scoured them. Enhanced that expression of extreme something. Mirth? Agony?

The eye sockets were huge cavities. Someone had scooped out those eyes. Someone had used an electric saw to take the top off that skull – a perfect circle. There would have been a cloud of sawdust, and splinters of red bone flinging off everywhere. And there would have been a smell – worse than the meat section at the market.

Someone would have grubbed out the brain – they'd have cut the spinal cord and tried to lift it out in one flopping mass. The brain wouldn't have been firm from being in formalin, like in dissection class. No, it would've been mushy and disintegrating, like a jellyfish on the beach, and it would have stunk like a jellyfish too.

But somehow someone had got that skull and those bones nice and clean and white. That's what the Australian medical student wants – white bones.

She started to take the bones out and arrange them on her bed. She felt like wearing gloves but didn't have any. No-one used gloves to handle bones. What a woos you'd be. Nurses might wear gloves, but not med students.

Vertebrae – seven cervical, twelve thoracic, five lumbar, and the sacrum. All present and correct. Clavicle, sternum, scapula. Ribs – only seemed to be eight but that probably didn't matter. Pelvic bone – narrow brim – yes you could tell it was male. Humerus, radius, ulna and an articulated hand. This was a left side. Yes, she was sure of that. Femur, tibia, fibula, articulated foot. Something weird – perhaps this was the substandard part – the fibula was bent over like a violin bow, and so was the tibia. She held the fibula up to her left leg.

Yep.

Poor bloke.

The box needed a good dust-out. She upended it and gave a little shake then leant back and turned her head away as a cloud of straw dust followed.

There was a residual swishing in the box, so she turned it back over. Something was caught under the join in the plywood. It was a piece of paper, the same colour as the wood easy to miss. No, it wasn't a piece of paper, it was a very thin book. A small book bound in cream cardboard, creased and stained, powdered with grey dust. The faintest of words on the front in sepia letters.

GITANJALI

A slight smell of vinegar. She turned the little book over, nothing on the back. Then leafed through the pages – an old book on rough paper. Looked like a book of poems. In English.

GITANJALI

Rabindranath Tagore

First published by the India Society, London 1912

Published by Macmillan and Co Ltd, London 1913

This edition published by Hawakal Publishers, Calcutta 1922

Bloody hell. This was something – India. The bones had come from India. Why else would there be a book printed in Calcutta in there? But who put the book in the box?

She sat down at her desk and looked properly at the book. Someone had underlined some of the words in the index at the back.

Poem 74: The day is no more, the shadow is upon the earth.

Poem 86: Death, thy servant, is at my door.

And circled some page numbers – 7, 10, 17, 20 – and more.
And half-underlined some other words.

And they'd written something as well:

TRIVEDI

CALCUTTA.

And then below that:

H E L P

Faint brown letters like dried blood. No doubt about it.

'Well mate,' she said to the bones. 'That's something incredible to discover. I'm going to find out more about all this, Box of Bones. Yes, that's what I'll call you, B-O-B. Bob. Shelley felt as though she was lacking air, but didn't feel panicky. No, she felt as though she had things under control. 'I'm going to find out where you came from and how you got here.'

'Now I'd better put you back in your box or I'll be late for dinner shift. Question is, where will you fit? Don't want you too close to my head, no offence. Don't want to get any diseases. We'll try in the corner.'

The chairs outside the Dean's office were comfortable and made of quality fabric, and the carpet was deep and soft, celadon green. The plant in the Japanese pot looked remarkably healthy, and Shelley touched it to see if it was real. No, it was not. Bad sign.

The Dean had selected some fascinating reading material. Should she browse through the University of Australia Annual Report, or the Research Report?

She heard a door sweep open over the carpet.

'Ah, Miss Conway, come in.'

Dean Thompson guided her past the secretaries, who were surveying Shelley as if she were a criminal, and on into the inner sanctum.

Shelley watched out for the tissue box sign which would tell her how much trouble she was in. If tissues were in the room but not too prominent, you weren't in too much trouble, but if a tissue box was right in front of you, well then you were in deep shit.

The tissue box was there all right, but on top of a polished wooden filing cabinet. Not too close.

Everything was swishy and quiet.

'Miss Conway, I've asked our Registrar, Mr Smith, to take notes, just so we have an accurate record, you understand. You've met Mr Smith I believe?'

Shelley had met Mr Smith. She couldn't forget that face – a bandicoot, an obsequious bandicoot, one who would research and report. The Dean was powerful and imperious – had many enemies but no predators. Like a wombat, no, one of those ancient mega-wombats – a diprotodon, that was it. Professor Diprotodon.

'Miss Conway, the last time we met was when I offered you special entry into our medical school in view of your particular circumstances. I was enduring a great deal of arm-twisting from the Vice-Chancellor. Diversity. Complete rubbish in my opinion. Diverse doctors, what a nonsense. But the Vice-Chancellor thought that it was important we have one diverse student. Do you remember all that, Miss Conway? I told you the conditions were that you pursued your studies diligently and made satisfactory academic progress. But I don't think you've been pursuing your Anatomy studies diligently at all.

'We've adjusted some of the requirements, but that does not mean we can let you sail through the course. I had serious doubts about your ability to handle the basic sciences, but we had a lot of pressure from the Vice-Chancellor's office – a lot – as Mr Smith knows only too well.'

He glanced at the Bandicoot, who flexed his sycophantic lips. Preparing for an attempt at a smile perhaps. An 'I-told-you-so' smile.

Dean Thompson was sitting in a vast leather chair with an equally vast portrait of himself behind. Bound theses on the shelves. Two bronze plaques. A desk set with a gold pen, and a large blotter housed in green and gold leather. A pristine blotter. How she would love to deface it with a plump heart. 'Thompson L. Thompson'. And an arrow of course, right through the middle.

'I've seen the result from your Anatomy examination.' The Dean did not seem happy, funnily enough.

'Yes, I—'

'No excuses – you need to rectify this situation, Miss Conway, as a matter of urgency. Your performance at the bones table was particularly regrettable. You need to get right into your box of bones and learn them.'

'Yes, Dean Thompson.'

'What I am wondering, however, is this: why did you disrupt Professor Redlich's lecture last week?'

'Because he told a sexist joke, and that came as a terrible shock.'

'That is impossible for me to believe, Miss Conway.'

Shelley wasn't sure whether to say 'yes' or 'no', so said nothing.

The Dean was rotating his gold pen in his soft fingers. 'May I remind you that you are studying medicine, not history or anthropology.'

He paused and glanced at the Bandicoot who responded with a smirk. Good one, Dean.

'No, these signs are not good signs, Miss Conway. I can say this confidently, based on my years of experience with students just like you.'

Dean Thompson paused. Rotated his pen in the opposite direction.

'I will be watching your progress closely, Miss Conway. You may be a mature student on paper, but I will be looking for evidence of actual maturity. And satisfactory academic progress. A genuinely mature student who does not disrupt lectures and does not make hysterical claims.'

'Yes, Dean Thompson.'

'You may go.'

'You pompous prick,' Shelley said, but under her breath.

Shelley wasn't keen on dissection. She'd always preferred live people to dead ones. After all, the reason she was doing medicine was to stop live people from turning into dead people.

Truth was, she hated dissection.

She hated the smell of the formalin – rotting her nose and eyes and lungs, seeping into her skin and mouth, turning her insides into molten wax. She could taste it sharp on the tip of her tongue and gaggy at the back of her throat, even before she opened the dissection room door. It was like breathing in lighter fluid. Explained why med students looked half-embalmed.

She hated arriving in the dissection room, with its pale white light, a light filtered through frosted windows. On one side of the glass normal life was playing out, and on the other, peoples' mortal remains were being pecked over by a bunch of teenagers.

She hated the first glimpse as you walked in – the tables of students crowded around the bodies, four a side, like a scene from a macabre old painting. One of those paintings in the fancy gold frames. She wouldn't be surprised if she saw a top hat or a frock coat. And now it's centuries later and there were so many more students. Everyone was so squashed in they couldn't avoid dragging their sleeves, or their books, or their hair, in the cadaver.

She hated the secrecy. As if they were in a cabal. No chance of anyone peeking in. The public outside oblivious to the grisly tableau just a few metres away, behind those opaque windows. A timeless world, a world of never-never.

She hated the purr of gossip as the students scraped and scrutinised, and snipped and split, and she hated the bursts of laughter as someone told the latest crude joke.

Most of all she hated the inspection of her, Shelley Conway. The new girl, the old girl, the country girl, the weird girl, the unco girl. Dissection brought out the worst of the bearbaiting. And today the inspection would be more prolonged and more intense, because she'd been detained by the Diprotodon and the Bandicoot.

Her table, Table D, was the farthest from the door, and she could feel those aristocratic medical student eyebrows going up as she threaded through the cadavers, trying not to brush her leg against drapes and bits of corpse. Everyone was perving at the strange girl with the shells dangling from her backpack, the one who'd had the run-in with Redlich. The one who was older – well at least twenty-five, my God. What was she doing here, when everyone else was a normal age, like eighteen? The one who started the course late. The one from the country and that's what got her in. Talk about weird.

She was finally there at Table D. It was the smallest table, and the other students had dubbed them 'The Dregs'. It was just Shelley and two Asian students – but it was definitely the friendliest table. Shelley tried to put on a cheerful show after the ordeal of walking through the dissection room.

'Reporting for duty, Professor Kumar Jeffrey Sengupta, Professor Wang Jun Xian Eddie Wong.' Shelley liked to make a genuine attempt with Eddie and Jeffrey's real names, unlike the Anatomy demonstrators who thought the name of any Asian student was bizarre. They either ignored such a student completely when they marked the roll, and just ticked any foreign name as 'present' or made a great song and dance about it. 'Mr Wang or is it Wong, Jun or is it Juan, Exian or is it – oh I give up.'

And they always put a great emphasis on the 'Miss' of Miss Shelley Conway, as if having a female in the medical course was some sort of bizarre mistake.

'Good try, Shelley, but you still haven't got my name quite right,' said Eddie, without looking up. 'I'll give you another lesson one day. I'm just wrestling with this thenar branch of the ulnar nerve at the moment.'

Eddie had a part-time job as a theatre orderly and had picked up a few tricks of the trade from his heroes, the surgeons. He could do single-handed knots, he held his dissectors in a certain surgeon-like way and chatted without taking his eyes off the work. Looking at Eddie, anyone would think that this was a life and death battle for the cadaver.

Shelley swung her backpack to the floor, shells chinking, unzipped it and felt inside for her dissection kit. She looked up at the hooks – there was one gown left, and it was even more filthy than usual – sleeves stiff and yellow from formalin, shreds of muscle all over the front, not to mention the odd strip of blood vessel or nerve, and the self-tie missing – no wonder it hadn't been taken.

'Sorry, Eddie. Yes, I need further tuition. Good morning, Methuselah,' she said to the heap of tendon and bone they'd been working on for three months. 'Is Eddie looking after you?'

'Yes, I am as a matter of fact,' said Eddie. 'There's that branch.' He held a tiny white thread up for view in the crook of his dissectors.

He could be drawn as just a few oblongs, Eddie – a stocky vertical oblong for his body, if he were standing up, or two angled oblongs if he were sitting at the dissection table, and a small horizontal oblong for his glasses. You'd also have to draw a little diagonal spike for the *European Journal of Cardiac Surgery* sticking out of his coat pocket – a most unusual item for a first-year medical student to be carrying around. Some might accuse Eddie of showing off, but Shelley knew he was just focussed. Focussed to the point of being completely unaware of what other people might think. His clothes were neat – cardigans in ochre or maroon and a striped tie, the tie exhibiting multiple colours, but not ochre or maroon, and a sharp crease ironed into his jeans. He was probably the only eighteen-year-old in Australia who ironed creases into his jeans and polished his shoes, Shelley thought. The only other people Shelley knew who wore shiny shoes were ASIO. The gold tie pin was a special present from Eddie's parents to ensure that his tie didn't fall into the cadaver.

'It's so good to see you, Shelley,' said Jeffrey. 'We were worried you'd been kicked out.' Jeffrey was tall and elegant and had a smile which could be seen from outer space. He spoke with rounded vowels and crisp consonants, and always chose his words very carefully. 'Kicked out' was high slang for Jeffrey, and Shelley was a bit surprised.

However, she didn't reply immediately because they were being drowned out by a conversation from the table next door. Her nemesis, Table C. She could have given them a name beginning with C, but she didn't want to insult any part of the female anatomy, or offend Eddie, who was religious, so she'd made do with the good old 'Turds'.

The Turds were speaking deliberately loudly, anyone could tell.

'Hey, she's made it to the other Dregs,' said one of them.

Laughter, and the other Turds followed the lead. Rich joke-making possibilities here.

'One day those two Asians will go back to where they came from. Surely.'

'Yep. They're needed over there, wherever it is.'

'One's from India. The other – God knows where.'

'But what about the weird chick. Where's she going to end up?'

'Probably some hippie commune.'

Louder laughter.

'Better be near the coast so she can go shell-collecting.'

Raucous laughter.

Jeffrey and Eddie had selective hearing loss and were not reacting to any of it. They'd been perfecting that hearing loss all their lives, Shelley knew that.

'Glad you could make it, Shelley,' said Jeffrey. 'What with your busy schedule – meetings with the Dean, and so on.'

'Well, Thompson's put me on notice.'

'The Dean's put you on notice? So what's happening? What's happening with Redlich?' The boys were keen to hear the latest.

Shelley turned her back on the Turds table, so they couldn't eavesdrop. 'Thompson's gagged me, the bastard. Redlich's been telling that Venetian prostitute joke for years, and Thompson can't see anything wrong with it. He's a creep – they're both creeps.'

'You'll have to be a good girl for a while,' said Jeffrey. 'A whole new Shelley.'

'Fuck that for a joke. Sorry, Eddie.'

Jeffrey and Eddie continued their exploration of the fascinating thumb region while Shelley surveyed the room. The twenty or so tables, their yellow cadavers in various stages of dissection, all brown muscle and stringy white tendons. The sagging bellies and the slack skin. And under the trolleys the scraps buckets, each labelled with a body number. The cadavers, straight and stretched and on display – except for their genitals, which were covered up with ridiculous modesty towels. For God's sake, cadavers were not troubled by modesty. Were students supposed to respect bodies at one end while destroying them at the other? The cadavers could have their bloody faces peeled off, their eyeballs popped from their sockets, but they couldn't have their willies out. Honestly.

'Jeffrey and I have been talking about you, and we feel we should teach you how to stay out of trouble,' said Eddie. 'That's why we invited you onto Table D. D for diplomacy. You need to learn diplomacy before you can change the world.'

The three of them laughed.

Nearby tables looked around to see what was so funny. Asians didn't have a sense of humour, and nor did weird girls.

'The Dregs are in good form today,' said a Lesser Turd.

Top Turd – he of the blow-dried hair and tucked-in shirt – was apparently lowering himself to speak to her. Top Turd always sounded like he'd just swallowed a large oyster.

'Off to Venice, are we?' Top Turd asked solicitously. The Lesser Turds fell about in hysterics. Fawning sycophants.

'Piss off,' said Shelley.

She felt a tap on the shoulder. Oh God, what was it? Look around slowly. Don't fall off the stool. Yes, a hacked-off finger.

'Fuck off.'

'Got a problem, Spazzo?' said Turd Minor.

'What did you call me?'

Jeffrey and Eddie both stood up. 'Leave her alone, you big bully,' said Eddie, making no allowance for the fact that this particular Lesser

Turd was pretty short, maybe five foot three if he was lucky. But then Eddie was only five foot two.

Shelley was stuck on top of the stool. 'Yes, just fuck off, you moron. And if you flick fat into my hair today—'

She turned back to Methuselah and the boys. 'Why do we have to put up with those arseholes?'

The five-foot-three Turd had retreated into the colony.

'Just ignore them, Shelley,' said Jeffrey. 'Try to calm down.' He changed the topic. 'So how are you going with your new box of bones?'

'You won't believe this—' she said.

'No, we probably won't – whatever it is, it's sure to be incredible, knowing you,' laughed Jeffrey. 'What's happened?'

She started by telling Eddie and Jeffrey about her new set of bones and how her skeleton was called Bob. 'Though maybe he should be Half-Bob.'

The boys generally laughed if they thought Shelley had made a joke, even if it was incomprehensible to them.

'And the poor bloke's got something wrong with his tibia and fibula – they're all twisted, so he wouldn't have had much of a life.'

'Did you get a discount?' asked Eddie. Typical Eddie.

'Yes, actually. A big one, twenty dollars off.'

'That's very good, Shelley,' said Eddie, tucking his tie behind his tiepin.

'But listen to this – I found an old book in the box – a book of poems from India. You'll be interested, Jeffrey – it was published in Calcutta.'

'Well, that is interesting. In Hindi?'

'No, English. The author's name is, or I should say was, somebody-or-other Tagore.'

'Tagore. I know who he is, most definitely. Rabindranath Tagore, Bengal's poet. Won the Nobel Prize. Well, that's most interesting. Is it poems?'

'Yes,' said Shelley. 'There's some writing in there too. I'll bring it in to show you. I need to know more about it.'

'Uh-oh,' said Eddie, 'I can feel a new cause coming on. Detective Shelley's on the case.'

The two boys laughed, and even Shelley joined in.

'Definitely show me the book,' said Jeffrey.

Shelley had to make the best of things; she knew that. But there were some things it was very hard to make any best of.

Take her so-called room in College. It was remote from just about everything else, and even accessed by a different staircase – the old servants' staircase on the side of the building. Shelley didn't like walking down the laneway to the stairs, especially at night. It was hard to tip-toe safely through broken glass and dead rats.

The smell in the lane was bad, but the smell inside not much better – mildewed jock straps was the best way she could describe it.

She remembered her first viewing of the bedroom a few months ago, and how her heart had sunk. Dusty floorboards, and a frayed Axminster carpet square for a rug, a tiny bed with half its complement of wooden slats and a thin foam mattress. A plywood wardrobe with two straightened-out metal coat hangers – looked like something for nicking cars, but surely not in a gentleman's College.

The bathroom at the end of the hall was a bacterial green, with the odd colony of black mould. She'd wondered if she might be able to do some microbiology research in there. Penicillin and all that. Could be her first Nobel Prize.

Living here was going to feel like being on a forgotten planet. Pluto she'd call it – Pluto. Cold, dark, forgotten. No-one would have a clue she was there.

But since then, she'd improved the décor no end with a new quilt and a few shells here and there, a rickety desk and an old chair, both of which she'd found in the lane. She'd also cleaned the bathroom.

And now she had a roommate.

Shelley got into the habit of retrieving Bob's box from the corner at night and then getting out the bones she was trying to learn. She was concentrating on upper limb at this stage, because that's what they were doing in dissection. Her favourite bone was the radius, it was true. She loved that neat and tough head, so different from the ulna. The ulna was free form, organic, flamboyant. Looked like someone made a drastic mistake when they designed the ulna – they'd just flattened out some random bit of plasticine. Not like the radius – minimalist and functional – the radius had been designed by an engineer.

Now she had to learn all the attachments and articulations, so she was ready for Smiling Death when the end-of-year exam came. She'd show him, the permafrost bastard.

She was getting used to Bob but had moved the box as far away from her head as she could, which, in a broom cupboard, wasn't very far. But sometimes at night she'd hear a very faint high-pitched set of notes over and over. At first she thought it was wind in the old chimney above the blocked-up fireplace, then she wondered if a drunk College gentleman was playing the bagpipes out in the middle of the park, but then it occurred to her that it could be Bob crying.

Phil Donnelly was up himself, that was for sure. He spoke so loudly Shelley had to hold the receiver away from her ear.

'You're ringing me in September for Anatomy books? Expecting me to drop everything and go down to the med school and get you a second-hand textbook just like that?'

'No, I—'

'Because you've been too slack to get one before now?'

'I'm sorr—'

'Left it just a tad late, don't you think?'

Don't tell him the real reason – that she'd got into the course late. Special entry. That she's older, from the country. That she ticks more than one box under 'disadvantaged' so they can meet their targets. No, keep below the radar so these shits don't peck her to death.

'I'm really sorry, Phil, to trouble y—'

'Well, listen, you might just be lucky, because I happen to be in a good mood, and we do have a couple of Anatomy books left, most unusual for this time of year.'

'Oh, tha—'

'And I happen to be going into the med school this afternoon.'

'Oh, goo—'

'Five o'clock. Common room. Down near the kitchenette. Don't be late – I've got training tonight. And bring correct money. They'll be twenty-five or thirty bucks, depending.'

Depending on what? But he'd hung up.

Shelley propped her bike on the ti-tree fence outside the med school at exactly five pm. This was an important ti-tree fence because it bordered the Vice-Chancellor's Garden. Shelley thought it was good for the unimportant people like her to know where the top person could be found in case of emergency.

The University of Australia was always boasting about being in the top four hundred universities in the southern hemisphere, but the judges clearly didn't inspect the students' common rooms. Walking into the entrance of the med students' common room was like descending into the nocturnal exhibit at the zoo. There was the general gloom, and then there was the fauna – the fauna that congregated at the lockers in between lectures and at the end of the day – the Peters, the Davids and the Pauls – cramming their stuff into lockers – their dirty white coats, their stethoscopes, their photocopies, their smokes, their footy boots, their orange frisbees, their old school ties.

Shelley walked down to the kitchenette, which would not pass any food premises legislation anywhere in the southern hemisphere.

'Would you be Phil?'

'Certainly would.' Phil eased his white-as-white shoes off the table and butted out on a plate.

Shelley put her backpack down against the wall, and, when he heard the jingling, Phil raised his eyebrows.

'Shells,' she explained.

'Shells,' Phil repeated.

'Seashells.'

'Seashells. Of course. What was your name again?'

'Shelley.'

'Ri-i-ght.'

She could have been a specimen in the Pathology museum, the way he was looking at her now.

'And do you plug yourself in every night?'

'Huh?'

'To get your hair like that.'

'That's a bit personal.'

'Just joking, Shelley. Gotta take a joke.' Phil said this without even a hint of a smile, and in a voice that needed a muffler. She felt like asking had he ever considered plugging himself in at night. Might be able to work the volume dial.

He pulled his jeans down from his crotch. He had the massive thighs of a footballer. He must have trouble getting that plump wallet out of the rump pocket, Shelley thought.

'So, we've got three books left – a Gray's, a Cunningham's and a Last's. I recommend the Gray's of course, and the Cunningham's for dissection.'

The Cunningham's was transparent with fat.

'Now don't forget two dollars from every sale goes to the Med Students Society. Helps fund the PFAs. Pleasant Friday Afternoons, better known as Friday night piss-ups.'

'Yep.' She had been to one PFA. One was enough. She had never seen so many people so drunk.

Phil brightened up. 'You should come this Friday. And then I could give you a personal Anatomy tute.'

'No thank you.' Some things were beyond contemplation.

'C'mon, mate, you've gotta take a joke. Med school is med school. Doesn't matter how old you are.'

Phil went over to the lockers and came back with a small blue book and a pen.

'Phil?'

'Yep?' He was looking for a clean page in his book.

'What year are you in?'

'Fourth, why?'

'Well, I've got a question for you.'

'Uh huh?'

'You know the boxes of bones? Where do they come from?'

'The bones? I've got no idea. Some country.'

He looked at her more closely.

'You should leave off the questions and study more. You'll have Smiling Death in the Anatomy oral. He'll destroy you on bones for sure.'

Shelley decided to keep her encounter with Smiling Death to herself.

Phil was trying to get his pen to work. 'He hates females. Calls them a waste of space,' he said, full of cheer.

'Oh, good.'

'What school did you go to? He'll ask you that.'

'Wonnegurra High. A while ago though.' She gave a short laugh. Seemed like for ever ago. Beyond living memory.

'Wonnegurra High? Is that a school? You're kidding me.' Phil let out a roar like a bullock. 'That's the funniest thing I've heard all day. Don't say that, whatever you do.'

'What should I say?'

'Oh, MLC, PLC. One of those.'

She had no idea what they were.

Shelley could hear people coming in through the front door. Table tennis starting up. A can rumbling out of a soft drink machine.

'Five-thirty,' said Phil. 'Gotta get a move-on.'

Loud male voices, and lockers opening and closing. Some music – Creedence.

Fortunate Son.

Phil hummed along. 'Like Creedence?'

'Yep. Not this song, though.'

'Why not?'

'Fortunate sons.'

'You don't like fortunate sons?'

'No, I don't.'

Pause.

'Go to demos do we?'

'Maybe.'

'Read – what's it called, that student rag?' Phil was working himself up.

'*Farrago?*'

'That's right, *Farrago*. Read it? No, don't tell me, you write for it.'

'Sometimes.'

Phil clapped his massive hands on his massive thighs and shook his head. He opened up Gray's *Anatomy* and looked for something. He'd found it. 'This is what you should read, Shelley, instead of *Farrago*.'

She looked. *The Anatomy of the Male Genital Tract.*

She slammed the book shut. The sicko. Shelley put three yards between him and her. All she wanted to do was get out.

Phil laid his hands flat on the table. 'Jokes aside, Shelley, you radical woman you, we'd better get down to this transaction.' He gave himself a business-like shake before picking up the receipt book again, flipping through to a fresh page and patting the carbon into place.

'Put your name, address and phone number there please. Press hard.'

Shelley sat down to write. Phil closed up his locker.

He was back behind her, watching her writing. She sensed him bending over, and then his hot laughter was in her ear. 'Press harder, Shelley.'

Shelley was tempted. The words were on her lips. Fuck off, Sleazebag.

But no point in upsetting him more. She'd be out of there in a couple of minutes. Try to stay below the radar, Shelley.

Phil continued standing over her, arms folded. 'My advice is to know your bones. Shells and spells won't get you through Anatomy.'

He took his book back and smacked it on the table. 'There's a lot worse than bones in this course. Just you wait.'

Shelley pulled a twenty and a ten out of her jeans and put the money on the table.

'Thank you.' No more chit chat.

Phil signed the receipt book, started to tear out the top page and then stopped. 'Shelley Conway. Shelley Conway. Hang on a sec – that's a familiar name – how do I know that name? Ah – I know who you are – you're the one in trouble, aren't you? You're the chick who took on Prof Redlich.'

'I might be.'

'Sounds like a yes to me. So, what the fuck happened?'

'Just a minor disagreement.' Not this again.

'So, what's going to happen to you?'

'Don't know. Have to see the Dean on a regular basis.'

'Sheesh.' Phil shook his head. 'You're such a rebel. Don't you want to be a doctor?'

'Of course I do. But this shit's not about being a doctor – it's sexism. And as for the bones, I actually care. Unlike everyone else.'

'You're right there, Shelley. Nobody else cares. Nobody gives a stuff. Fact is, everyone else is sensible.'

Dissection came around quickly – far too quickly in Shelley's opinion. But she'd had time to think things over.

'So, Shelley?'

'I'm tired, Jeffrey. Jesus I'm tired. It's this fucking College maid job. Eddie, I'm sorry, I meant, well you know what I meant.'

'It grieves me when you take the Lord's name in vain, Shelley.'

'I apologise for taking Jesus's name in vain, but Jesus wouldn't like this job either. Waiting on those silver-spoon types. Getting treated like shit, working hours and hours just for board. No money. Seriously, I'm so tired at night I can't study.'

'Maybe you should think about some other job,' said Eddie. 'Maybe at one of the other Colleges, where they pay more respect to Our Lord Jesus Christ, like the Baptist one.'

'It's a thought.'

'What about that soup kitchen you go to?'

'What about it?'

'Well, what do you achieve down there?' said Eddie. 'You don't get paid. You don't help those characters, and they don't help themselves. See, we're a bit worried about you, Shelley, now that the Dean is on your case. You're wasting your time down there, Shelley.'

'We do help them. Get them something to eat. Get to know them. Not their fault. You two should come down some time.' Jeffrey and Eddie would never join her at the soup kitchen. Not in a million years. It wouldn't help them in their exams.

Eddie was stripping the skin off the fingers using his patented scraping technique. This involved removing the blade from his scalpel and using the handle as an instrument for blunt dissection. It worked for Eddie, but neither Jeffrey nor Shelley had had much success.

'And have you been learning your bones? Now you've got your own?' Eddie was keeping an eye on the operative field, while still chatting.

'Yes, how's Bob settling in?' Jeffrey gave a bit of a chuckle.

'Yeah, not bad,' said Shelley.

Table D was silent for a few minutes.

'What about the rest of society? Have you saved that yet, Shelley?'

'You're not being sarcastic are you, Jeffrey?'

'No, Shelley. Would I be sarcastic?' Jeffrey was staring up at the high windows.

'I'm not a sideshow.'

'No, never, of course not,' said both the boys in reassuring tones.

'Having a social conscience isn't like having a virus you know. You can't just throw it off.'

Jeffrey returned his gaze to Shelley. He was looking concerned. 'We're simply asking you what you've achieved with all your efforts. And we're worried now that the Dean is coming down hard on you. We don't want to lose you, do we Eddie?'

'Certainly not,' said Eddie. 'There's no-one like you, Shelley. You're more mature than anyone here. But you'll do more good as a doctor than as a social worker.'

One of the demonstrators popped his head in between Eddie and Shelley and asked if they needed any help. Nice of him, Shelley thought. Must be new. Eddie said no, they were fine.

'Well, thanks you two,' said Shelley, but I'm not going to forget my principles because some antiquated prick of a Dean thinks I should shut up. No way. I'm going to speak out about injustice when I see it.'

'That's where we think you're wrong, Shelley,' said Jeffrey.

'Well, I appreciate your advice.'

Quite a long period of silence.

Shelley thought of a new topic. 'You know how I organised a blood drive last week? I thought that my fellow med students might see it as a good thing to do – to give blood.' She gave a snort. 'And I got the Blood Bank van to come to Uni last Thursday – you did know that, didn't you? It was on the boards before all the lectures.'

'I can't give blood,' said Eddie. 'Asian.'

'Same,' said Jeffrey. 'Well, South Asian.'

'That's not a reason.'

'It is for me,' said Eddie. 'It's not so much being Asian, it's having an Asian family. They think I'll get weak and won't be able to pass my exams and earn money and look after them in their old age if I give blood.'

'Same,' said Jeffrey.

'Well, I'll forgive you this time. At least you're telling the truth. I've had some doozies from the other med students: one had blood pressure – high or low – he couldn't remember which, just knew he had blood pressure; one said he played sport; one said it was a full moon; one was on a diet – I'm serious; one had their period; one hadn't had their period; one said she'd have to look at her astrology forecasts. This is all true. Someone else tried to tell me that med students and doctors are permanently exempt from giving blood.'

'You can't force people to give blood, Shelley,' said Jeffrey.

'I was just giving people the opportunity. You'd think that if anyone could see the need it'd be med students.'

'Sounds like you were giving them the third degree,' said Eddie.

Shelley held her hands up in defence. 'I wasn't forcing anyone. Anyway, guess how many med students in our year gave blood. Out of a possible two hundred.'

Eddie shook his head. 'No idea.' Unusual for Eddie.

'Fifty?' said Jeffrey.

'Five. And they could only get half a pint out of me, so that's four and a half.'

'See, Shelley,' said Jeffrey, 'that's what happens – now you've got no blood left.'

Shelley laughed. 'I've got plenty left. D'you know there were more donors from Arts and Commerce and even Engineering than Medicine? Per capita I mean.'

'Four and a half pints is better than nothing,' said Eddie.

'Not much better. You wouldn't be able to do any cardiac surgery if you only had four and a half units of blood available, Eddie. You wouldn't even be able to open theatre.' Shelley had no idea if this was true, but it sounded convincing.

Eddie sat back from his dissecting and looked at Shelley. 'Shelley, back to the main issue. You're here to learn how to look after sick people, and you'll do a lot more good if you commit to that. You're not going to get a degree in protesting about the war, or blood-collecting, or for calling lecturers sexist pigs.'

'Thanks Eddie, but fact is the big problems in the world are social. It's social injustice that's responsible for most health problems. Not to mention fucking war.'

'Shelley.'

'War.'

'I would submit, Shelley, that it's better to save one person from something you can treat, like meningitis, than trying to save millions of people but getting absolutely nowhere.'

Shelley didn't answer. Eddie just might be correct.

If there was one thing worse than dissection, it was physiology prac.

'How are you, Shelley? And how's Bob?' Eddie was getting ready to pith a toad. Shallow tray with layer of Ringer's solution. Toads in a bucket. Selection of hat pins. Chopping board.

'Yes, how's Bob settling in?' Jeffrey gave a bit of a laugh.

'Well boys, poor Bob's giving me the heebie-jeebies. I can't bear to have him under my bed, so I've put him in the furthermost corner of my room, which is about a yard from my head. I keep wondering about that boy. How did he die, who killed him and who got the flesh off the bones? And where is he really from? There's no label as far as I can see. Just a name in the Indian poetry book. I'll show you.'

Shelley pulled the little cream book out of her backpack. 'See this? See the underlining?'

Death thy servant is at my door and

'He will go back with his errand done leaving a dark _shadow_.'

'And a whole heap of numbers circled.'

'And there, see the words "TRIVEDI" and "CALCUTTA"?'

Eddie was choosing a toad. He called out to Jeffrey.

'Jeffrey, you should know all about this. Aren't they supposed to be from India, the bones? Shelley, which toad should we go for?'

'Haven't a clue.' Jeffrey shrugged his shoulders. 'Wouldn't be Hindus.'

Shelley was becoming aware of what Eddie was doing. The toad was on its stomach, with its arms and legs stretched out. Eddie was running his fingers up and down, looking for the small depression at the top of the spinal column. This looked like his second go. The toad kept jerking out of place.

She turned her head the other way and stared through the window of the lab into the cream brick wall of the Biochemistry building next door. She just could not watch that poor animal splayed out on the board, jumping and twitching as Eddie tried to pierce the bottom of its brain. She had to say something.

'The poor thing, it's still moving. Eddie, do you know what you are doing?'

'There's no way of knowing if it's pithed or not. So I'm trying to make doubly sure.'

'But it's reacting when you stick the pin in. Oh no. Eddie, why don't we ask the demonstrator for help?'

Shelley spotted a young woman standing near the bench. She seemed to be deliberately facing the other way, and so had to be a demonstrator. She had on a long-sleeved pink shirt with cuffs tightly buttoned around her wrists, plus a string of pearls. Ready for work.

'Excuse me – excuse me—' Volume increasing. 'Could you help us, please? My friend's having a bit of trouble.' Shelley raised her voice even more. 'Excuse me.'

Eddie glared at her.

'Oh, sorry, I didn't hear you. I'm afraid I can't. I'm no good at pithing,' said Pearls. And then, as Shelley stared at her, 'I'm a Biochemistry demonstrator really. They've just roped me in today because they're short-staffed. I hate this sort of stuff,' she laughed. 'Give me test tubes any day.'

'But how can you laugh? This creature is suffering. How do we know we've done it properly and the frog won't feel any pain?'

'Toad,' said Eddie.

'All right, toad,' said Shelley.

The toad gave another twitch.

'Looks like you've had enough goes,' Pearls said to Eddie. 'I'd assume you've anesthetised it and go on with the experiment.'

Even Eddie looked a bit startled.

Pearls continued. 'You have to pin it onto the board and take the skin off the leg.'

Shelley started to feel sweaty, and a black curtain was coming down in front of her eyes.

'Are you all right?' she heard someone say, possibly the woman.

'No, I think I'm going to—' She felt herself sliding off the stool like a coat. 'I—'

No words would come out. The world was black and she was going to be sick. Pearls was trying to sit her up, but Shelley had to lie down.

There was something splashing on her face. She opened her eyes and could see Jeffrey and some other people peering down at her.

'Stop the experiment,' she tried to say. It didn't sound right. Her words slurred into each other. 'Everystop.'

The demonstrator had one of her arms and Jeffrey the other, and the demonstrator was dragging her. Felt like her shoulder would dislocate. Pearls kept tugging her until she was stumbling out of the lab. Shelley's left foot was twisting. She could hear the pink and black lino squeaking under her sneakers as they dragged her into the foyer.

Pearls was trying to force her to take her weight.

'She can't stand.' That was Eddie. 'She'd better just lie on the floor. You shouldn't stand up if you've fainted. Postural hypotension.'

'Use my lab coat.' That was Jeffrey.

'Here's a chair,' said someone.

The demonstrator's long nails were digging into her arm pit. Shelley could see the chair. There was a black circle around her field of vision. There's the chair. Fabric and metal. Pearls pushed her at it and Shelley felt herself topple. Her arm hit the metal arm of the chair, bang. It hurt. She was spread all over the place like the toad.

'She's looking all right,' Pearls said. 'She'll be okay to go home in a minute.'

'I don't think so. She's not right at all,' said Eddie. 'Look at her, she's grey and sweating.'

'I'm right,' Shelley tried to say. But her attempt was incomprehensible, she knew.

'Maybe we should get an ambulance?' someone said.

'Take her to Student Health.'

'Or over to Casualty.'

'Now everybody, back to your experiments. What's your name? Eddie, is it? We'll leave you in charge, Eddie. Everyone else back to your bench.'

Shelley made a big effort to speak. 'No, no. Everyone stop. Stop the experiment.'

She pushed herself up a bit. 'The frogs are in pain, and you know it.'

The College maids' phone wasn't working, so Shelley had to use the phone box out in the street, the one that smelt like fish and chips.

'Mum—' Sound of coins clanking down. 'Mum, it's Shell.'

'Shell! We've been wondering when you'd ring. Jack! It's Shell!'

Shelley could picture her mum calling her dad. He'd be in the lounge room giving the newsreader a hard time. If pressed, he would always agree it wasn't the newsreader's fault, the state of the nation, but it made him feel better to tell her off.

'Jack! It's Shell! Trunk call! Quick!'

As if Dad could get anywhere quickly.

'It's all right Mum, no hurry—'

And then Mum's echoing voice was back again. 'So, how are you, Shelley?'

Mum always cupped her hand around the mouthpiece and shouted as if she was yelling from the South Pole.

'Fine, Mum. I hate everything, but I'm fine.'

'You hate what?

'Everything – med school, College. I hate waiting on all these little princes.'

'Princes?'

'Yep, princes. Born to rule. All called Simon.'

She was in a bit of a mood, she had to admit. Hoped no-one was listening outside the phone box.

'I don't think you should hold that against them.' Her mother saw good in the weirdest people. Even Simons.

Her father had picked up the phone in the den. 'What's this, Shell? Not happy?'

'I stick out like dogs' balls here, Dad. Sorry, but it's true. I'm trying my best to fit in, but – you know. I'm old. I didn't go to private school. I'm not rich. I walk funny. I come from the country. They can't cope with any of that. I'm a complete nobody.'

'That's ridiculous,' said Mum. 'Medical students aren't all snobby, surely. Anyway, you can't be both a nobody and stick out like, like, you know what, at the same time.'

'Well, I can. And they don't care about anything.'

'What do you mean?'

'Like experimental animals. Just awful. And the fact that everyone has to buy bones – human bones – from God knows where, and no-one asks any questions. I wasn't expecting that.'

'Well, bugger me,' said Dad.

'Don't get your father all worked up now,' said her mum.

'Well, I didn't want to tell you. But you should see my box of bones – it's a fifteen-year-old boy. And in the box there's a book of poems, all about death, with a name in it. Or looks like a name. Don't you think someone should ask some questions?'

'Someone, maybe,' said Mum. 'But not you, Shelley. You don't have to be the one all the time. What sort of name?'

'I'm not sure – it's hard to read, but it was printed in Calcutta.'

'You wouldn't think they'd have poetry books in Africa,' said Mum. 'But Shelley, you've just got to put things like that out of your head. They've probably got more dead bodies than they know what to do with over there.'

'Mum, I can't put things like that out of my head. But everyone else can. They just go on with their lives – ski holidays and all that—'

'Maybe it would have been better if you hadn't started medicine.'

'What do you mean?'

'Well, if you'd just got a normal job like everyone else. A trade. You could have finished an apprenticeship by now. Earn while you learn. You don't have to go to university. None of us did. Look at Wendy. She's loving her hairdressing apparently. Not that that would have suited you, with your hair—'

'Or nursing,' said Dad. 'Have you thought about that, Shell? You might fit in better.'

'I'm going to be a doctor. That's my thing. I've told you.'

'Yep, we know that, Shell.' Dad was trying. 'But you're up against it, mate. Those bloody types, to the manor born, never done a day's work in their lives. Parents own half the country. Your Baillieus, your Holmes à Courts – they're all there. Born with silver spoons in their mouths. A whole bloody silver spoon collection, like your mother's.'

'Now, calm down Jack. Don't start on my spoons.' Mum's spoons came from all over Australia.

'Dad, I wouldn't know those people if I fell over them. Anyway, College is just temporary I've decided – I'm going to get a job to pay rent somewhere else. It'll help me if I live in some other joint. Meet some other students.'

'What sort of job?' asked Dad.

'Not sure – waitressing probably.'

'Do you really need to meet more people? Could you even manage waitressing?' Her mum was dubious. As usual.

Before Shelley could answer, her dad said, 'That'd be United Workers Union. Make sure you sign up straight away, Shell.'

'It'll be okay, Mum, I'm working it all out. And yes Dad, I'll sign up. Long as it doesn't cost too much. It'll be about my third union.'

'And don't worry about the bones,' said her Mum. 'That's not your job to worry about them. I'm sure the University has everything under control. They don't want bad publicity.'

'Mu—'

'You're always so melodramatic, Shell. Yes, she is, Jack. She should just be trying to fit in.'

What would Mum know? But she was always going on as if she did.

'Now, why don't you come home for a weekend and we can talk about all this,' said Mum. 'I'll do a roast. The twins are dying to see you.'

'Yep, I'll try, Mum,' said Shelley. 'Hang on, there's the pips.' Shelley scrounged around in her backpack and found two twenty-cent pieces. Wonders never ceased. She put one in.

'Skye wants Ballerina Barbie—'

Now a bloke was waiting to use the phone. Looked hard up.

'Sorry to interrupt Mum, but—'

'—and Rory wants a green football cake, so don't know how I can combine those—'

'Mum, I'd better go, someone else wants to use the phone. I'll call you soon – promise – bye—'

Check if any coins were left in the tray – no, but she'd got that other twenty cents. 'Here you go, mate, here's twenty cents. All yours. No worries. See ya.'

'I've always thought the humerus had something to do with being funny – what do you think Bob? It does look a bit like a cartoon bone, the humerus. Now why is it called humerus? Must look that up. Not exactly humorous for you, is it Bob? Nice and smooth, not too complicated. Those nice condyles at the bottom. And some of the names – like "bicipital groove" – that's the tunnel that the biceps tendon runs down. Sounds like a piece of jazz music. Is it the long head or the short?

Better check. But that's why it's called biceps, Bob – did you know that? Because it has two – bi – heads. "Ceps" means cephalic, and that means heads. Helps when you understand what the words mean. They should tell us that.

'Though the shoulder joint – I don't know about that – none too stable. I think the Great Engineer should have made the cup deeper so the head of the humerus is less inclined to pop out. She's relying too heavily on the poor old ligaments there, the Great Engineer is.

'Yes, I think you and I could improve the shoulder joint, but we won't say anything to Smiling Death about that, will we? Or maybe we should.'

Shelley laughed.

Shelley loved the ride to her new job. She felt so free as she sailed through roundabouts and bumped over kerbs – streamers flying, shells dangling and bell jingling. How she'd love to live in this little terrace house with the black and white tiles on the porch, or this one with the two-seater stroller out the front, or that one with the jasmine flooding the fence.

And she liked the glimpses into other worlds on the way: the world of skateboarding under the housing commission high-rise; the world of the Greek grandmothers in their wrinkly black stockings, bent over like question marks; the world of the Italian *nonnas* with their bulging shopping trolleys; the world of the *nonnos* in their bars and amongst their cards, coffee and smoke.

And there was the added bonus of getting out of College for a few hours – away from the charming gentlemen with their vomit in the bathrooms and farts in the hall.

Trois Bouteilles was altogether fancy. Three bottles hanging out the front and red checked tablecloths. She'd never heard of most of the dishes before, let alone the wine. However, it was surprising what you could get away with if you gave a bit of a smile, and she'd ended up with quite a few tips.

Tomas the chef told Shelley he cooked what he knew, and they could call it what they liked – Italian, French – didn't matter to him. It did matter that she knew he was To-*mas* and not *Tho*-mas, and it did matter that she knew her garnishes.

Tomas was tall and pale with yellow tips to those sprigs of hair which ventured out from underneath his chef's hat. Maybe he had malnutrition – the greenish tinge was probably iron deficiency, and the cracks in the corners of his lips – that was a sign of B12 deficiency, wasn't it? And he was so thin – almost looked like he had beriberi. Not a good sign in a chef.

'You cut up the lemon like this, and then you dip one side in parsley or paprika.'

'Right.'

'Parsley for the fish and paprika for the escalopes.'

'Right.' What was escalopes?

'Now we have two blood assure today—' He stopped and looked at her. 'Is there something wrong?'

'No, I'm working out the French, Tomas.' She had to remember that *blood assure* was *plats du jour* which was *on special*. 'Just making sure I remember it all.'

'Well, you must concentrate – carelessness is the cardinal human vice – do you know who wrote that? No? Of course not. It was Kafka, Franz Kafka.'

'Oh, I've read *The Trial*, Tomas. I loved it.'

'Read it? Loved it?' Tomas looked disbelieving.

'And *The Castle*.'

'You read *The Castle*?'

'Yep. Just finished it actually. I'm trying to improve my knowledge.'

Tomas was scrutinising her face. 'You are better than Franz then. He didn't finish *The Castle*.'

'Oh.'

'But it is good that you are improving your knowledge. Very good.' He could almost be smiling, Shelley wasn't sure.

Tomas looked over to the stove. Something was bubbling. He was so tall he had to fold and unfold himself like a Jacob's ladder to get underneath the palisade of implements and back to his pots.

Shelley parted the ladles to continue the conversation. 'Do you come from Czechoslovakia, Tomas?'

'Yes, I do.'

'I've never met anyone from Czechoslovakia. But I like the stamps. The triangle ones.' How the twins would love some of those stamps for their collections.

Tomas didn't take the hint. 'Just make sure you can carry three plates.'

At the end of the first two shifts Shelley gave Tomas half her tips. When you thought about it the customers were tipping the food as much as the service, and Tomas was under much more pressure than she was. Besides, she felt sorry for him – he seemed lonely. Sometimes he wouldn't be quite all there, and other times he could be cranky and irritable. Maybe this gesture might smooth relations a bit.

Tomas was shocked.

'You are a good girl. And you are not even strong. Not like a Czech girl. Tall and straight, Czech girls.'

'No, but I'm a good worker, Tomas, and I never complain.'

Tomas had turned away. She'd drop another hint about stamps another time.

'Bob, it's a beautiful day. Sunday. You and I might go out on the lawns. People will stare if I take your whole box down, so I'll just take your clavicle and sit on a rug in the sun.'

'There. Now Bob, I'm just thinking about your clavicle. It's the most commonly fractured bone. I suppose it's useful – it acts a strut between the shoulder and the sternum, the book says. But you'd have to say it is not exactly effective if it's the most commonly fractured bone. I think we should re-design the clavicle, you and me, Bob. Make it straight for a start. That curve is asking for trouble. So "clavicle" means little key because the clavicle rotates like a key when you straighten out your arm away from your body. Two joints – sterno-clavicular and acromio-clavicular. Now how can I quickly tell right from left? Got to check that out and learn all those muscle insertions.'

'You okay?' the boys enquired when Shelley arrived at the next dissection class.

'Were you ailing for something?' asked Jeffrey.

'It was the toads – you both know that. How disgusting. No-one knew if they were properly anesthetised or not and the demonstrator couldn't care less.'

Jeffrey looked abashed. 'Yes, I agree Shelley, it wasn't very nice.'

'Wasn't very nice? It was totally barbaric.'

'Well, maybe we'll have more success next week.' Jeffrey didn't sound too confident.

'Might have a better demonstrator,' said Eddie.

'You're joking, I hope. There's not going to be a next week. I'm going to write to the Physiology Prof about this. Or maybe Diprotodon Thompson, I haven't decided yet.'

'Shelley, no. You'll be expelled for sure. You're on the brink already.'

Shelley decided not to answer – for a minute anyway.

At least the cadavers were genuinely dead. No twitching from Methuselah. She'd never imagined she'd be grateful for dead bodies.

18 Sep 1970

Dear Professor Dawson-Walker,

I wish to register a protest about the pithing of frogs and toads. Nobody knows how to do it properly – not even our demonstrators. This means that the animal is held down while someone tries repeatedly to jab a hat pin through its spinal cord/hind brain. By the end of multiple attempts, we still don't know if the animal is anaesthetised or what. Our demonstrator could not help us and was even more hopeless than us. Considering the frogs are used for muscle and nerve experiments it is unbelievably cruel if the frog can feel pain.

I believe a video of the experiment would serve the educational purposes you have in mind.

Could you please send me a copy of the Ethics Committee approval for medical student pracs involving live animals?

Do vets ever inspect the experiments?

Yours sincerely

Shelley Conway

'So, Shelley,' said Eddie. 'How's Bob?' Was Eddie trying to get her worked up, or was he making intelligent conversation?

'Bob's fine, thanks Eddie. Just wishes he was where he should be. Like alive and in another country.'

'How do you know that? What's the difference between bones and a body anyway? Why the fuss about bones?'

'You're joking, I hope, Eddie. At least Methuselah is donated and presumably Australian. And he's a hundred, not fifteen. And most likely died of natural causes.'

Eddie was about to say something, but she hadn't finished.

'These bones have been sent from some poor country. Hundreds of skeletons, thousands, sent all over the world, year after year. So how do they get them? Shouldn't med students ask that question?'

Table D was silent for a few minutes.

'And that gives me the creeps. And knowing someone has put a message in the box.'

'Message?' said Eddie.

'Yes, in the poetry book. I'm sure there's a message there. And that address means something. I haven't worked it out yet. But I am trying to learn my bones, or I should say Bob's bones, if that makes you feel better.'

'Good,' said Jeffrey. 'I'd forget about the poetry book – it won't be on the exam. Smiling Death won't be asking you to recite poems.'

'Now, what else are you trying to save at the moment, Shelley?' said Eddie.

'Are you both stirring me again? Is this a campaign?'

'Yes – bones, the war, frogs – you're into so many causes, Shelley. It's too much.'

'Well thanks you two, but I'm going to speak out about injustice when I see it. All my life, I hope. Whatever I end up as.'

'That's where we think you're wrong,' said Jeffrey.

'Well, that's so kind of you both.'

She instantly felt bad. The boys were trying to help her, but they didn't get it. 'I'm sorry. I didn't mean to be sarcastic. People are making a difference, Jeffrey. They wouldn't be withdrawing troops from Vietnam if we hadn't had the moratoriums. And I wasn't on my own. There were a hundred thousand people at the last moratorium.'

'Maybe yes, maybe no,' said Eddie, 'but there will always be wars, Shelley.'

'You're right there, Eddie,' said Jeffrey.

Dissection class was over, and the Grey Ghost was hovering.

The broom cupboard. The desk. The far corner. Shelley rolled back on her bed on Sunday morning to consider her guest. Who was grieving for him and where? Was there a mother in India who never knew what happened to her son? Did he just disappear one day?

Maybe he'd died of an illness, and was buried, then dug up. But they didn't bury people in India, did they? She'd have to read up on that. Go to the State Library. And maybe look up that poet at the same time.

She needed to address this matter properly. Shelley sat up and spoke directly to the box.

'Bob, I'm sorry, Bob. Whatever happened, you shouldn't be here. Someone must have loved you at some time in your life, and then something bad happened. I know you couldn't have had a happy life, or you wouldn't have ended up here in this room with me. I am really sorry. I'm going to try and make it up to you. I don't know how, Bob, but I am.'

The box didn't answer.

'Anyway, it's the scapula today, Bob.'

Shelley put the box on the bed and opened it up.

There was the book. GITANJALI – what would that mean? Jeffrey didn't know – said he didn't speak much Hindi. And the author, someone called Rabindranath Tagore – who was he? Jeffrey had said he'd won the Nobel Prize and that was the sum total of her knowledge. She turned to the index of first lines and wondered why again why some were underlined.

'It's pretty mysterious, Bob. Not too sure myself. Mist and Old and Stormy and Rare and Year and Wild. What could all those words mean? And some other things underlined as well. Now I'm going to give you a view. We are going to put your skull here on the windowsill, with the book just there so you and I can read it. You'll be able to see what the outside world is like. Different from wherever you come from. I'll get some nice things for you to be next to, like some shells. There, that's better, isn't it?'

She turned the skull this way and that until Bob's skull had the nicest view possible over the courtyard to a few gum trees. It took up almost the entire width of the window.

'I'll see if Tagore has anything relevant to say. Here we go:

Trees are the earth's endless effort to speak to the listening heaven.

'Oh. Trees are the earth's effort to speak to heaven. That's profound. I've never thought about trees like that.

'There. And we'll keep the scapula out and close the box and put the rest of you under the bed after all. So, scapula means trowel – did you know that Bob? And how complicated is it? There are eighteen bloody muscles involved – twelve originate from the scapula and six insert. And there are two joints – glenohumeral and acromioclavicular. And most of the muscles are there to stabilise the shoulder joint. We know the shoulder's a pretty tinny joint, don't we Bob? Seriously why did she make humans so complicated? Oh, here's something interesting – platypuses and echidnas have separate coracoid processes, like dinosaurs. Smiling Death might ask me that if I get into an Honours oral.'

Shelley laughed aloud. 'Honours oral? What am I thinking of?'

29 Sep 1970

Dear Professor Dawson-Walker,

I wish to register a strong protest regarding the disgusting experiment we had to do today in Physiology Prac – the decerebrate cat. Firstly, the brain surgery on these cats is cruel and especially cruel when done by amateurs. Secondly it is very distressing to see the cat stumbling around, falling over and bumping into things. Thirdly, our experiment didn't even work so that the cat didn't right itself and fell onto the floor. There was no veterinary supervisor and I am amazed that the University vets ever allowed this experiment to go ahead.

If it is really important why do you not have a video of one cat prepared properly and humanely.

This is the most cruel and revolting experience I have ever had. All the other students felt the same, but probably do not have the courage to write.

Would you send me the Ethics Committee approval for this experiment?

Finally, I am very disappointed that you did not answer my letter of 18 Sep on cruelty to frogs and toads.

Yours sincerely

Shelley Conway

6 Oct 1970

Dear Miss Conway

Would you kindly attend the office of Dean Thompson at 11 am on Mon 12 October.

Yours sincerely

F. Smith

Registrar

Shelley thought that the triumvirate of Faculty secretaries would be getting used to her turning up to see the great man. But no, there was no hint of recognition from any of the trio when she arrived. The junior one told her to sit down, and then nobody spoke to her for fifteen minutes. They just click-clacked away. Eventually the most senior one took off her glasses and sashayed into the inner sanctum. Shelley could hear her voice. Sounded fake.

'Professor and Dean, Miss Conway has arrived.'

Senior sashayed out.

'Ah, Miss Conway, we've been waiting for you. Do take this seat, would you?'

The Diprotodon was standing near the door in his full regalia – purple bow tie and pants that didn't know if they were meant to be over or under the expansive tummy. Tuffets of grey-green hair growing out of ears and eyebrows. Fertile soil obviously.

Shelley's chair was placed in the middle of a stretch of pale green carpet between the desk and window. Small table next to Shelley's chair with a pink tissue box. Junior Secretary should have ordered a green box – better match. Thompson moved back behind his magnificent desk and blotter. Views to the vivid green trees outside.

There was a gentle murmur of traffic from Royal Parade, and the tappety-taps of the three Remingtons just outside the door.

Shelley wondered if the office really was sumptuous, or just seemed so in comparison to the rest of the medical building.

'You will know Professor Dawson-Walker.' Dean Thompson indicated a small man sitting to his left whom she'd overlooked. Hadn't stood up.

No, she didn't know Professor Hyphenated. Never seen him before in her life. But that might be because she'd missed a lecture or two, so best not to say anything.

Professor Dawson-Walker fixed his gaze on Shelley for a moment, so Shelley looked right back at him. He possibly moved his lips. Hard to be sure, but a gold tooth flashed. He had those forward-facing eyes that can spot mice from two hundred feet. Professor Daryl Dawson-*Wanker*. Perhaps the name was some compensation for his short stature.

Was it credible that this background person with no manners was a sadist, responsible for the murders of so many animals? If Shelley added it up, it would be thousands of frogs, toads, rabbits, cats, mice, rats and dogs every year.

Well, he did have those eyes.

'Now I believe you have written to Professor Dawson-Walker regarding physiology practical sessions? Yes? And I believe you not only left the session, but you encouraged, no, *harangued*, other students until they did the same? So that not only you, but all those other unfortunate students will forfeit the marks for that prac?'

'I didn't harangue anybody. Everyone thought that experiment was disgusting.'

'Despite my asking you specifically not to be disruptive?'

'Dean Thompson, those cats were in pain and utter misery. They were stumbling around like this.' Shelley got up and staggered blind and helpless around the office, lifting her feet up high, like the poor brainless cats had. She bumped into a filing cabinet and fell on the floor. The carpet cushioned her fall. It was a soft as a slipper. Quality carpet.

Professor Dawson-Walker leaned forward and pointed to Shelley's feet. 'You haven't got that gait quite right. It's an ataxic gait that they get.'

'Oh, I fully agree, I haven't. I should also show you crawling on my belly, meowing in pain after I was dropped from a height and failed to right myself. Shall I show you that?'

'That's quite enough, thank you. Get up please.' The Diprotodon was concentrating on getting his papers into a perfect pile, no sheet out of line. And the sadist, Professor Dawson-Wanker, was regretting showing interest in the gait demonstration, and now was checking the ceiling lights. Any tubes need replacing, mass murderer?

Shelley took her seat again, pushed her hair off her face, looked at Professor Dawson-Wanker. 'And Professor Dawson-Walker, you didn't reply to my letter about the torture of frogs and toads.'

The Diprotodon picked up his sheaf of papers and tapped them on the desk. Regaining control. Order, order. 'Miss Conway, just because you are a mature student you do not have a licence to harass and intimidate. I am not sure whether you realise that your letters could be interpreted as threatening? Insofar as you have asked for Ethics Committee documentation. Such matters are hardly within the purview of a first-year medical student, and threats would be a matter for the police, you know.'

'Dean Thompson, I did not make any threats. I just want those experiments to stop.'

'I see. Well, if every student got what they wanted it would be a very strange curriculum. I'm sure Professor Dawson-Walker would agree.' The wanker nods and glints.

'And, moreover, you have jeopardised both your own physiology marks and those of your colleagues who left the practicum.'

Nod, nod, nod from the Wanker.

'Professor Dawson-Walker and his team produce results of international significance, and their research is admired around the world. Professor Dawson-Walker is one of the stars in the University of Australia firmament.'

The humble star put up his hands and protested. 'No, no.'

'And you students are privileged to have such a teacher.'

Star? Privileged? Teacher?

'I am going to ask you one final time to concentrate on your studies. You are very fortunate to be in in the course – you know that. We were pressured by the Vice-Chancellor, and we agreed on the condition that you kept up. You do realise examinations are coming up? And I will be personally scrutinising your papers, as will Professor Dawson-Walker, and all the other Professors in fact. You will be given, shall we say, special treatment. And if you fail, you will be asked to leave the University. You do realise that?'

All was silent for a moment. The typewriters had stopped – strange – but Shelley could hear a helicopter going overhead in the direction of the Children's Hospital. Whenever she heard those helicopters, she thought of the tragedy that must be occurring.

She could still remember the pain in her leg, and the nurses making her scream, and that pale blue light coming in from windows so high you couldn't see out of them – but she knew they'd saved her life, the Children's. That's why she wanted to do all this – to save lives, not to torture cats.

Shelley brought herself back to the great man and his portrait, deciding what angle to take, what to say. She took a breath and adopted a friendly smile.

'Thank you, Dean Thompson. I do appreciate the time you've spent with me but I'm afraid that certain aspects of the course cause some students great concern. Not only cruelty to animals. Take trafficking in bodies for example.'

'Trafficking in bodies? Whatever are you talking about?'

'Our boxes of bones. Where do they come from? Do you know, Dean Thompson? Shouldn't you know? What would the public think? Killing people – it's generally frowned upon.'

'You have more pressing matters to be worrying about Miss Conway. As I said, just because you are a mature-age student—'

'Nothing could be more pressing. And maybe you need a few mature-age students around to see the right and the wrong. I'm going to find out where our bones come from. I've heard it's India. India. That sounds a bit colonial, don't you think?'

Dean Thompson's face was now suffused with a purplish wash, the same colour as his bow tie. Looked like he was being strangled.

'That is precisely the sort of activity you should not be doing. A complete waste of time.'

'Waste of time? What about wasting the time of students who can't hack the medical course because they've actually got feelings? The few that care about people and animals? That's why they get psychological problems.'

'What a lot of claptrap. The University of Australia medical degree is one of the world's finest, and the best in the southern hemisphere. The curriculum has not changed in over a hundred years. You are privileged, very privileged to be studying this course.'

'Yes, Dean Thompson.' Be docile some of the time. Confuse him.

'I want to make one or two things quite clear.' Dabs the illustrious forehead.

'Yes, Dean Thompson.'

'If you don't pass your exams you will be sent down as an outright fail, no right of supplementary examinations or repeat.' Keeps looking at Shelley over his glasses. Dabs again.

'And if I find you've been engaging in any subversive activities, I repeat, any, I will send you down under Section 12 (f) of the University Statutes. Vice-Chancellor or no Vice-Chancellor.' Doesn't take his eyes off Shelley. 'Do you have that down, Mr Smith?'

'Yes, Dean Thompson,' squeaks the Bandicoot. Talk about Uriah Heep.

'Miss Conway, Section 12 (f) deals with Deliberate Student Misconduct. That would cover many of your activities I believe, including interference with other students' rights to access to educational materials. That is bones, Miss Conway, bones. You have now been officially warned.'

The Dean was giving his gold pen multiple revolutions.

'Dean Thompson, there is actually something missing from your famous curriculum.' Shelley stood up.

'And what would that be?'

'Humanity.'

'Humanity? What are you talking about?' Thompson had stood up too. 'I don't think humanity is a science, do you Professor Dawson-Walker?'

'*My refuge is humanity*. That's from Tagore. Nobel Prize-winning poet, from India. You should teach humanity.'

'It just keeps coming doesn't it?' Professor Diprotodon said to the Bandicoot. 'The mumbo-jumbo.'

Enthusiastic nodding from Uriah Bandicoot.

'You're talking complete rubbish, Miss Conway. Goodbye.'

The Bandicoot didn't bother to stand.

Typewriters silent. No doubt about it – she was the morning's entertainment for Professor Diprotodon and his secretaries.

As she strode down the corridor, she heard the two old farts laughing.

'She'll probably come back as a Hare Krishna.'

'Have to shave off that hair.' Two big laughs and three delicate titters.

The shits. Shits and fuckwits. Humanity? They wouldn't have a clue. It only takes one letter to turn human into humane, gentlemen.

Shelley liked to give Bob an update when she got home. She'd wheel the bike into the College bike shed, then clump upstairs, unlock her door, lock it behind her, turn Bob's skull around to face the bed, plonk down and have a chat.

They'd sit in the darkening room, listening to the birds roosting for the night. Cockatoos and kookaburras making a commotion, starlings making a buzz. The only birds she didn't like were pigeons. They were ugly, incessant and had gimlet-eyes.

Today she'd bought a Passiona from the drink machine downstairs to help her calm down. She just had about thirty minutes before she had to put on her maids' uniform and report for work.

Hoped the young gentlemen had settled down since last night. The serving of the soup was quite something. A dildo had come winging over from the next table. The pink dildo spinning in the mushroom soup was a sight she'd never forget.

She just didn't know how much more of that witty frivolity she could take.

And the run-in with the Dean today had added to her general crankiness.

'So, I've put them on notice, Bob, the Dean and the Prof. They know I'm on their case about the cats and frogs. I'm going to report them to the RSPCA.'

Bob was interested, she could tell.

'Only problem would be if they kick me out of the course.' That was the one big downer – getting expelled. Or they could just make sure she failed every exam. Then the opportunity would be lost. She had to play her cards carefully, and not lose sight of her main purpose. Might have to do some study.

'I do want to achieve my goals, Bob, but I'm not going to let them get away with everything. It's our duty to speak up when we see cruelty, isn't it? I'm sure Tagore will have something to say – let's see—'

No civilised society can thrive when it has victims whose human-ity has been permanently mutilated.

'That's a good quote from Tagore. How can we be a civilised society when we completely ignore the humanity of our victims? We must treat humanity with humanity. This demonstrates that the word humanity can refer to people, or an attribute. I like that. Nice one, Bob.'

It was then that she saw a white envelope slide slowly under her door. Strange, no-one ever came to her room – it was so far off the beaten track.

And whoever it might be was taking pains to be very quiet, because she could normally hear every step on the floorboards outside, and right now she could hear nothing.

On the front was written 'MISS S. CONWAY' in slightly childish capitals

Inside a folded sheet of paper with individual letters cut out of a newspaper:

Dissection class was twitchy today. As Shelley walked in, she could hear the scraping of stools and a general heightened noise level. They were moving onto head and neck which meant everyone was crowding round the tops of the cadavers and re-arranging stools. Getting a good spot.

Eddie and Jeffrey already had the three stools organised – one advantage of being a small group.

'Hey, Shelley! You're going so well,' said Jeffrey. 'We're going to make it impossible for the Dean to fail you.'

'Thank you, Jeffrey.'

'How are you faring with your bones?' asked Eddie.

'Well, I did the humerus last night. That's a straightforward bone, isn't it? Predictable. But I'm feeling a bit depressed.'

'About?'

'Bob. My bones. His background story. We're mates now. He gets to look out over the trees and we have chats.'

She wouldn't tell them about the note under the door. They'd freak out.

'Chats?' Eddie and Jeffrey spoke in unison.

'Bob chats. In his own way.'

'Shelley, this is ridiculous,' said Jeffrey. 'Look at me, I'm Indian, and I'm coping. I'm not going crazy. You are. You're being completely stupid. Get over it.'

Well. That put her in her place.

He changed the subject. 'Shelley, the face is too small for us all to dissect at once, so we're taking turns. I'll show you where we're up to. That's Wharton's Duct there, you know, the sub-mandibular duct? Well, we have to dissect that out and not cut it.'

'Or the lingual nerve,' said Eddie. 'You cut that nerve and you get sued for a million bucks. Anyway, we learned this mnemonic from them.' He indicated the Turds, then stood up and cleaned and straightened his glasses.

'The lingual nerve:

Took a swerve
Around the hyoglossus
Well I'll be fucked
Said Wharton's Duct
The bastard's double crossed us.'

'Excuse my French. That's how you remember the lingual nerve.'

'I'm shocked Eddie,' said Shelley, 'and when there's a lady present too.'

'Lady, what lady?' said Jeffrey.

General laughter. Stares from tables A, B and C.

She took her turn at the head and neck, dissectors in her right hand, Volume 3 of Cunningham's (Head and Neck) in the left. She tried to fathom the course of the lingual nerve, the nerve which would have enabled Methuselah to taste his vitamised vegetables. She was no Eddie: she found it hard to concentrate on the job at hand and keep an ear open for the gossip at the same time.

Eddie was in a fawn cardigan today, with a diamond-patterned tie in orange and teal. He was holding court with fascinating tales from the front – his theatre orderly job. Eddie knew all the jargon and was even on first-name terms with some of the doctors.

'We've got a new med reg, a woman—'

'What's a med reg?' asked Jeffrey.

'Medical Registrar. You know, senior junior doctor. So this huge fellow with tatts everywhere calls the med reg over and says, "Nurse, can you get me a bottle?"'

'You should have seen her. She was ropable. She said, "I'm not a nurse" and marched off.'

The two boys laughed.

Eddie turned to Shelley. 'Shelley wouldn't appreciate being called a nurse, would you, Shell?' Both boys laughed again, hoping for an entertaining rejoinder.

'You're wrong there, Eddie,' said Shelley, putting down her dissectors and her book. 'I wouldn't care what I was called. But that doctor – her attitude needs to change.'

'But you wouldn't want people to think that because you're female, you must be a nurse?' said Jeffrey. 'What would Germaine Greer say?'

'I couldn't care less, Jeffrey. How dare she be offended because she's been called nurse? Does she think she's better than a nurse? What an arrogant—'

'Calm down, Shelley,' said Eddie. 'You'll cut something you shouldn't. I just assumed—'

'Well don't.'

Eddie looked crestfallen.

'Sorry, Eddie. I didn't mean to attack you. Go on with your story and I'll shut up.'

She mustn't react every time someone baited her. Keep in everyone's good books, that was the thing.

The session finished at four pm and as the boys packed up Shelley asked the demonstrator if she could stay back to revise the course of the lingual nerve. His jaw nearly fell off its hinges. Eddie gave Shelley a thumbs up, and Jeffrey flashed a joyful smile. Shelley was pulling her finger out at last.

'So long as you don't cut that lingual nerve,' said the demonstrator, 'and you'll have to be finished by five – Mr Jones will want to close up then.'

Jeffrey was on his way out when he called back to her. 'Oh yes, Shelley, want to come with us to the pathology museum tomorrow? Nine am? We're supposed to be searching for musculoskeletal pathology.'

'Okay, Jeffrey. Thanks.'

At quarter to five Horrie came in to get the cadavers back in their formalin wraps. Like putting chooks away, thought Shelley.

'There's m'little mermaid,' he said to her chest. 'Now it's not Sandy. No, it's, it's – it's Shelley, that's it.'

The rash on Horrie's face seemed to be worse – not only blotchy, but violaceous. She'd always been wanting to see a violaceous rash, this would be violaceous, she was sure of it. She must look up what the diagnosis might be.

Shelley adopted her most winning manner and asked if he minded if she spent a bit of extra time in the dissection room over the next few weeks, catching up. She'd missed out on a bit because she'd been ill. Could she perhaps help him now with the clearing up?

'Yes,' he said to her boobs. She'd have to put up with that for the greater good, and that good was Shelley Conroy's exam results.

The Pathology museum was, for Shelley, the embodiment of hell. The walls were lined with shelves of ghastly pathologies in specimen pots. Foetuses with deformities, organs with huge cancers, whole heads with leprosy, malformations of every kind in every organ. Group D for Dregs headed to the skeletal system section and took notes on the various afflictions. Severe curvatures of the spine. A disease that fuses all the joints. An osteosarcoma necessitating amputation.

And a very small person, maybe six years old, with each of his shortened legs bent into curves like cabriole legs on a Victorian chair. 'Polio,' said Eddie and moved on quickly, Jeffrey also took just a quick look. 'Come on, Shelley you don't want to look at that. So depressing.' The boys were almost too considerate at times.

She told Bob about it later. 'They'd decided to stand him up, Bob, with his little walking sticks. The label said: "Poliomyelitis, severe contractures, age unknown, India. Acquired 1969." Countryman of yours, Bob. Nothing else. No acknowledgement of the fact that polio's a completely preventable disease, or that by 1969 new cases of polio were unknown in Australia. He's just a collectable. An artefact from the exotic east. We know all about that, don't we Bob? Should I write a letter, Bob? Or am I making a fuss about nothing? Will they just add it to their "Shelley Conway Troublemaker" file?'

When Shelley walked into the lecture theatres now, she found people made room for her. Lots of room. Like a whole row. Lectures were such a waste of time anyway. Simply a challenge to write down everything on the overhead slide before the lecturer changed it. And if he did move on too quickly there'd be a large sigh from the fifty per cent of the students who were still awake. What a bloody useless waste of time.

The squeaking of the drop-down desks. The continuous murmur from the back rows. The occasional teasing remark from the lecturer – 'And I do strongly recommend you learn this formula' – implying that it might be on the exam. Maybe. You couldn't trust them.

That drowning feeling which made Shelley feel like a floundering fish, a flapping bottom-feeder about to suffocate. The Great Loneliness of the Lecture Theatre.

If the seating plan for the lecture theatre were an official subject Shelley would have got top marks. She'd analysed it to perfection. Two rows up the back for the boys who went to the prestigious Presbyterian School, then two rows for the prestigious Anglican school. A few Baptists and other strange sects claiming to be Christian were in the next couple of rows down. Then three or four rows for the Catholic schools, with their own sub-hierarchy. Jesuits were above the rest – that's all Shelley knew about Catholics. The front rows of the lecture theatres were reserved for the Asians and Jews – boys like Eddie and Jeffrey sat here. And then there were a few spots for people from even more unfortunate places like Government schools, or extremely weird places like the country.

The boys in the front rows were the only ones who listened – the boys in the private school rows up the back took advantage of the elevation and spent their time throwing paper darts.

Girls were uncommon, and could distribute themselves where they liked.

Except for Shelley. She had a whole row to herself. She couldn't really care less, but it was extraordinary that two hundred students could treat a fellow student as if she was carrying the plague and walk right past even though she was sitting all by herself in the row. And these people were headed for a career in caring. She couldn't do that to another human being. No way.

There was only one row in which other students might talk to her on the odd occasion that they showed up, and that was the 'weirdos' row'. There was Feather with her caftans and feathers and eyes that never quite connected, and Trace from Outer Space who was rumoured to be in a cult. That was a popular diagnosis for anyone a bit different – Shelley had heard them say that about her. It might just have been true of Tracey.

The bloke Shelley liked best was the one she called Puffing Billy, for obvious reasons. Lately he'd been doing less weed and more hard stuff, which she was anxious about, and so the joke had turned into a line about staying on the rails no matter what, and not being tempted to leave the rails like Tootle in the *Little Golden Books*. Billy said he'd always liked the picture of Tootle frolicking in the meadow with a daisy chain in his boiler. Shelley said that wouldn't get him through the exams, frolicking in the meadow. And then couldn't believe she'd said that. How self-righteous she'd become! But she did worry about her mate, Billy. And even though she'd started the course after him, she had more of a clue about what was going on than Billy did.

'I'm nowhere near the rails today, mate.'

'Where are you, Billy?'

'I'm astral travelling in a beautiful space meadow.' Billy was leaning back in the blue seat with the drop-down desk down, his eyes closed and a euphoric look on his face. His blonde hair hung down in ropes.

'Okay.'

The Biochemistry lecturer was now ten minutes late.

'What've you been up to, Shell?' He hadn't opened his eyes.

'Oh well, the same old. I'm trying to find out where they get our boxes of bones from. Don't you think it's terrible that we don't know?'

'Guess so. Hadn't really thought about it. We're all made of stardust, Shell.'

'Stardust? That's not much help if you've been turned into a box of bones.'

Puffing Billy sat up, fire in his eyes. 'But don't you see Shell – we're all connected. Astral travelling's amazing, especially if you're stoned. Amazing, Shell.'

'Oh?'

'Yeah, mate.'

He resumed his former position of travel.

Shelley could smell something that had travelled from Bali on his tie-dyed T-shirt, or maybe it was from Nepal on the yak wool jacket.

'Billy?'

'Yeah, mate.'

'Billy – what shit are you on?'

'Weed, babe – hash – smack. Whatever I can get, y'know.'

'Oh. Is it hard to get, mate?'

'Well used to be there was plenty of grass but nothing else. Now it's easier to get H. I'm not complainin'.'

'You'll have to show me mate.'

He opened one eye and looked at her. 'You into it, Shell? You're always at me to get off it.'

'Yeah, but you know, sometimes—'

'Yeah, right. Well, I'll come and help you with that soup kitchen one night, sure I will. Promise, mate.'

'That'd be excellent. Maybe we can hang out afterwards.'

'Most definitely.'

The lecturer had shown up. What a pity.

Puffing Billy had one last thing to say before he slid into the oblivion of the lecture. He tried to whisper but wasn't very successful. 'That Krebs' cycle,' he said, 'when you're on this shit, it's like pulsating man – like the cycle's coming right out at you, you know?'

'I'm Shelley Conway, Professor Lennard. A first-year med student. Oh, thank you.'

Shelley sat down in an old University armchair which must have been made before springs were invented. In any case she'd have a bugger of a job getting up. Nice décor. A cirrhotic liver on that window ledge, a row of heads in large cubic pots on the shelves. The liver was beige and stringy with lumps of gristle, and the heads all purplish with closed eyes and thick lips.

'Now, what can I do for you?'

'It's about an exhibit in your Pathology museum.'

'It's not about exam results then?'

'No, I'm only in first year. We haven't done Pathology yet.'

'Of course, of course. Well, that's a relief. Go on.'

'The one of the little boy with polio contractures. The one whose skeleton is standing up with the two sticks for crutches. He comes from India.'

'Ah yes, we only got that a year ago. It's a real find. One of our treasures I would say. Nothing like it in Australia, even in the U.K. I suspect.'

'Well, Professor Lennard, I'd like to know how you got it?'

'How we got it?' Professor Lennard's eyes glinted.

'Yes.'

'Well, that's something I'm not really able to discuss, Miss Conway. You will understand, I'm sure. We have our eyes and ears open of course for opportunities like this. Opportunities from which our students will benefit. Do you have a particular question about the specimen?'

'Yes, I do. I want to know how and why he got polio when it's a preventable disease? I want to know where exactly he came from? And how you got his skeleton? Was his corpse stolen or was he murdered? Just that sort of thing, Professor Lennard. Professor Lennard? Are you okay?

'I'll leave it there, Professor Lennard. I'll be writing to you in the near future just to follow up.'

Puffing Billy kept his word and came into the soup kitchen one Friday night. Shelley didn't even realise he was there – partly because she was busy, and partly because, well – she just didn't recognise him.

The caravan was down near the river, under the neon signs for Allen's Sweets, which meant that everyone and everything including the soup was alternating orange and blue. They had a few fold out tables and chairs and some white fairy lights strung around which made it friendly enough.

Serving the soup didn't take much time, but talking to the customers did.

There was Harry the Hirer who had a whole hardware store hanging off his piercings and had a big heroin problem and Stewart who was always trying to crack onto some poor woman or other. Shelley listened but wondered whether she was encouraging a pervert. Then there were Doris and Ida, the two sisters who both had intellectual disabilities and laughed loudly at anything resembling a joke. And George, a big block of a man. The hungry Hungarian, they called him because he was always as hungry as all get-up. Opinions were divided as to whether this was due to dope, or just normal hunger. Always had thirds and fourth servings, if there was enough, and a lot of butter on the bread please. Shelley noticed his eyes were red more often than not, so thought she knew the answer.

And then over the counter who was there, but Billy. He looked terrible.

'It's Puffing Billy. Great to see you mate, come to help?' Maybe not. 'Like some soup? It's chicken and veg.'

'No, mate. I'm strung out. Bad.'

He was much skinnier than last time she'd seen him, and was sweating and shaking, with pupils big as saucers. He was strung out all right.

'Shit, mate – you look terrible. Hang on a minute.'

Shelley took off her hat and apron and came out from the caravan. She put an arm around Puffing Billy's shoulders and took him over to an empty table. It turned her stomach to smell him, and turned her heart to feel his bones, his shaking bones.

'Where's your jacket, mate?'

'Sold it.'

'Oh.'

70

'Mate,' said Billy, 'Can you lend me a bit of dough? I'm desperate.'

'I can see that. I'll have a look. But Billy, wouldn't it be better to get some help. Like go to The Lighthouse. Or Central Clinic. They can help you there, get off stuff you know.'

Billy looked like a bird flapping on the side of the road. A pigeon that's been run over. The neon sign flashing orange and blue didn't help.

'I'll take you there now, right away. Taxi. I'll pay.'

The rattling was starting again. Must be his teeth.

'Billy?'

He stood up. 'Don't worry. I gotta go.'

She reached into her jeans and took everything out and put it on the table. 'Who's your contact, mate?'

'No contact.'

'Where d'you go?'

'Vine Street.' Billy looked at Shelley. 'Why d'ya wanna know?'

'Oh, just wondering.'

'Well I don't know his name. Says he's got friends at Uni, and he can arrange to get me failed.'

'Bullshit.' Shelley was picking out a few coins for her train fare home. 'No-one can get you failed. You can have all this Billy, but I'm going take you down to Central Clinic now. They've got stuff can take away all the shaking and pain. Help you get off the hard shit.'

Billy was either coughing or spewing on the ground – she couldn't tell which.

'Hey mate Billy, we gotta get you back on the rails, okay?'

The shaking was getting worse.

'C'mon, let's go. I'll just tell my mates.'

She stuck her head through the caravan door and told the guys she had to leave – emergency, sorry she couldn't help with the clean-up – but she'd be there next Friday night as usual.

When she turned around the money had gone, and so had Billy.

'Rails, mate, rails,' she said to no-one.

'Yeah, mate. Rails.' That was George speaking. He was tucking into number three.

'You can't get into trouble on the rails, George. No choices to make.'

'Yeah. You sound like you know what you're talkin' about, Shell.'

'The pelvis. The pelvic cavity blah blah blah.

'My God Bob, how they make something so interesting sound so boring. We'll have to wait 'til after Christmas to finish the pelvis.'

One Friday night after work, Shelley had an almost irresistible urge to walk down Vine Street, it was a very long time since she'd been there, and she pulled her beanie down real low, even though it was a warm night.

The same old crowd was hanging around the supermarket and the car park behind. Someone begging just there, someone looking wrecked on the bench. Nothing had changed.

'Chasin'?'

She looked up, stunned for a moment.

'No, mate, no.'

'I seen you before?'

'No mate, I'm from interstate.'

'That's funny. I could swear—'

She couldn't hang around, that was for sure.

She stopped outside a shoe shop window and could see a reflection from across the road. It was Billy, stumbling down the street. She turned around to watch him. He stopped a couple of people. Knocked back once; the other person gave him some coins. Then he veered off into a side street and she saw him pause for a couple of minutes trying to get his hand into his jeans. He was having trouble, even though his jeans were hanging off him. Very shaky. He eventually got his hand into the right pocket, and he pulled out a lot of notes. Counted them, took a while. Passers-by looking at him. Put some notes back. Walked further up the lane to a parked car, an old Falcon. She couldn't see any details in the dark, but maybe a brown colour. A window was rolled down, the old one-two, in-out.

Billy lurched up into the dark of the lane. But Shelley knew there was a toilet block with a light at the back of the carpark and that's where Billy was headed.

It was December 23rd when the second note arrived on Pluto. This time she was asleep, with the door locked and double-checked. But something had woken Shelley – a footstep maybe, or some rapid breathing from someone who'd just climbed the stairs, or the rustle of an envelope on a dusty floor. Her tiny window had no functional curtains, and the moon was just rising so there was enough light to reveal an envelope.

Shelley felt a surge of fear. Who was this person who could come so close to her, and wish her such harm?

She stamped out of bed, flung some heavy books on the floor, unlocked the door and flung it open.

'Fuck off!'

There was no-one out there, no-one. No-one to hear her.

She saw the name on the envelope – same childish lettering. Maybe done with a non-dominant hand, that'd be it. And the folded note inside, same cut-out letters:

Shelley couldn't sleep for the rest of the night.

The next morning she went to see the Security Supervisor for the College. He was a bulky ex-Army man with a crew cut, and short sleeves even though it was cold.

'I think someone's coming into the maids' quarters at night.'

'Well, we've tried and tried with you maids. Every time we put new locks on the outside doors or new security you just disable it. It's either your blokes, or you maids letting blokes in. There's nothing more I can do. Just lock your door at night.'

'But people are outside my door.'

'Well, I'm sure they're not after you, so I wouldn't be too worried. Anything else I can help you with? No? Now you have a good Christmas and I'll see you in the New Year.'

On Christmas Eve, Tomas pulled something out of the pocket of his houndstooth pants. It was a little brown velvet box with a cream satin ribbon around it. Looked old.

'Open it this evening, Christmas Eve.'

Shelley had a gift for Tomas hidden behind the trays. Tomas unwrapped the present and then just stood gazing at the hardback copy of *The Castle*.

'You are a good, good girl,' he said.

'Look inside.'

Tomas found the inscription she had written in the front, in fountain pen.

To Tomas, Happy Christmas

From Shelley xxx

'I have spent all my life resisting the desire to end it.'
– Franz Kafka

She thought that quote might be of general relevance, but when she re-read it she wasn't so sure.

Shelley managed two nights at home with the olds. She opened Tomas' box on Christmas Eve, as instructed, and found a gold brooch like a branch, with leaves and deep red stones. The gothic-looking writing on a manila card inside the box read:

Garnet, Praha, belong to my mother, Eva Novotny.

Tomas Novotny

Shelley kept her promise of an outfit for Skye's Barbie. Shelley had made it herself, put it in a box, and labelled it: 'Revolutionary Barbie'. She'd made a minuscule Viet Cong flag, a little T-shirt with a tiny slogan – 'SMASH US IMPERIALISM' – some jeans, and a Mao cap.

Skye gave Shelley a hug and said no-one at school would have a Barbie outfit like that.

'Morning, Bob. How's your leg? Mine's giving me hell today. You and I are going to do tib and fib together. And that will be very interesting for both of us. I'll be able to see what effect those poor weak muscles have had on your bones.'

'Well for a start, your fibula's about three centimetres shorter than it should be and the tibia is twisted. And all your muscle markings are pretty unimpressive. And I can see how your knee and your ankle are both partially dislocated. You would have been limping behind all the other kids, Bob. Easy prey.'

Images of a living Bob came to her every time she opened the box. Was he the same age as Shelley when he somehow died and was boiled down? How do they get the flesh off? What about his family?

And why did no-one care? No-one ever asked, or if they did, the responses were always the same.

'Where do they come from?'

'The bones? Oh, don't worry about it, just India. Or someplace like that.'

Did no-one else worry about these things?

'How come everyone's so quiet today?' The dissection room was like a morgue. No-one talking, no jokes. Weird, Shelley thought.

'Haven't you heard?' said Eddie.

'No, what?'

'That boy that you call the Train Engine, or whatever—'

'Billy?'

'He died at the weekend.'

'Oh no. No. Died of what?'

'OD. Well, that's what everyone's saying, It's about the third one on campus this month apparently.'

'Poor poor Billy.'

No-one seemed to care too much about Puffing Billy. She couldn't find anyone who knew anything about a funeral. There wasn't a death notice in the paper, not even in *The Sun*.

If only she'd caught up with him more, maybe she'd have found some stuff out, helped him, stopped him dying. Shit.

Now there'd be absolutely no-one to talk to in lectures. Maybe the boys would let her sit in the Asian section.

Shelley had started to help Horrie with his tasks at the end of the day. As long there were some good songs on the radio the task was almost bearable. She'd persuaded herself that the end justified the means – the end being discovery of the origin of the bones.

One Tuesday afternoon when no dissection classes were scheduled, they were turning some new bodies in their formalin baths. 'When I Die' was on the radio, in between Race 5 and Race 6 at the Valley. Horrie was serenading the cadavers along with Blood, Sweat and Tears. Horrie was tone deaf, but that didn't dampen his enthusiasm.

He'd had made up his Special Embalming Potion this morning and was in a grand mood. Twenty litres of pine oil, phenol, di-hydroxyethoxy-methane and formalin, in the right proportions, for each bod.

'There, that looks right,' he said, and then came up close and whispered in her ear. 'Preparation is the key, Shelley lass.'

'I believe you, Horrie.' Moving away, not showing any interest.

The next song turned out to be from Woodstock.

'You all right, Shelley?'

'Yes, Horrie.' Reminded her of Puffing Billy.

The bodies went into the fridge for months and underwent The Spray in a special rotation of Spray One and Spray Two. Shelley wasn't yet inducted into the Order of The Spray but she had found out what the secret ingredient was – Dettol.

'We never get mould now we use Dettol – but mind you don't tell anyone now.'

And who on earth would she blab these secrets to? Everyone she knew would run a thousand miles if she started talking about that sort of stuff.

But she did have a matter to discuss with Horrie. She hoped she'd accumulated enough brownie points.

'Horrie,' said Shelley, 'you know the bone boxes?'

Horrie placed a stray arm from 70-062 back into its bath and looked at Shelley. At least she thought he did.

'I've just been wondering how you get them. I mean we buy them from you, but where do you get them from? Just wondering.'

Horrie had finished cannulating and held out his hands over the tub to let the formalin run off before he took his gloves off. 'Shelley lass, you'll get into trouble one day.'

'No, well I wouldn't say a word to anyone if I did know – I'm just curious that's all.'

Horrie was washing his hands.

Horrie was drying his hands.

Race 8 was about to start, and she shut up. Horrie had his form guide and his blue pen out and sat down on his stool near the body bath.

But 'Troubador' didn't get a placing, and Horrie was disgusted. 'She's a bloody good horse and perfect track for her. Crooks the lot of them.' He threw the newspaper in the bin.

'Shelley, you need to stay right out of it.' His leery eye was drifting all over the place. 'Get me?'

'Yes, Horrie. I get you. But Horrie I've got another question.'

'Yes?'

'My Dad's given me a couple of bottles of good whisky. Single, double, I forget. But he says it's good. Would you be a whisky drinker?'

'Now you're talking,' said Horrie.

'Bob, this is about your skull. It supports the structures of the face and provides a protective cavity for the brain. The skull is composed of two parts: the cranium and the mandible.

'Functions of the skull include protection of the brain, fixing the distance between the eyes to allow stereoscopic vision, and fixing the position of the ears to enable sound localisation of the direction and distance of sounds. In some animals such as horned ungulates, the skull also has a defensive function by providing the mount (on the frontal bone) for the horns. It's got twenty-two bones, and I have to learn about every one of them.'

'Shelley lass, you've come to help me?'

Horrie stood up rather quickly, opened his desk drawer and threw the sheet of paper on his desk into it.

'Yes, Horrie.'

'Ah, that was such a nice drop you bought me.' He gave Shelley one of his leery smiles.

She thought she should buy a white T-shirt and put a big arrow on it pointing upwards to her face and write: 'My face is up there'.

'Not a problem, Horrie. I can get you more if you like.' Regardless, she would avoid any sort of top or dress from now on. She'd stick to massive long-sleeved numbers. Something like a burka or a habit, that would be good.

'Aye, girlie, that would be a comfort.' He turned away from her and put both hands on his desk. 'Here lass, I don't know where the bones come from. The Prof handles all the invoices and pays the accounts.'

He looked at her again, but there was a grey glint in his eyes and Shelley knew he was lying. He also knew she was on the prowl for information.

'We don't want our little operation to stop.' He said this softly. 'You understand?'

Shelley wasn't stupid. She nodded.

'Now, Shelley lass, I must attend to the bods. He ushered her out of his office, with a hand on her back. A stroking hand.

'Just got to lock up.'

Shelley waited while he went down the corridor to room 420. That single sheet of paper was in that drawer. She ducked into the office, opened the drawer, grabbed the document, stuffed it put it into her pocket without looking at it, closed the drawer, and returned to the corridor, heart hammering.

In a few seconds Horrie was there again and standing just that bit too close. Time to go.

She forgot all about the piece of paper, and it was only when she arrived home to Pluto that night that she remembered it.

It was a carbon copy of docket, with a big diagonal slash across it, and the word 'PAID'.

INVOICE

TRIVEDI BROS

CALCUTTA

INDIA

To: H. JONES

UNIVERSITY OF AUSTRALIA

Natural human skeletons	50000 R
half-sets 100 boxes @500 R	
Shipping 4 kg per set @ 50 R	5000 R
Grand Total	55000 R

Terms: 30 days

Agent: Odyssey shipping, Australia

Shelley asked Jeffrey in their next dissection class.

'Jeffrey?'

'Yes, Shelley?'

'How much is five hundred rupees in Australian dollars?'

'Bit under ten dollars.'

'And fifty rupees?'

'One dollar, obviously.'

'So five hundred and fifty rupees is about eleven dollars?'

'Yes, of course, why?'

'Just wanted to make sure of something.' But to herself she said, 'We've all been totally ripped off.'

The General Post Office was, for any capital city in an Australian state or territory, the testament to the city's belief in its own importance. This one had columns of such stature that you were transformed into a reverential state of worship for the city before you even entered. Inside, there was that echoing sound which denotes a really historic building. Shelley didn't even have to look up to know that the ceilings would be a long way away and painted in green and grey with touches of gold.

Now, which desk? Poste restante? Parcels? Philatelic supplies? General postage? Try that.

'I'm just wondering if you would have a phone book for Calcutta?'

The thin-faced woman behind the counter was trying to be helpful.

'Calcutta? That's in Africa isn't it still? Hard to know these days. Do they have phones there?'

'I'm actually after an address.'

'I'm sorry, we don't have books of addresses. I don't think we can help you. We have lots of phone books – over there – but they're all normal places. All I can suggest is that you ring International Directory Assistance. You can use one of our phone booths. It's free, until you get connected that is.'

The phone booth was stuffy and smelt of sweat and cigarettes. It was lined with that white soundproof Caneite with little holes, which gave Shelley something to do while she was waiting. Put her pencil in every hole.

'India? Hold the line please.'

'Calcutta? You might have some problems getting through there. Hold the line please.'

'Trivedi – how do you spell that? Do you have an initial please Madam? Not residential. You should have said so. Business. I shall try our *Yellow Pages* for you.'

'What type of business Madam? I beg your pardon? Human bones did you say? I'm a busy person, Madam, and I don't like pranksters. Something scientific? Well we'll try that. Here is Trivedi Bros Anatomic and Scientific. Does that sound right? You want the address? Do you have a pen please Madam? And what is the weather like in Australia?'

Trivedi Bros

104 – 106 Kalu Ram Road

Calcutta. India

Dear Trivedi Bros,

I am interested in buying a human skeleton as I am a medical student. Do you have a price list or catalogue and could you send it to me? I would be happy to pay for the postage.

Yours sincerely

Shelley Conway (Miss)

Coming home to her little hidey hole wouldn't be too bad had it not been for the envelopes. Shelley would leave the desk lamp on if she was going to be late, and give Bob a 'hoy' as soon as she got in.

'Bob, whatcha been up to? I'll turn you around now. It's getting dark and you can't see out of that window. There, now you can watch me studying, got to do a whole lot of work tonight, Bob, like oxidative phosphorylation and stroke volume and God knows what else.'

Death is not extinguishing the light; it is only putting out the lamp because the dawn has come.

'That's Tagore, Bob, but you know that.'

On the first of February Shelley received her third note. This time she heard the post boy. It was three am and she woke to the quietest footsteps on the landing outside her room and the softest breaths.

Only a couple of yards away from her.

Sounded male.

Sounded heavy.

Sounded cruel.

A male who was trying to be ultra-quiet, but failing.

Trivedi Bros
104 – 106 Kalu Ram Road
Calcutta. India

Dear Conway Miss,

Thank you for your letter. We do not have a catalogue as you request. Our range of the quallity
human skeleton products and education products is
available from Mr H. Jones, Anatomy Department,
University of Australia. We emphasis that our products are all natural human material.

We wish you success in your schollaly endeavour.

Yours sincerely

Trivedi Bros

There, proof of address and proof of crime. She had all she needed.

'Bob, I'm buggered, truly I am. But, guess what, I've paid for my tickets to Calcutta. Fair dinks. It was a good deal with Student Travel. They think I'm off to find a Swami. Nope. I'm just going to call in on Trivedi's and ask a few questions, assess the situation. I might be tilting at windmills, Bob. That's from *Don Quixote*. Yes, it might all be hopeless, but at least I will have tried. And if I do confirm my suspicions, I don't know what

I'll do. But at least I can make it public knowledge and maybe people will boycott the sale of human bones. That seems do-able. What d'you reckon, Bob? Let's ask Rabi—'

You can't cross the sea merely by standing and staring at the water.

'That means I must go, mustn't I? And I might even be able to visit the home of your old mate Tagore while I'm there, and yes I will pass on your regards.'

'But Bob – I'm not telling too many people, especially not Horrie, okay?'

'Mum, it's Shell.'

'Shelley, darling, how are you?'

'Good thanks Mum, how're you and Dad?'

'Fine. Your father's at a party meeting. A young chap picked him up. Nice of him. Wants pre-selection of course. So, what's news?'

'Everything's fine and I'm going away for a short while.'

'Going away? Where?'

'Well, you'll be surprised, but it's India.'

'India?'

'Yep.'

'Why on earth—'

'I'm doing some research. Part of the deal.'

'Research into what?'

'Into where our sets of bones come from, you know the ones we have?'

'What's that got to do with India?'

'Well, that's where they come from.'

'So you know the answer already then.'

'That's just the point, Mum. India is not a sufficient answer. It's appalling that people think it is.'

'Well, I think it's a sufficient answer – do any of the other students worry about where their bones have come from?'

'That's just it. No, they don't. It's amazing. I've asked heaps of them, well quite a few, and they just say "India". As if that explains everything.'

'Well, doesn't it? I mean there are too many people in India, and they've probably run out of places to bury them.'

'I think you might feel a bit differently if it was your relative.'

Brief silence. Mum thinking. Shelley hoped there wouldn't be tears because then she'd feel really bad.

'Is anyone going with you?'

'Well one of the students in my group, Jeffrey – he's Indian, Kumar is his real name, he's from Calcutta – he's getting his cousin to meet me and show me around.'

'Calcutta? Where the Black Hole is? Shelley, that doesn't sound like a very safe place.'

'I'll be fine, Mum, I won't go anywhere near the Black Hole, I promise. Besides, I'll have Jeffrey's cousin with me.'

'What's his name, Jeffrey's cousin?'

'Mr Mukherjee – or something like that anyway – he speaks good English. Jeffrey says he's got political leanings like mine. He works in his father's export business, silk.'

'I don't think I want to know about political leanings. Silk sounds all right I suppose. But what about money? And your job?'

'I've saved up. I've put all my pay from the restaurant into one bank book, and that's what I'm using. I might bring you back something nice – a caftan maybe—'

'Oh Shelley—'

'What Mum?'

'I don't want a caftan. I don't know how the authorities can let you do these risky things. And I don't know how your father will take it.'

'Well, it's my life, Mum.'

'We've heard that before, Shelley, and, and—'

'And what?

'Well, we've seen the consequences, let me put it that way.'

'What d'you mean?'

'Just be careful. I hope everybody knows what they're doing.'

'Everybody?'

'You know what I mean, Shelley. The – the Government, the police, everyone.'

'Yes, Mum.'

'And don't drink or eat anything.'

'No Mum, I won't, I promise.'

Shelley couldn't possibly tell her Mum that she did feel a touch nervous going to India. After all this was a quest based solely on a hunch.

She'd had her vaccinations. Cholera, typhoid, tetanus and tuberculosis. She could hardly move for days. Just as she decided she'd received the live cultures instead of the vaccines, she recovered.

She was packed a week before leaving. She had her travellers' cheques, and she'd photocopied the Calcutta Sightseeing section from *Fodor's Guide to India*, which amounted to half a page.

She'd requested some material from the Department of Foreign Affairs, and she now knew about one thousand times more about India than she'd known three weeks ago. Some of it she'd rather not have known. There were warnings for the whole of Bengal and the situation was 'volatile'.

But when you thought about it, they probably always said that, and, besides, it wouldn't affect a medical student from Australia. Just so long as Mum and Dad didn't find out.

Calcutta

S helley hadn't been too convinced by the results from her research on India, particularly the information on temperature. She'd decided the temperature was going to be much the same as home. But it turned out *Fodor's* was correct, and India was hot. Seriously hot. The short walk from the plane to the New Delhi airport building just about killed her. How on earth do people live here? So many of them, too. Maybe that's why it's so hot – all these bodies.

Inside, things were hotter still, even though it was near midnight. People shouting. Lights. And soldiers with large guns – machine guns. Shelley couldn't stop looking at them. She'd never seen a real machine gun before. Then she thought that this might look suspicious, so she tried not to look at them at all. Did she now appear even more guilty?

She'd put on a clean T-shirt in the plane toilets just before landing. Rolled on some deodorant and brushed her teeth. She still felt terrible. Exhausted and sweaty. Total waste of effort. And a waste of a clean T-shirt. She only had three T-shirts for the whole trip. Her jeans felt like thick wet cardboard. She was so hot.

Long queue at Immigration. She let a family with five adults and five children go through before her. The interaction between the family and Immigration involved many loud adult voices. The children were silent, just watching with large, unblinking eyes.

Eventually her turn came. She had all her documents neatly arranged. The official seemed to be able to feel his way around the documents without looking at them, thereby allocating one hundred per cent of his gaze for Shelley. A very special stare which made her nervous. She'd already decided not to mention the bones project. No, the best strategy to explain her short trip to India would be to provide detailed decoy information. She regaled the official with her life story and her reasons for coming to India. She was here to organise a future placement. She was a medical student who wanted to help India. She had always wanted to come to India, to Calcutta in particular, to do some voluntary work with Mother Theresa. Why, she, Shelley, was even known as Mother Theresa at her medical school back in Australia. She visited the homeless at a soup kitchen each week, usually vegetable, but sometimes chicken and vegetable. Bread rolls and butter too. It was very popular, but she supposed that there wouldn't be soup kitchens for the homeless here, just too many of them. And most people would be vegetarian, wouldn't they? She organised blood donation drives too, but people in Australia were so lazy or selfish, she didn't know which, and they were medical students too, you wouldn't believe it. She knew Indian people would be much more community minded.

The official looked at Shelley as if she was a new species of cockroach, not to be imported under any circumstance. Then, still staring at her, he gave her passport a punitive thump, and held the stamp down for a good minute. Got that cockroach, all right.

Shelley's suitcase made it all the way to Calcutta. Remarkable. The little case, covered with stickers, had somehow weaselled through both Singapore and New Delhi airports. Dear square suitcase, a present from her grandparents one Christmas. A bit old-fashioned now. None of those wheels like some people had, but it worked fine at holding stuff together. Plus, it told a life story – a few peace stickers, five different anti-Vietnam War stickers, a 'Hey, hey LBJ' sticker that was no longer current, but had a certain authenticity, and her latest, a large 'Stop Apartheid' sticker, with a picture of a leaping deer, and the word 'Springbokke' with a cross over it.

Just as she pulled the case off the luggage cart, she saw a broad-shouldered young man in a long-sleeved white tunic, long white pants and sandals striding down the concourse. He was looking to left and right and carrying a sign: 'MRS SHELLEY CONWAY'.

'Mrs Shelley?'

'Yes.'

'My name is Amit Mukherjee.' He slipped the signboard under one arm, put his hands into a prayer-like position in front of him and bowed. 'Namaste. Welcome to Calcutta. I am the son of Mr Aman Mukherjee, and the cousin of your friend Mr Kumar Sengupta.' He had earnest brown eyes, and spoke gently but deliberately, giving every syllable equal emphasis.

'How do you do, Mr Mukherjee,' said Shelley, holding out her hand. 'And by the way it's just Shelley, Shelley Conway, no Mrs.'

Amit paused for a couple of seconds, looked a little nonplussed, then did another namaste. Shelley wasn't sure if she had committed some sort of faux pax to do with handshaking, or a cultural offence by being female and single, or something else entirely. Now she thought about it, she did recall something about left and right hands. She converted her handshake invitation into the same prayer-like gesture with a small dip of her head. Hoped that this covered all the essential courtesies.

The airport was noisy and echoing and there were dozens of people in all sorts of robes and headgear circling her. Maybe wanting to take her in their taxis. Mr Mukherjee waved them away.

'And you must call me Amit.'

'Certainly, Amit.'

'You will be very tired after such a lengthy journey.'

It was hard to hear, and she found herself shouting.

'I am a bit tired, but it's very late for you too – to be picking me up, I mean. Isn't it about three am?'

'Picking you up? No, no, I am picking up your suitcase.' He laughed as he took the suitcase from Shelley, and then examined all the stickers in turn. Shelley waited, feeling self-conscious. After his appraisal Amit gave Shelley an approving look. 'I shall guard this with my life. Now we must get into my father's car.' He led the way out through the airport doors into a roadway of hooting cars and orange lights which flared against the dark sky. Amit was able to carry Shelley's case with one hand and protect her with the other, and also create a passage through the crowd like Moses and the Red Sea. Or was it the Dead Sea? Shelley just knew she didn't want that sea of people to close over her again, and she stuck to Amit as closely as seemed respectable.

There were cars everywhere, mostly black or yellow, but all the same old-fashioned shape, like something out of a fifties movie. All honking their horns, every one of them. Amit asked Shelley to stay right there, exactly there and please don't move, and vanished into the suffocating air with her case. She was standing on a strip of broken ground surrounded by puddles and rubbish. There didn't seem to be a footpath at all, and she felt like she was standing in the middle of a road in peak hour. Would Amit come back to her?

After ten minutes or so, just as she was beginning to wonder, one of the horn-honking black cars stopped next to her and blocked a lane of traffic. Amit jumped out and held open the front passenger door for Shelley. The car seemed to have cooling, thank heavens.

It didn't take them long to leave the airport. Almost immediately they were in what she presumed was downtown Calcutta. The sky was now rust-coloured. Shelley could make out a few higher buildings, but the road seemed to be mostly lined by ramshackle huts which looked like they belonged in a rural village. She could also see occasional large tree trunks with huge battlement-like roots. The little shanties were all lined up and open to the road like shoeboxes on their sides, and there were people everywhere – lying, walking or sitting in circles playing some sort of game, maybe cards. Each little shoebox had a single dim lightbulb glowing, and it took a while for Shelley to work out that these were in fact shops with built-in dwellings, and were open for business in the middle of the night.

Amit drove like everyone else – with his hand permanently on the horn, swerving and dodging. Shelley could feel her pelvic and thigh muscles clenching against each potential collision. The only time Amit braked was when a huge beast loomed without warning out of the dust and darkness. Everyone slowed down at that point, and the honking stopped, just for a moment.

'This is our airport area,' Amit shouted. 'It's not as busy as the rest of Calcutta.' He gave a particularly long blast on the horn and moved violently into the right lane, just missing another black car.

By an inch, Shelley thought. She tried very hard not to gasp, or show any sign of alarm or panic, although her body was tense all over.

It occurred to her that there were no women to be seen.

'Mrs Shelley, my father has asked me to impart to you his very, very sincere apologies for not greeting you himself, but unfortunately, he has had to go to his brother's house in Kerala. Calcutta is very dangerous right now.'

She nodded. Calcutta did look dangerous.

A bicycle with a frame upon which were suspended about thirty clay pots, wobbled across in front of them. It wasn't entirely clear if there was a rider. A large smooth-coated cow with long ears materialised out of nowhere. The car stopped suddenly, and Shelley was thrown forward.

'Not safe?' said Shelley, who was beginning to feel almost tearful.

'No, it's not,' said Amit. 'My father tried to get a message to you, but nothing is working here. There is no mail service at the moment, and no telephone service. That is why I have taken the liberty of arranging your accommodation in a very nice but inexpensive hotel. I know you were going to go to the Salvation Army hostel, but it is unsuitable.'

Mr Amit Mukherjee was gesturing as he said this, taking both hands off the wheel and twisting his palms up, demonstrating how unsafe the situation was. 'We have a lot of fighting – the Islamists are out to kill all Bengalis and all Hindus. It's going to be as bad as our 1948 killings. Maybe worse.'

'Oh.'

'There are millions of refugees from Pakistan here – a very political situation. A powder keg and a tinder box, you might say. I am very sorry.'

Shelley felt like she'd been hit. She'd possibly come all this way for nothing. 'What do you recommend I do?'

'Well, Mrs Shelley Conway,' said Amit, 'that depends on what you are here for.' The car was slowing down. 'I suggest we talk in the morning. We are at your hotel. You will be safe here. May I suggest I meet you at ten am in the lobby?'

'That would be fine,' said Shelley, relieved to have arrived somewhere. She was starting to feel quite sick.

'Mrs Shelley, here is your home away from home.'

Shelley saw a small white building. Anup International Hotel. It looked like a cross between the Leaning Tower of Pisa and Luna Park.

Shelley looked around the room and decided she might possibly survive. Hard to tell in the dark. The kerosene lamp did give a certain ambience. Could be scary or could be exotic. She decided to go for exotic, at least until morning. She'd be able to do her exercises. A small doorway through to a tiny shower, and a small hand basin. Next to it, on the floor, a porcelain bowl with a hole in the bottom. No idea, but must be something to do with the toilet. Luckily, she didn't need to go right now; she was probably in renal failure. She brushed her teeth at the hand basin and used the tap water to rinse her mouth. Bugger! She had totally forgotten. Don't put the water in your mouth without treating it. She'd probably die now. Sorry Mum.

She put some Puritabs in her water bottle and filled it from the tap. She checked again that the door was locked, lay down for a moment on the bed – at least there was a sheet – and conked out.

Shelley woke to muffled light. There seemed to be fuzzy sunshine through the window, a grey-orange light reminiscent of bushfire days at home, but without the smell of smoke. Must be very early, or maybe it was foggy. Or maybe that filmy look was due to pollution. Cream walls. High windows. Some green wooden slatted doors on the windows – they could be shutters. Traffic noise wafting up, along with drafts of diesel. Around the bed some brilliant orange sheer curtains, slightly shredded at the bottom.

Time to get up and try that shower. See if she can get rid of the sick feeling in the stomach.

She was in the lobby of the hotel, ready to meet Amit at ten am. Ceiling fans made the air almost bearable. The tea was spicy, sweet and milky, and came in terracotta beakers. Just the ticket. The furnishings were huge, and Shelley felt Lilliputian as she sat on a heavy leather Chesterfield armchair, with a large glass and a wrought iron coffee table between her and Amit, under an elaborate chandelier. There was also a greater-than-life-size Santa Claus figurine proffering an arrangement of exotic fruits, vivid flowers and burning incense. Strange sight in July.

Shelley certainly felt a lot better – the shower may have been only a trickle, but it was still wonderful. She'd put on a green dress she'd bought specially from that Indian shop in Lygon Street. Well, the shop claimed to be Indian, and it did have incense and brass teapots. Shelley had presumed, therefore, that this dress would be suitable for her trip. But the material was sticking to her thighs and making her feel hot. The tea had been brought by a young waitress in a sari with a sleeved top underneath, and Shelley had become acutely conscious that her own arms were bare. Bloody fake-Indian shop. Why would anyone bother faking Indian stuff anyway?

Amit beckoned to Shelley to sit next to him on the mountainous couch. He looked fresh and cool in a white cotton tunic and trousers. 'There is ample space, and our conversation will be more private,' he said, glancing over at the concierge's desk.

Shelley knew then that Jeffrey must have told Amit about her mission, even though she'd asked him not to say anything. Otherwise, why the secrecy? She hadn't wanted anything to deter Amit from meeting her. Wanted to explain it all herself. Disappointing, but there was no indication that Amit disapproved, not at this stage anyway.

From the couch she could see an astonishing vista through the glass front door. It looked like a metropolis struggling to function after a natural disaster. A confusion of poles, wires, and cables up high, a commotion of engines, people and cows below, a constellation of neon and hectic wooden signs in between. And everything black with dirt. Shelley couldn't be sure if it was harmonious order or complete chaos out there. She suspected the latter.

'Well, it's a long story.' Shelley tried to rearrange her dress so she wouldn't stick to the couch quite so much. The ceiling fans only seemed to cool her while she was calm. Or perhaps it was the tea making her feel hot. 'But I'd like to clear up something else first, Amit. The reason I am not Mrs is because I am not married. So just call me Shelley, please.'

Amit reacted to this piece of bad news by placing a gallant hand over his heart. 'My regrets. I am sure you will be married very, very soon, to a suitable husband.' And then dazzled her with a brilliant smile.

'Thank you.' She wasn't sure whether to reciprocate with an expression of sadness, rapture or hope, so decided to just plough on. 'Now I will tell you the reason for my trip to Calcutta.'

Amit listened without demonstrating any emotion. Sipped his tea. 'Life here is different, Shelley,' was all he had to say. 'But may I ask why your trip is so brief when your purpose is so important to you?'

'I have exams soon, and then lectures starting in four weeks, and I must be home for both, otherwise I fail my medical course. And in a few weeks, we will have our third big moratorium in Australia – against the Vietnam war, you know. I want to be home for that – to stand up and be counted.'

'Do you?' asked Amit, sitting forward.

'Yes, I do. I've been at the other two, and I can't imagine missing this one.'

'No,' said Amit, 'no you can't.'

'And there's another reason.'

'Yes?'

'The Faculty – that is the University – is completely opposed to me investigating the bones, and in fact have threatened me with expulsion.'

'Expulsion?'

'That means losing my place at University.'

'I know that,' said Amit, 'but that seems like a very harsh punishment.'

'Yes, I've had even worse actually. I've had death threats. Anonymous threats to me and my family.'

Amit nodded. 'In India, it would be the other way around. Losing a place in a medical course would be regarded as worse than death.'

'Oh, that's a bit different from us,' said Shelley. 'But there is no doubt that the longer I stay here, the greater the risk that my University will kick me out.'

'Kick you?' said Amit, with consternation in his eyes. 'This is part of the punishment?'

Shelley laughed, just for a moment. 'I'm sorry, Amit. That is an idiom, you know, a figure of speech. I mean the University might turn me out for ever.' Shelley looked out at the street view and paused. 'But, Amit, now I am here – I have to admit I didn't realise about the troubles in Bengal. Now I learn from you how bad things are, a part of me thinks I should leave as soon as possible, so I don't take up your time.'

'And the other part of you?'

'Well, I know I appear like a busybody, an interfering do-gooder—'

Amit nodded. He seemed to agree.

'But I really think it's shocking that the medical schools of the western world could be responsible for grave robbing. Or even murder. And that there's money being made out of it.'

'I've no doubt about that,' said Amit. 'Money will be being made all down the line. Even if you prove it, you're going to find it hard to intervene. But you seem like a very determined young woman, I must say. Why don't you wait a little before you make any decisions?'

Sounded like her Mum.

'Would you like more tea?'

Really sounded like her Mum.

Amit tapped his beaker and waved to the waitress who disappeared into the rear of the lobby.

'Let me show you our Calcutta, while you think about what to do.' Amit pronounced it 'Coolcatar' with the emphasis on the first and last syllables, rather than the middle one. 'Come,' he said. They got up and he steered Shelley to the lobby window.

She tried to make sense of the goings on. There was a massive wall of buildings opposite, all very old and very ornate: Whiteaway Laidlaw Co., Kuver Bank, Ruddy's Tea. All had seen far better days. They were decrepit dowagers, laced up in corsets of wrought iron, and festooned with black soot. Peeling paint, decaying signs, strings of clothes hanging out to dry. Visible layer of grey dust on everything, including the washing.

A cow was chewing its cud on the footpath directly opposite them. Other cows ambled along beside the scurrying rickshaws, cars, buses, army transports and little green and yellow three-wheelers. Amit said these tiny ones were called tuk-tuks. Motorbikes buzzed in and out, often carrying what seemed to be whole families, and honking non-stop. There was no apparent official delineation between the motor traffic and the human traffic. No footpath. Just a river of people lining the road and crossing it willy-nilly – no breaks in the traffic, no traffic lights. People wanting to cross the road launched themselves into the current, disappeared, and then, by some miracle, reappeared on the other side.

Over that way was a man in a brilliantly white long top and pants going somewhere important, and just here was a woman of firm foundation in a green and gold sari holding tightly to the hand of her little daughter in a red and white checked pinafore – on her way to nursery school perhaps. And over this way was a man in grey rags just standing. Just standing – on a piece of cardboard.

'He's guarding his square. That's his home.' Amit had been following her gaze. He swept an arm across the view. 'It's an intriguing panorama, is it not?'

'It's—it's—well, I can't believe anyone can cross the street and live.'

'No, but they do.'

'I've never seen anything like it.'

'Of course, there are many beauty spots in Calcutta, and had we time, I would have shown them to you. Our Hooghly River, our Victoria

Memorial, our Marble Palace – but we have more important things to do than sightseeing.'

'There's really only one thing I would like to see, Amit, if it's possible. Apart from the bones, of course.'

'And that is?'

'That is Mr Tagore's house.' She was not at all confident about the pronunciation of the first name, despite some instruction from Jeffrey.

'Rabindranath Tagore? You like Tagore?'

'Very much.'

Amit bestowed upon her a million-rupee smile. 'That is as commendable as it is unexpected. You had better not go home too soon then.'

Their fresh tea came in new beakers, and they sat down again. As they moved away from the windows the honking outside diminished to the level of a gaggle of one thousand geese.

They were attracting the attention of various visitors in the foyer, including a plump woman in a startling pink and gold sari, with jewellery that might even have been real rubies and diamonds. The woman obviously felt it was her duty to keep Shelley under close observation, and was fluttering around them like a butterfly on a sampling journey. Shelley wondered if she'd even come and sit on their laps. Amit stood up and asked her something in Bengali (or so Shelley presumed) and she flitted off.

'Let me give you some information on grave robbing in Calcutta,' Amit said. 'The burial ground is not guarded properly anymore, and there are many grave robbers. They come from a very low caste, the Dom people, the same as the grave diggers.'

Amit seemed to be discussing such sensitive matters in such a casual way. Could this mean he wasn't taking her cause seriously? Or was life just not valued here?

'But I do take your cause seriously. And I value all lives. We Hindus believe in re-incarnation, but we still value life. May I ask what you are trying to achieve exactly?'

'Well, the horrifying thing for me is that my medical school insists on the purchase of these bones – says that it is compulsory for their medical students to own them. And they buy and sell them as well. So, the University is complicit in this trade, and makes a profit out of it, which is terrible. I've come to the conclusion that there must be a pipeline of bones from Calcutta to Australia.'

'So, why do you need the proof? What difference will it make?'

'I'd like to do something to stop it. At least from the Australian end.'

'And what is it that troubles you so much?'

'It is that no-one in Australia seems to care. "Where do the bones come from?" someone asks. "Oh, *just* India," someone else answers. As if that's a sufficient explanation – as if Indian lives are worth less. That's what horrifies me.'

'Uh-huh.'

'Don't you think it's horrific, Amit?'

Pink Sari was back on her rounds. Shelley glared at her.

'Yes, yes, I do, of course. But you should know, Shelley, that it may not be illegal here to procure and export bones.'

'It isn't?'

'It may not be. I agree it's not ideal, immoral possibly, but it may not be illegal. There's probably no actual law banning grave robbing. There might be, but our legislation is so far behind where it should be.'

He drained his tea.

'And, besides, all Hindus are cremated.' This last was said with a nod.

'So, you don't think it is evil? To rob graves? Because they're not Hindus?'

'I didn't say that. I'm just giving you the context, from my point of view. There are so many cultures, so many perspectives, in India, you see. But murder – that's another matter entirely. Murder is reprehensible of course, no matter what or whom.'

At least they agreed on that point.

This morning Amit had a driver, and Amit got into the back seat with Shelley.

'Where shall we start?' said Amit.

'Well, one of the staff at the University, he has access to the bones invoice book, but wouldn't give me the information. But I managed to find an invoice. This one.' Shelley had the poetry book in her shoulder bag with the documents folded inside, and she showed Amit the invoice.

'See. Trivedi. Trivedi Brothers, well Bros actually, Calcutta. Then I went to the post office and rang India and got them to look up the Indian phone book, and they found an address. So, I wrote to them and got this letter back:

Trivedi Bros

104 – 106 Kalu Ram Road

Calcutta. India.

'Well, well.' Amit looked impressed. 'You've done a lot of research.'

'Yes.'

'And what do they charge for the bones?'

'Well, you can see there. Five hundred rupees per half set, plus fifty rupees for the shipping.'

'And back in Australia?'

'What do they charge, do you mean, at my University?'

'Yes.'

'Ninety-five dollars. That's for a half set plus skull.'

'Ninety-five Australian? So nearly one hundred? Which is about two and a half thousand rupees?'

'Yes.'

'Per box?'

'Yes.'

'Someone's making money.'

'And I have one more piece of evidence.'

'Yes?'

'Well, when I opened up my box of bones, I found this in it.'

She pulled the poetry book out from her cotton bag and passed it to Amit.

He leafed through it. 'This is a little treasure, Shelley. It would be the first printing in Calcutta. See how it was printed in London first, in English, and only later in Hindi, even though the poems were written in Hindi?' Amit laughed. 'English always trumps everything.'

'Sorry about that.'

'Not your fault.'

'But see,' said Shelley. 'There's the writing – TRIVEDI BROS – and then there's this underlining and circling of numbers.'

'Interesting.'

'Well, it does definitely say 'TRIVEDI' doesn't it?'

'Yes, but I wonder what all the underlining means,' said Amit. 'Mist and Shadow. Sounds ominous. And the numbers – 7, 10, 17, 20 – and so on. Might be some sort of code. Or just their favourite poems. But I don't think they've chosen the best ones.'

He gave the book back. 'Someone needs to write all that down and study it.'

All the traffic from last night seemed to be still on the roads, and even more rickshaws – rickshaws pulled by donkeys, rickshaws pulled by horses, rickshaws pulled by cyclists and rickshaws pulled by people on foot. Barefoot. All of the pullers, whether animal or human, were emaciated. Then there were people trotting along with trays of oranges on their heads, trucks loaded with workers, and buses so crowded that they looked as if they were about to topple over. Weaving and dodging through all this were swarms of motor scooters and tuk-tuks.

Shelley saw that what had appeared like a row of small shops last night was in fact a maze of little structures – little structures made of corrugated iron, plywood, thorn-tree branches, hessian sacks and tarpaulins, with laneways criss-crossing, like an ant farm. Every few yards there was a glimpse of domestic life. A man having a piss, a child having a shit, a woman washing clothes at a tap, some boys bending over a game.

There were families clustered around small cooking fires. Their mother was doling out what seemed like tiny quantities of food onto banana leaves. The children were sitting in silence. Some of them looked very pale with large eyes. Starving, Shelley knew. Anaemic. Some of them had the dry ginger hair that indicated malnutrition. The babies were crawling in the dirt. Where else could they crawl? They all had large stomachs and very skinny legs.

Here and there she saw a crater where the ant farm had been cleared away, and a huge hole dug out. In each of these construction holes Shelley could see workers clinging to flimsy bamboo poles – that was their scaffolding. Swaying. No hard hats, no shirts, no work boots, in fact no shoes at all.

The driver made a sudden turn to the left and they were in a narrow street lined by three-storey buildings with elaborate iron balconies and green shutters.

'Dalhousie,' said Amit. 'This is where the British lived in the time of the Raj. In these mansions.'

Shelley couldn't see any mansions.

TRIVEDI BROS SCI & ANAT was located down one of the even-smaller side streets. The Brothers occupied a large double-storey building. The high stone walls had once been rendered in cream, and before that in brown and pale green, judging by the peeling layers. Most of the Hindi letters in the sign had survived, whereas the English letters had not. Symbolic, Shelley thought. The front entrance was closed off with cyclone fencing and barbed wire, and the steps behind were caked in dried mud. There was no gate. The porch was completely overgrown with creepers and ferns, and a goat peered at them through the jungle.

Trivedi Bros had gone out of business.

'Well, that is interesting,' said Amit.

'Interesting?' said Shelley. 'It's a disaster.'

'But shouldn't you be pleased the bone traders might have gone out of business?'

'Yes, but, but have they? How do we know they're not trading somewhere else? Someone's trading.'

'I was just testing your resolve. We'll have to go to Writers'.'

'Writers'?'

'Writers' Building. It's the Government offices and it is the most frustrating place in the world. It is almost certainly not open today because today is whatever day it is.'

'Oh.'

'But we will go tomorrow to find out where the Trivedi Bros have gone. For now, let us have a cup of coffee.'

Shelley couldn't help but wonder if Amit really cared about the bones. Part of her felt he couldn't care less. Maybe because they weren't Hindu bones, or maybe he had bigger tragedies on his mind.

The Indian Coffee House was the second home for intellectuals in Calcutta, according to Amit. 'In fact, one cannot be a writer unless one has had coffee at the Indian Coffee House.'

'Oh?'

'And right here is another famous Calcutta landmark – College Lane.'

Shelley looked around and realised they were walking through a maze of books. Neat walls of books were stacked directly on the pavement. Millions and millions of books on every conceivable topic, in thousands of tiny stalls. Cheats and study guides to the books on every topic known to mankind. Cheats on using cheats. But also, chemistry, geology, engineering, metallurgy, management, accounting – medical books too, in dozens of languages including English – in amongst piles of smashed chai cups and dogs feigning death.

'Dogs are good actors,' said Amit.

Eventually Amit indicated a doorway as dirty as all the others, with a large sign above: 'Indian Coffee House'. They went up two flights of stairs to a large room, with waiters bustling and coffee brewing. Shelley was having trouble avoiding touching things – the banister, the stairs. All so filthy. The round wooden tables were clean, however, and there was a lovely light coming through the paned windows. Almost like an eighteenth-century coffee palace in London, she thought. The waiters looked professional in their white uniforms with wide green sashes, their toques having the appearance of collapsed souffles.

They took a table with a view onto a huge flame tree, the red blossoms just at the tail-end of their glory.

'Look around. You might see Amartya Sen. Or Satyajit Ray,' Amit said, as he pulled the heavy wooden chair out for her.

'Oh?'

'You don't know who they are, do you?'

'No,' said Shelley, and they both laughed.

'I have a lot to teach you,' said Amit, with a soft touch to his voice. 'This is where famous writers, filmmakers, poets come for *adda*.'

'*Adda*?'

'Intellectual conversation.'

'What a nice custom,' said Shelley. She'd never match up, that was clear.

Amit ordered two coffees, no mention of milk or sugar. She hoped they boiled the water but could hardly ask the question. It would sound rude.

Amit leaned forward on the table. The hairs on the back of his brown hands emphasised the whiteness of his long-sleeved shirt – as white as snow on the Himalayas, she thought. How Amit, or anyone else, kept their clothes so spotless was a mystery.

'Shelley, may I ask you something?'

'Of course.'

'Could you tell me about your political alignment please? Just a summary, so I know we are in the same wave.'

Shelley wasn't expecting this – an opportunity to impress, maybe? To earn her stripes? All right. She just had to imagine she was at a demo, although demos seemed a world away.

'I'm a Maoist, Amit. I believe that wealth should be re-distributed from the elite to the poor. I believe that intellectuals and workers must act together to achieve change in the world.'

There. The demo leaders at home would be proud of her. Hoped Amit would be impressed.

'Sounds a bit like rote-learning,' said Amit. 'But please go on. I am listening intently. What is your position on the need for armed struggle?'

'Armed? What sort of armed?'

'It shouldn't matter what sort of armed. I am asking you this because I know you are a comrade, and I know you believe in the struggle. I too am a comrade, a Maoist. You cannot call yourself Maoist if you don't believe in bloody revolution.'

'Oh, yes, right.'

The coffees came. Black, bitter, no sugar, no milk. Serious coffee. Like the politics.

'Do you know the four pillars of Maoism, Shelley? No? Well then you cannot call yourself a Maoist, can you?'

No, she didn't suppose she could.

'It's my duty to check your credentials, to make sure you are not a spy, to make sure you are who you say you are. We get all sorts here. Secret police from all over the world, people investigating crimes that have nothing to do with us, people who are just using us. I have to make sure you are not one of those people.'

'Yes, I see. I don't know how I can prove all these things to you.'

'Sometimes it just comes down to trust. And I think I trust you, Shelley. But we will see.'

'Well, I'm not a spy, that's for sure.'

'As I said, we will see. For now, let us enjoy our coffee and *adda*.'

'Good morning, Miss Agatha Christie. I hope you slept well.'

'Good morning, Amit. Actually, I lay awake worrying that we wouldn't be able to find the Trivedis and that my whole trip would be a waste of time. Not to mention a waste of your time.'

'But it's not a waste of time to meet a new comrade, surely?' Amit laughed. 'Also, I have a favour to ask you. If you do me the honour of the favour you will more than repay me.'

'Favour? Certainly. Just tell me what it is.'

'I will ask you in due course. For now, we must concentrate on surviving Writers'.'

Writers' was built to subdue the natives and bolster the Raj, Amit said, and was now used to bamboozle the proletariat. Shelley thought it was an impressive building – several storeys tall in red and white stone. Almost like a French chateau.

But, inside, well that was a different matter. They walked up a flight of stone steps to the front doors, and into what seemed to be the main reception area. On a large desk was a sign in Hindi, and underneath was an English translation: 'HELP'. Truer word was never written, thought Shelley, once she had glimpsed the situation within.

She felt like she was looking through layers of surgical gauze. Everything behind the desk was hazy. The morning light was pushing its way through some high windows, revealing millions of dust motes just hovering in the air, suspended for the moment perhaps, but about to drop onto the filing system below.

The filing system consisted of piles and piles of foolscap folders which seemed to have been left where they dropped. They were orientated in higgledy-piggledy fashion, presumably to make the stacks more stable.

No-one had left any passageways so there'd be no way you could walk between the piles. Shelley could see a layer of grey dust on the top file of each stack. She imagined picking that file up – the shower of dust you'd cause, the coughing and sneezing, the grimy feeling on your hands.

At the very back of the floor there were huge windows with black lead-lighted glass. The main staircase ended in a landing at this point, and then separated into two further staircases, which branched off to the left and right. The files were piled all the way up these stairs as well.

She wondered what was at the top of the stairs. Clearly no-one had walked up there for centuries. Perhaps there was a file for heaven – file number H0000000001.

Shelley was reminded of Franz Kafka, and then thought of Tomas, and then felt homesick, just for an instant.

There was no-one at the 'HELP' desk, and so Amit and Shelley walked up the public front stairs, calling in at each level, trying to find the West Bengal Land and Property Directorate. On the first floor they found an office full of passports – some in piles, some in boxes, some just strewn around the floor. Must have been thousands, the sign at the front saying, 'PASSPORTS. HELP'.

On the second floor was an office with two employees in white kurtas lying on their backs on the desks, mouths open – hard to be sure whether sound asleep or poisoned by carbon monoxide.

On the third floor, they struck gold – a living and awake person. Shelley could have kissed the young clerk with his neat shirt and glasses.

'Property records? I don't think I can help you.' Shelley just knew this was what he was saying in Bengali. But the conversation was going on and on, and there was gesturing, and exclaiming, and then a map was produced, and finally a handshake and two smiles. Oh, and a few banknotes. Amit must have had success.

'He's a cousin,' said Amit. 'He has no record of the Trivedi Bros moving, and he cannot help us at all.'

Shelley felt the smarting of disappointment, and she turned away.

'Do not fear,' said Amit. 'We will find a solution.' He started to walk down the steps again. 'If there is one.'

They went downstairs to the entry doorway again and Amit pointed out something shocking in the distance – an expanse of green grass.

'The Maidan,' he said. 'Would you like to walk there?'

Together they crossed the first of several roads. Shelley gripped Amit's elbow and closed her eyes as they plunged into the traffic.

They made it to the other side, and, after three more terrifying road crossings, arrived at the Maidan.

'That beautiful building is the Victoria Museum,' said Amit. 'We in Calcutta admire Queen Victoria. Now, we might just sit on this seat for a moment.'

The wooden bench was located next to a round garden exploding with red salvias and other bright flowers. They were shaded by two flame trees. A fountain was spraying, and beyond there was a palatial white building with a large dome, and beyond that again the green parkland. Did not look like Calcutta at all. Not the Calcutta she'd imagined.

Why were there no beggars here? No people making homes with their little pieces of cardboard? Where was everybody?

Amit answered the questions before she could voice them.

'The Maidan is reserved for cricket, and one other activity. We love our cricket and so all this grass is sacred. Poor people are not allowed here. And the building – that's the Victoria Memorial – well, it's beautiful is it not?'

Shelley nodded. 'One other activity? What activity?'

'You'll have to work that out for yourself,' smiled Amit.

Strange.

'You recognise the building of course?'

'Umm. The home of a famous filmmaker?'

Amit laughed. 'No, no. Can't you see? It's a replica of St Paul's Cathedral in London.'

And so it was. How could she not have seen that? Amit must think her so stupid.

'This is a good vantage point for us, Shelley.' The bench was comfortable and well-worn with a rounded back and iron legs. Amit sat quite close.

'If only we had an umbrella,' he laughed.

Strange remark, considering there was no sign of rain.

'Yes. This is a good place to tell you about the two Calcuttas – one Calcutta for the rich and one for the poor. There are millions of people here in West Bengal who have no land, no income, no food and no clean water.'

'Yes.'

Amit had such deep brown eyes. Black really. Like Omar Sharif.

'We have had a Marxist-Leninist Communist party for years here, but they oppose the idea of violent struggle. I am a Maoist like you, Shelley, but I am a true Maoist. A militant Maoist. A Naxalite. We are working towards revolution, and blood must be spilt.'

'Oh.'

And perfectly shaped lips. She didn't want to think about blood.

'One is not a communist until one's hands are coloured with the class enemy's blood. We are all prepared to die for the cause.'

'I see.' This all sounded a bit serious.

A little monkey was swinging up and down the tree while its mother looked on. A baby with the face of an old man. Perhaps he knew something about Calcutta?

'Hello, baby,' said Amit. He opened and closed the fingers of one hand, like a baby learning to wave. He looked at Shelley. 'You must keep this information to yourself. We act secretly. Indira Gandhi is trying to exterminate us. Her Home Minister has ordered that we be annihilated.'

And she'd thought Mrs Gandhi was a goodie. She gazed over the lawns to the huge white building. She had so much to learn. So much that had nothing, absolutely nothing, to do with bones. And so little time.

'But why are you telling me about it, Amit?'

The monkey was swinging directly overhead.

'Don't encourage it, Shelley. They carry diseases. Because we need support now from the west. I know from my cousin that you are left wing. I saw the stickers on your suitcase. I hear what you tell me about your political convictions. We need people like you to tell the world about us. So few westerners come here.'

Shelley now understood. Amit wanted to use her for public relations. She would be the bearer of knowledge and information which would support the Naxalites' cause.

The monkey seemed determined to come down to them. It was attracting the mother's attention then chuckling and pointing at the visitors. Perhaps that's why Amit had wanted an umbrella.

Amit spoke faster. 'There is something planned for next week – I think it will be just before you leave Calcutta – so you'll be able to see it, and then escape quickly.'

'Escape?'

'Shoo to you, monkey. We're going to attack Dum Dum Central Jail – there are two hundred Naxalites in there and we're going to get them out.'

'Oh. Right. How?' She was starting to get some loud noises in her head.

'We have a lot of explosives.'

Shelley contemplated this information. The monkey had swung over to the other tree. So adorable but carries diseases.

'Isn't that dangerous?' Turbine noises. Danger signs. Keep calm, Shelley. Deep breaths.

'Some of us will die. Those may be the lucky ones. Some of us will be taken to Gupta's house. That's a torture facility, with the most up-to-date methods.'

Amit's voice was going very slowly, like a record on the wrong speed. She couldn't say anything.

'Or we might be shortened by six inches, Prime Minister's request.'

'Shortened.'

'Beheaded. "Shortened" is the term Mrs Gandhi uses. It is her little joke. She keeps the guillotines busy.'

'Horrible.'

'I agree. We are planning everything in the next seven days. I would like you to observe what you can, Shelley. That is the favour I'm asking of you.'

Shelley was starting to feel as if she had lost control. She was floating above her body again, looking down on everything. Amit's voice was the voice of an ogre, getting louder and louder.

Amit seemed to have noticed. 'Don't worry, Shelley, you won't be in the front line, and I myself will not be in the front line. I am an undercover Naxal. To the world here, I am a businessman, the son of Aman Mukherjee, silk merchant. I must keep that cover as long as I can. That way I can do the most good.'

Amit moved an inch towards Shelley, took one of her hands and placed his own over it. The little monkey was now snuggled up to its mother.

'But I must be frank and tell you I have a slight foreboding about this small protest. I am anxious, and that is unusual for me.'

'Oh?'

He returned Shelley's hand. 'Yes, just a slight foreboding. Perhaps your presence has unstabilised me.'

'Destabilised,' said Shelley.

'Yes, that as well.' And then he darted a kiss onto Shelley's left cheek. Just like that.

Amit looked abashed. 'Sorry, Shelley, I couldn't resist. Lovemaking bubbles up when I am on the Maidan. That's why I should have brought an umbrella.'

Shelley wasn't completely sure she understood what had happened, and whether discussing umbrellas meant your companion was a good girl or a bad girl. She really didn't know how to react, and decided to try and look as detached and dignified as possible.

The baby monkey threw some seed pods at them and laughed.

Amit asked Shelley if she'd like to see his father's warehouse.

'But I must warn you, we have to drive through the slums to get there,' he said. 'These slums are what Calcutta is known for. It's why Mother Theresa is here. But they're not random squalor – they're communities. The people know how to live in them and how to survive. They may have one latrine for fifty families, but they manage to share. They may have one tap for twenty families, but, again, they have their times to wash their clothes, their dishes, themselves. The children are never naughty. They simply cannot misbehave. If you watch them, you will see they are always observing and helping.

'And people go to work from these slums. They have their work clothes. They shine their buttons.'

'That is, well, astonishing,' said Shelley.

'Yes,' said Amit. 'Exactly. Your mission here is important for more than one reason, Shelley. You understand that the slum dwellers of India are people. They are not just bodies, body parts, bones. They are people.'

'Yes, of course,' said Shelley. 'I know that.'

'I know you know that. Some people don't.'

'I know that too. But what about Mother Theresa? What does she do?'

'That is controversial,' said Amit. 'The main thing she seems to do is convert the dying to Christianity.'

'From what?'

'From whatever. Maybe Hinduism, maybe Buddhism, maybe Islam.'

'What good does that do?'

'Yes,' said Amit.

Shelley could not say much for quite a while. Eventually she had to ask. 'Is there any solution?'

'There is a solution. Something that is valued in Calcutta more than anything else.'

'And that is?'

'Education, Shelley. In Calcutta education is the way out of the slums.'

'Yes.'

'But the solution for India? That's different. The only solution for India is revolution.'

Amit's silk factory had a large, open and well-lit showroom. The shelves were bursting with bolts of fabric and the colours were magnificent.

'That blue is the blue of the peacock's tail,' said Amit. 'That is the green of young rice fields, and that red is the red of Chinese lacquer. That is what we aim for.'

Amit directed one of his staff to tie a sari for Shelley. The young man asked Amit to choose a colour, and he said white. The employee then embarked on a procedure involving the folding back and forth of five metres of white fabric. In the end the fabric was draped over Shelley's head so that just a few of her curls were showing. She had to admit that in the mirror she looked special. The lustrous white silk brought out the whites in her eyes and teeth. Amit was staring at her, and she blushed.

Shelley did not purchase a sari, but she did buy some carved elephants for Rory – a little family of three – and silk robes for her mum and dad and some necklaces for Skye. She was wondering about Tomas, and Amit suggested some spices. He sent his staff member away and he brought back three small packets.

Shelley had no idea what to do with them, but Tomas would know. They looked so exotic – ochre, orange and gold.

'Ginger, turmeric, saffron,' said Amit. 'The gold is the saffron – gold from the foothills of the Himalayas. In autumn the fields are purple with crocus flowers. Each flower has only three fragile red stamens, and the tiny point of those stamens – that is the golden spice.'

Shelley wondered if Amit exaggerated sometimes, or was India in fact one huge exaggeration?

That night, Shelley slept until someone from reception knocked on her door and said she had a visitor downstairs. She wasn't showered, and she wasn't properly dressed.

'Good morning, Miss Agatha Christie. I see you have slept well.'
Amit gave a small bow.

'Oh yes, thank you.'

Amit looked over his shoulder, then spoke quickly, in a low tone,
even though, as far as Shelley could tell, the foyer was empty. 'Today I
go to visit one of the local camps of our movement, and I am wondering
if you would come, please.'

'Your movement?'

'Yes. What I was telling you about yesterday. I can't say exactly where
we shall be going, but it's a long way from here. There are many refugees
on the road, so we must leave soon. You'll need some suitable shoes and
clothing for walking in the jungle.' He spoke as if he was referring to
the dress code for a garden party.

'In the jungle?'

'Please keep your voice quiet, Shelley.'

'And the bones?'

'They won't go anywhere.'

She was offended by Amit's apparent lack of concern about her
reactions, and the peremptory tone of his voice. 'I might wear my green
ensemble. Shall I bring a plate?'

'A plate? No, that will not be helpful. In fact, do not bring anything,
not your passport, not your purse. Leave those with the hotel please.
Now, I must go to my father's business briefly. Could you be ready in
forty-five minutes?'

Amit left Shelley, and was just about to open the heavy front door
when he turned and came back into the foyer. 'We are going to visit
a special place on the way. I think it will meet with your approval –
it's a polio home. It's a fine place, and there's a young health worker
there. A therapist – a rare thing in India. She's about your age, and very
impressive.' He nodded and was off.

'We're going to the polio home first,' said Amit, who was at the wheel this morning.

In the end she'd worn her white harem pants, as nothing else seemed remotely practical. She couldn't wear shorts, no-one did, nor her dresses from the Indian shop. She'd die in jeans, she knew that. That left the rayon harem pants with elastic cuffs at the bottom. Probably be hot but couldn't be helped. Plus her new white sneakers, because that was all she had apart from some ridiculous leather thongs.

They twisted through several miles of alleged roads, really just rivers of animals, vehicles and people, and eventually came to a large area which might have normally been a clearing, perhaps a market square. But now it looked as if someone had raked up a whole lot of rubbish into a pile. Only thing: the rubbish was humanity.

On the edge of the heap was a cluster of drab buildings with corrugated cement sheet roofs, a cow byre perhaps. Amit managed to drive around the square by honking and nudging. As they drew closer, she could see a network of low bungalows arranged like a crossword, with vegetable plots and papaya trees in the spaces. It looked cool and peaceful, at least at this early hour. Roosters were crowing, and chickens foraging. There was a fence constructed from upside-down stakes, stakes which were already sprouting bright green shoots. A live fence. A yellow sign with paintings of a Christian cross, some Hindi words, and a little boy with several large red tears on his face and crutches was hanging from a fence post. Something had kept the great tide of people at bay – she wondered if it was the fence, the sign or the cross.

Amit drove up to a gatekeeper in a baggy cream wrap who undid a chain and dragged open a pair of wrought iron gates, one side at a time. The ground was neatly raked even under the mango trees, and there was the dusty blue haze and smell of cooking fires. A wheelbarrow and rake stood at duty, and through some long dangling spirals of vines, Shelley could see women in blue habits, gliding along the paths with baskets in arms and bundles on heads.

Then about two dozen boys in shirts of school blue hobbled out from the shadows under the verandas, almost like a choir about to perform. They were neatly dressed, hair parted, grey shorts without holes. Shelley wondered what time they had got up. Almost all were propping themselves up on wooden sticks and displayed the whole gamut of deformities – short legs, withered legs, twisted legs. Two boys with no legs at all sat on wheeled platforms. A few wore massive iron callipers which would be as heavy as they were. In the background some nuns carried children on their hips. From the corner of her eye she could see a boy walking on all fours.

There were no wheelchairs.

Amit parked the car and went to the boot, then waited while the little invalids approached him.

The shadows behind the boys were deepest blue and the smoke from nearby cooking fires was a grey-blue, so that everything looked a bit watery. The boys didn't hustle like street beggars but stood quietly, faces open, eyes earnest. Amit spoke to them, and then indicated Shelley. The boys lowered their eyes for a second, and then looked at her face and hair, and her legs.

Amit had some large baskets in the back of his car and beckoned the boys over. Shelley heard the excitement and saw flashes of brilliant orange being passed around in the blue shadows – it was citrus fruit.

'Oranges. It's only because you're here,' Amit said to Shelley. Two little boys came up to Shelley and said something in unison, and Shelley realised, with a little stab of pain, that they thought she'd brought them.

'They are a treat.' The boys had all squatted down under the verandas and were helping each other peel the fruit. One of them sat with the crawling boy in a corner and helped him peel the orange with his mouth.

'Do you mind helping me carry a basket or two?' said Amit. 'We're going to see Kavita now.'

Shelley's basket was covered with a cloth and was quite heavy. She put it down at a doorway in order to remove her shoes, and as she picked it up again, she saw it contained long bars of yellow soap. No wonder it was heavy. She followed Amit, who was carrying three baskets, through a corridor and up to the entrance to a small room.

Amit stopped and stood watching at the doorway, and Shelley peered over his shoulder.

The only furniture was a small bed and a mattress with a piece of ticking on top. It was still early, and the drifts of smoke coming through the small windows made the room a milky blue, except for the iron of the bed which was etched black. Shelley thought the scene looked like a Vermeer painting, until she realized what was happening on the bed. A young boy, maybe eight, was lying on his back, his legs bunched up. A slim woman was supporting one leg gently under the thigh with one of her hands, while slowly straightening and bending the leg with the other. Her hair was plaited loosely at the back of her head, but some had escaped and brushed the little fellow's legs as she leaned over him. Shelley could hear crackles like someone crushing up cellophane. The boy's face was contorted but he didn't make a sound. After a series of loud cracks, the young woman put the leg down, lifted the boy's head gently, wiped his tears with a small cloth, and then kissed his forehead.

Amit put down his baskets and the two knew then they had visitors. The woman stood up straight and turned around. When she saw Amit, her expression changed from one of sadness to one of joy, just like a magic slate. It was then that Shelley noticed her bright orange kurta and royal blue pants. A bird of paradise. She turned back to the little boy and said something which made him smile bravely for Amit. The young woman smiled too, a flash of lovely teeth. She said something to Amit which made them both laugh – he in his sonorous voice, and she in a voice like nectar. Amit came over and kissed Kavita softly on one cheek, then the other. He held Kavita's head against his chest just for a second.

Shelley felt something inside her die.

Amit introduced them. 'Kavita, Shelley. You are both good-doers.'

Kavita offered her hand, but her face was now serious.

'And this is Mandip.' The little fellow on the bed had covered his face with his hands but was peeking through his fingers.

'I've just brought some soap and rice and a few more books for the boys,' said Amit. 'We haven't got much time I'm afraid.'

'That's wonderful, thank you,' said Kavita in English now, and then, to Shelley, 'you're a medical student, aren't you? Amit told me.'

'Yes, that's right, just first year.'

'So, what has made you travel all the way to Calcutta at this time?'

Shelley gave her the short version.

'What you have done is very brave. I hope you can do something about that bone trade.'

'I'm not sure what I can do now. The people seem to have closed their business. For the moment anyway.'

Kavita was stroking Mandip's legs. 'They will rise again, Shelley, no doubt about it.'

Shelley didn't know if that was good news or bad.

'May I suggest something you can possibly do in Australia – for living people – could you search out a doctor? One who might come here and do some surgeries for us?'

Shelley knew her expression was not one of confidence, let alone enthusiasm. An Australian surgeon, come here?

'Doesn't have to be a surgeon, I know we'd never get one of those. But a good-hearted general doctor. We have so many cases. Like Mandip – see his contractures? I put him through a full range of passive movement every day, but he's getting worse. You doctors are lucky, you can do something. Make a difference to someone like Mandip who—'

Mandip had taken his hands away from his eyes and Shelley could see tears.

'—who so desperately needs tendon releases.'

Shelley could see the contracted tendons.

'Amit and I think we can set up an operating theatre, don't we?' Kavita looked to Amit, who nodded.

'There's only so much that physical therapy can do.' Kavita stroked Mandip's crooked legs. 'He's a brave boy.' She said something to Mandip, who gave a small smile.

Shelley wished she had something to give the little fellow. Amit had crossed over to the other side of the room and was examining a loose shutter while simultaneously hiding behind it and giving occasional glances outside. He must be worried about being spotted. And anxious about the mysterious destination perhaps.

'You're at the University of Australia? I trained in therapy at Christian Medical College, Vellore, on a scholarship. It was from The Fair and Lovely Foundation.' Kavita gave a pretty laugh, like an arpeggio. 'We used to meet the medical students in Anatomy. I am so glad I had that opportunity.'

Shelley nodded.

'Has Amit told you about our polio home? No? This is a Christian charity, run by the Sisters. Amit is Hindu, of course, as am I. But the nuns welcome anyone who can help. Our children are very needy, but we have the generosity of people like Amit and his father.'

Shelley nodded again.

'But that is enough about us.' Kavita smiled.

Fair and lovely, thought Shelley, very lovely. And valued her education. And she, Shelley, took her education for granted.

Mandip was looking from Kavita to her in an eager way. Did he think she could relieve his suffering somehow? Shelley quickly looked to the window. She didn't want to cry. She turned as if to take in the view into the courtyard. She could see two nuns out in the yard carrying a heavy basket towards rows of clotheslines on props. The lines were already full of washing. They looked about seventeen and were laughing as they struggled with their load. They'd been up early, she thought. All those little blue shirts. Tears were coming. It was all too much. She turned her body further.

She didn't want Mandip to see.

Kavita came over and put her arms around Shelley's shoulders. 'Don't get too upset, these boys get the best care – they get food and love. More than you can say for most children in Calcutta. And good people like Amit and his father bring books and things for the school.'

She gave Shelley a squeeze. 'But the tragedy now, Shelley, is that there is no polio vaccination in India – none at all. Australia's had it for twenty years.' Kavita's voice had lost its musical tones and was now direct. 'They use the children of India for the trials – and then, once it's proven to work, they vaccinate the children in the rich countries, and ignore us.'

Shelley remembered that skeleton in the Pathology museum. Put there as an historic exhibit, as if polio was a thing of the past.

'It makes me so angry, Shelley. The vaccine companies and the governments, they never do the right thing. I wish they'd all come here and see Mandip.' Kavita spoke Shelley's mind. Perfectly.

They both glanced over to Mandip who was looking back at them.

Shelley hadn't noticed that another man had entered the room and was talking quietly to Amit.

'That's Amit's deputy,' said Kavita.

'Oh.' Deputy?

'So, you're here at a critical time. Was that planned, or a coincidence?'

'I've only come about the bones.'

'I see. But now you're here with us, what about Central? Will you come and help me?'

'I don't know anything about Central.'

'Oh, so you don't know. But Amit's told me about your politics. Shelley, I'm going to need help. Please come on Tuesday. We've got an important job.'

Kavita's dark eyes were looking straight at Shelley. There seemed to be no choice.

'I'll do what I can to help,' Shelley replied, thinking at the same time how trite that sounded, and wondering if she even meant what she said.

'Good. That's settled then.'

Most of Shelley's tears had been bullied away by an unheralded sense of responsibility, and only one or two lingered on her cheek. What a baby she was. She searched in the harem pants pockets for a tissue. No luck. But she did discover a periwinkle shell – it was the prettiest orange and blue, the same blue as the boys' shirts.

She walked over to Mandip's bed and, although the shell was small, held it out to him with her right hand. There was a smell of liniment.

'For you,' she said.

Mandip's eyes brightened. Kavita spoke to him.

'I'm telling him what it is,' she said. 'He's never seen a shell. He didn't know they existed.'

Mandip said something to Kavita without taking his eyes off the shell.

'He says the sea must be very beautiful.'

Shelley had the urge to say, 'I'll take you there one day, Mandip'. But she knew that wouldn't be fair. So she patted his arm, and said 'Rami rami', hoping that that was goodbye in Hindi.

Something swept through her. No polio vaccine in India? For fuck's sake.

Amit called Shelley over to the window. He stood behind the loose shutter and told Shelley where he wanted her to look. Behind the polio mission was a belt of confused vegetation leading down into a chasm. On the other side of the valley, arising out of the gorge, was a high stone wall. It was pinkish with parallel black lines of what looked like ancient lichen. The distance from the window to the wall might have been only three hundred yards or so, but Shelley imagined it would take you a couple of hours to clamber through the gorge. Could even be impossible, the jungle was so dense.

Along the top of the wall were guards marching along – guards whose tiny size gave a true indication of the massive height of the wall.

'That's the Jail.'

'Right. The Jail.'

If there hadn't been a wall, and if there hadn't been soldiers, and if there hadn't been those guard posts, the view could have been described as picturesque.

Amit asked her to look to the far right around the shutter, and Shelley could see the commotion and hear the distant hubbub, despite the early hour.

'The Dum Dum district,' said Amit.

Shelley was becoming used to the strata of urban India – the upper canopy being a spaghetti of power lines, then a layer of neon signs, then roofing materials ranging from asbestos to sacks to blue tarpaulins, and an occasional TV antenna. The next stratum was the transportation mayhem layer – yellow taxis, hand-pulled rickshaws and trishaws, horse-drawn hansom cabs, buses, trucks, a herd of goats, a little religious procession led by men with drums in white turbans and dhotis, the odd cow and every manner of bicycle. The last layer was the road surface – it was rarely glimpsed, but when seen was dusty, except for moist piles of this and that, and the odd heap which was probably a corpse, animal or human, you couldn't be sure. All this activity drained into the road which led up to the Jail.

'See the tallest building? That building with the white and red sign, and the green neon?'

'The one that looks like a—a wedding cake? Looks like it's about to collapse?'

'Yes. It's the old palace. It's condemned now. That's where you and Kavita will be. At the top.'

'I beg your pardon?'

'We have a room there with windows to the east and north, so you can see the activity in both RBC Road and Central Jail Road and the front entrance to the Jail. That's where the decoy action will be – the fighters with the cocktails. We want to draw all the guards to the front of the Jail. The weakest parts of the walls are either side of the front gate, and that's where the mortars will be aimed. We should get a lot of hits that way.'

'And the prisoners?'

'They know what is happening and when. They have explosives too, which we've smuggled into the Jail. Once they hear the mortar attack that's their signal.'

It was all as routine as a school excursion.

'What will be the most important things for you and Kavita to observe, do you think, Shelley?'

Shelley didn't know what to think. She hadn't been told about this event, she had no idea of the context or the justification, and no-one had asked her if she was happy to do it. Whatever 'it' was. And yet now she felt like an integral member of the team. How on earth did that happen?

It was dawning on her that there'd be deaths on both sides. Young resistance fighters. Young guards. It was also dawning on her that she might have been trapped. Seduced into skiting about her left-wing views and then compelled into being part of this violent protest. Otherwise, no hope of progress with her bones quest. You could say it was blackmail.

She turned to Amit with tears brimming again. 'I don't know if I can do this, Amit. Those people. They might be killed. I don't know if I can stand it. And I'd be an accomplice, wouldn't I? I might be guilty of a crime.'

'No, Shelley, no. You are not part of this. It's going to happen whether you're here or not. You're simply a witness, someone who can make sure the world hears about this event, so that it's not in vain. And then we can answer any accusations which might be made. For example, the Government might say we set out to use violence.'

'But aren't you?'

'No, it's a peaceful demonstration to highlight the fact that there are two hundred political prisoners in Dum Dum Central Jail. Two hundred men who have never been charged, tried, convicted or sentenced. Two hundred men who have committed no crime. Two hundred men who have been forced off their little plots of land by the rich zamindars. Two hundred men whose families are now starving.'

'But what about the petrol bombs and the mortars?' She wasn't even sure what mortars were.

'That is only if the guards use violence, unnecessary violence against us. We have surprise on our side – they don't know we're coming, so there'll be no time for them to amass troops. It should be a peaceful rally. But that, Shelley, is the key thing for you to observe. If there is conflict, who is the first to use violence and how much? You see why you are so important? Number and severity of casualties is very important too, but who initiates the violence – that's what we need. Do you agree?'

'Yes, I guess so.' Shelley's voice had thinned out to a watery broth. 'I guess so.' She wondered who would be interested in her evidence, who would listen and when and where, and how. And did they know she was a Troublemaker, capital T? Dean Thompson would be only too happy to tell them that. The old prick. He would blame her for all this. Would he find out and get her sent down from Uni? She wondered about Amit. On the one hand he appeared wise and controlled. On the other, he seemed to be masterminding an operation which had a predictable outcome of casualties, deaths even, and failure. And this was her test.

Kavita had been listening, and now came over. Another squeeze of the shoulders. 'I know you're going up to the camps today, Shelley, but maybe you'd like to help me tomorrow?' Kavita looked over at Amit, who must have been listening, and who must have nodded. 'Tomorrow, I go to the girls' home, which is only a short way from your hotel. Maybe Amit could send a driver?'

'Yes, good,' said Amit.

'Tomorrow then,' said Kavita.

Shelley didn't think she'd said 'yes', but maybe she had. And the bones? They seemed to be getting pushed further and further down the agenda.

The road was dusty, winding, slow and very crowded. Crowded with people walking along the side of the road. Dozens, hundreds, thousands. A never-ending stream. Women in dusty saris. Bundles on backs, babies on fronts, toddlers on hips, children on hand, a goat in train. Some men, but most were women. Some pushing carts. The kids with skinny arms, big bellies and bigger eyes. Wispy gingery hair. This must be malnutrition. Real malnutrition. The adults with gaunt faces. And whenever she and Amit stopped people gathered, murmured, pleaded – louder and louder. Like a swarm of bees getting closer and closer.

Amit had sacks of rice and large brown paper packets of thick square biscuits on the back seat. Shelley reached over into the back and grabbed five or so bags, and then as Amit slowed passed the bags out through her window. Amit told her to leave the back doors locked. After a minute or two he drove on before hundreds of people surrounded the car and scores of hands reached through the window.

'Otherwise, we'll be killed.' After twenty minutes or so he said, 'This is genocide, Shelley. Genocide in front of our eyes.'

'Genocide?'

'The West Pakistan Government is exterminating all Bengali Hindus. And any other people they don't like – intellectuals, academics, even other Muslims. We know this because we speak to these people, and they tell us their stories. Hundreds of thousands of men and boys have been killed – they have been rounded up and shot, or clubbed to death like – well, worse than, animals.'

This was appalling – more than appalling. 'Who's doing the killing?'

'The five generals – but the worst are the two Khans, and the worst of the worst is General Yahya Khan. *Kill three million of them, and the rest will eat out of our hands.* That's what Yahya Khan said.'

Shelley almost gagged.

'The other Khan, Tikka Khan – he is the Butcher. The Butcher of Bengal.'

Amit kept his eyes on the road, and spoke in an expressionless way, almost as if he were reading a news bulletin. 'The women and young girls – they rape then kill. These ones around us – they're the lucky ones.'

Shelley turned her head to look directly out her window. These same women, these same little girls. Hollow faces, dead eyes. Couldn't bear it, so looked ahead again.

'They went into Dacca University and killed everyone – students and staff, hundreds in one day. They beat all the male students and staff to death first. They had locked the women in the dormitories. The women heard the screams, and then they were raped and beaten to death. A whole university. In one day.'

'When was this?' She could hardly give voice to the words. They came out in a whisper.

Amit angled his head to hear. 'When? Twenty-fifth of March.'

'Just weeks ago?' Croaky whisper.

Neither of them said anything for a long time.

Amit stopped and they gave out more rice and biscuits. 'I don't even know how they will cook the rice,' he said. 'We have millions of refugees here in Bengal and as you can see, we cannot cope. India and the world have ignored East Pakistan, and this is what is happening. Indira doesn't care. She's too busy torturing her opposition at home.'

Shelley was trying to put it all together. Hindus, Muslims, India, the Pakistanis, Naxals. 'What is the Naxalite position?'

'That's a good question, Shelley, and one I don't have a ready answer to. It is something that causes me a great deal of anxiety. The Naxalites come from many political backgrounds. Most are farmers. Our people don't have sophisticated political views, they just want a livelihood, and to live in peace. But the leaders of the Naxalites – that is different – some are Marxist, some are Marxist-Leninist, some are Maoist – I expect you have these issues in Australia.'

'I don't really know too much about that.'

'Well, here it is complex,' said Amit, 'because we have many ethnic groups and even within Hindus there are multiple groups. This means we get a lot of political views – and that means there are a few Naxalites who side with the Pakistani murderers. Not many, but this is a matter of great anxiety for me.'

Amit had turned onto a larger, sealed road, where the crowds had cleared a little. She could now see that behind the fringe of people there was a continuous line of small dwellings. There were no front doors or windows or curtains, so Shelley felt like she was peeking into intimate dioramas of domestic life. However, every view was filtered through fine brown dust, so the tableau could have been hundreds of years old. Reminded her of a Brueghel painting. Wherever you looked there was a little story.

Some of the little houses doubled as shops, so there was a single bed, neatly made with a white coverlet, next to a glass cabinet of sweet cakes and bees, with flower garlands and dangling slippers in green and pink and gold. In front of this shop there might be a tap, and the male proprietor, for it did always seem to be a male, might be soaping his head and torso with a bucket. If she really peered, she might see a woman in a sari right at the back of the little shop, the sari possibly a vivid purple or yellow, but hidden.

Normal life was continuing within, and normal life was trying not to notice the stream of desperation at its front doorstep. For what could normal people do for the millions of women and children heading for Calcutta?

'That is why I spend a lot of time at my camps, making sure they get the right information. There are many insurrectionists in our region who would like to cooperate with us.'

'Like?'

'Like the secessionists in Kashmir, like the NLF in South Vietnam, like the Tamil Tigers in Sri Lanka. All militant left-wing groups.'

'Right.' That reminded her. 'Amit, you never told me about the four pillars.'

'But of course. I will give it to you word for word – this is how we learn it. Just a moment while I pass this cart.' They overtook a donkey and his thin driver, and Amit's voice became deliberate, measured. 'One, accept Mao Tse-tung as the leader of the world revolution and accept his thoughts as the highest form of Marxist-Leninism. Two, believe that a revolutionary situation exists in every corner of India. Three, area-wide seizure of powers is the only path of taking forward the revolution in India. Four, accept that guerrilla warfare is the only means of advancing the revolution.'

'Right.'

'It's quite a lot to take in.'

'It is.'

'Can you repeat it?' smiled Amit. 'I am not serious, but if you were to become one of us, Shelley, that is what you would have to learn in your heart, and say in your heart, and also truly believe in your heart.'

After an hour or so on the main road they stopped at a tiny store that sold soft drink bottles filled with yellow fluid. Shelley was learning to use her eyes and not her mouth. So she didn't ask. She kept quiet and then saw the bottles being emptied into the petrol tank. The proprietor must have been waiting for them, as five dozen extra bottles had been counted out and were ready to go. Amit placed these carefully in the boot where the food parcels had been.

They must be going a long way.

They left the main road and the human stream, and travelled on what was hardly a cart track, past thatched-roof huts, cows, rice paddies and maize gardens. Amit turned off the track without any warning, into a small farmyard and drove the car into a barn, barely slowing down until he braked hard. Shelley fell forward and almost hit the windscreen, and Amit's face showed both concern and shame. He brushed his hand tenderly over Shelley's face but was also clearly anxious and in a hurry. 'Shelley, I am so sorry,' he said in a very low voice, 'but could you get out of the car quickly, do not shut the car door, and please do not go outside.'

A man emerged from the back of the barn and opened the boot of the car. He started transferring the petrol bottles into a cart, with layers of hay between the bottles. It took a minute for Shelley's eyes to adapt to the dark, and then to notice he had lost one arm above the elbow. Maybe a farm accident. Or maybe the protests. The man was making slow progress with the bottles, partly because he had only one arm, and partly because he was trying to leave a space in the middle of the cart, and the bottles kept rolling in. Amit threw a carpet in and arranged it so the space remained free.

'You need to get in and lie down on the carpet next to the bottles. We have to cover you with straw. Don't worry, I'll be next to you, and you'll be able to breathe. You'll be quite safe.'

Shelley did as she was told, though wasn't at all sure that Amit was right. The bottom of the cart was hard despite the carpet. Her heart was beating fast. She could feel the bottles next to her and hoped there were no smokers around. It occurred to her that she might be murdered. As long as it was quick with no pain.

Amit got in beside her and held her hand. One-arm covered them in hay, then scraped some away from her face. She could just glimpse light, but closed her eyes, moved carefully onto her side, and turned her face down to stop the straw entering her eyes. She decided she was a bit frightened, and for a moment thought of her mum and dad. Then she felt a tear and realised she had to stop snivelling at once, or how would she wipe her eyes? There was soft talking and then some yelling and a donkey braying. The cart lurched and they seemed to be off. How long would this journey take? She was thirsty. And itchy. The cart was so hard and the track bumpy, or maybe it was the donkey, or whatever it was pulling them. She could smell manure and wanted to push up her nose to avoid the sneeze but didn't want to lose Amit's hand.

After an hour, maybe more, the cart slowed, and Shelley heard quiet talking.

Someone scraped away the hay and helped her out of the cart.

'Welcome, Madame,' said a low voice.

Shelley opened her eyes. They were in the jungle. Massive tree trunks backlit by watery sunlight, like a huge kelp forest. Roots like walls. A smell like mushrooms. Soft and sinking moss underfoot. Water drops flashing on the leaves. A dozen or so people in camouflaged shirts and pants. Mostly young. Some young men, some girls. Black guns, not glinting. Solid black gun barrels. Lots of them. A stash of guns against a tree, plus one on just about everyone's back. Shelley knew they'd be AK-47s. Slung as casually as postman's bags.

'Now, Shelley,' said Amit, 'we must do a, how do you say it, track? Like they do in the Himalayas?'

A Himalayan-style trek? In these pants and shoes? Her enthusiasm, what was left of it, disappeared entirely.

But no-one had the slightest interest in Shelley's clothing or footwear, or, for that matter, her state of mind. People were taking the bottles of petrol and strapping them in cloths on their backs. Others were pushing the cart into the trees. The donkey was tethered to a stake. A line formed, and then snaked off, Shelley behind Amit, people in front and behind them, and Shelley guessed that they were in about the middle of the line. They headed onto a narrow track through the jungle, over vines, creepers and branches. Muddy sinkholes between large, solid tree roots. Mostly uphill. How was she going to manage this?

After a while Shelley realised they were in fact climbing up a watercourse. Up and up many little waterfalls. Her sneakers were soaked. Everyone else had black sandals on. She was sweating like crazy. And thirsty as anything. She'd obeyed Amit's instructions and hadn't even brought a water canteen. Everything had been so rushed. She'd had nothing to drink for hours and felt like she'd lost litres of fluid. Initially she had looked around at the plants and trees, but soon ran out of interest. She was so hot. And thirsty. After a while she scooped up mouthfuls of water from the creek when she could, trying not to hold up the Indian file. A genuine Indian file. *'Don't eat or drink anything,'* Mum had said. Mum, I have to, or I might die.

Everything on either side of the creek looked dense and dark. Like a Rousseau painting without any flowers. She rolled her once-white harem pants up above her knees, so now she looked like a sort-of forest faun with massive thighs and tiny feet. Her hair would be plastered against her head with all the sweating. Might even look normal for once. She didn't care either way. The left side of her back ached, and sometimes she felt like she couldn't drag her bad leg up another inch. Once or twice, Amit lifted her body up a steep bit.

They did stop at the edge of a small ravine, which might have been picturesque any other time, and a water canteen was handed around. Most people refused the drink, and Shelley realized the water was for her benefit. Despite her thirst, she just took a small mouthful, thinking there was always the creek. God only knew which was worse, the creek or the canteen. She noticed a young man with a club foot, and another with no arms at all, just a few fingers sticking out from his shoulders. Nobody stared at him, and nobody stared at her.

After a further half hour or so, Shelley was starting to feel exhausted. It was becoming harder to lift herself up onto each new rocky ledge. Both legs were throbbing. Amit was having to help her more often than not. Shelley wondered how he kept so fit. Doing this, she supposed. Just as she thought she would have to ask Amit how much further, they veered away from the creek and into a clearing. Shelley saw fifty or more people in army fatigues. Men and women. Or, more accurately, boys and girls. Some sitting, some cooking, some cutting branches. Many of them ran up and greeted Amit with handshakes and pats on the back. A young girl in army fatigues and a red cloth around her head laid an arm around Shelley's shoulders and put a tin mug of something liquid into her hand.

Shelley was so relieved to be somewhere her emotions got the better of her and she started to cry.

But after her hot drink she felt considerably better. She decided she might survive after all.

Shelley's new friend had squeezed Shelley's shoulders and had said something in Hindi. It sounded kind, and Shelley presumed she'd been told to buck up, or maybe 'stop being a baby'. Maybe even a 'well done'. Someone had found her a tree stump for a seat, and she managed to look at her surroundings.

All around them were swathes of vines, like huge walls, with glimpses of red rockfaces behind. It was a real hideaway.

After a while another younger girl came and led Shelley towards a small pool at the base of the rocks so she could wash her hands, and then over to the cooking fires where there were large steel pots of vegetables and piles of fried bread. They all sat around the pots on stones and logs. The girl gave Shelley a tin dish with a large serving of vegetable curry and the savory pancake-things, saying something like *labra* – but she gave it back and indicated she just wanted a small portion. A lot of people here would be much hungrier than her. Some of them were still growing. A group of men and women sat closer to Amit than the rest, and talked earnestly, possibly giving him a report of their plans, Shelley thought. She recognised the deputy. Two young men were drawing a large map on the ground. Shelley sat with her head leaning against a tree. Kind young women, in camouflage pants and shirts, smiled shyly at her. They were all very pretty. And young.

The group had been training hard, Amit told her. After the meal, AK-47s were distributed. There were plenty of guns, and she wondered where they came from. Her companions took her to a cleared area around the base of the cliffs. There were targets cut out of tin which had been nailed to stakes. Shape of humans of course. The young shooters started at about one hundred yards and then moved back in waves. The targets started to disintegrate, and a halt was called so that more could be nailed up.

'Yes, you would think the whole of Bengal would hear us but they cannot, or if they can, they're not going to give us away. This whole region is strongly Naxalite,' Amit said.

'Do you think I could have a go?' asked Shelley. Amit looked dubious, but he handed her a semi-automatic rifle. She held it like a precious vase.

'It's heavy.'

'With a loaded magazine it weighs another two pounds.' Amit walked her over to a rough bench and got her to put the rifle down on it. A group of onlookers gathered.

'You're the entertainment,' said Amit. 'They are amused that you cannot shoot.'

He said a few words in Hindi to the crowd, and everyone laughed. Shelley gave the audience a big smile, which made everyone laugh again.

Amit picked up the rifle. 'Always assume a rifle is loaded. This is the most important part of your gun – the safety lever. It should always be pushed up. If it isn't, push it up. First thing. Now you try. Good.' He patted her on the back.

'How you stand is very important. You need to have your feet apart, have the left foot in front of the right – like this – or maybe try your right – and bend your knees a little, be on your toes and lean forward at the waist. I know it's hard for you.' He said another few words in Hindi, and the young revolutionaries demonstrated the stance in a trice.

'Then,' said Amit, 'you have to hold the weapon correctly. The butt should be in your shoulder pocket here. You push your shoulders up to cradle it – your cheek should caress the butt. You look through this hole here and find the rear sights. Those are the two outside ones. Not the front ones. You aim just below six o'clock. Don't force the trigger, let it surprise you. Just drop the safety lever, focus on the rear sights, squeeze gently and let it decide. Let it surprise you. Keep your elbows in, control your breathing.'

Shelley adopted the stance. It didn't come easily, and she knew she looked ridiculous. She had the gun in her shoulder pocket. She caressed it with her cheek. The gun was waving around a bit. The guerrilla fighters had all moved behind her. She aimed at the target, held her breath and let the trigger decide. It surprised her all right. There was a massive explosion in her ear, and she was knocked over.

But the young ones were calling and clapping. She had hit the target right in the chest. Amit picked up a shell casing. He was laughing. 'Here you are, Shelley's shell. You're a brave girl all right. Actually, you looked better than I thought you would. Almost like you've done it before.'

Amit took the AK-47 back and put the safety on. 'You might like to help make the cocktails – it could be useful for you in Australia.'

Some of the group were stuffing long strips of cotton into small glass bottles, and dousing them with petrol. A taper was left outside the bottle. Shelley was given the job of ripping cotton into strips. She didn't allow herself to think of the consequences of what she was doing. Or of what might happen to these boys and girls in just a few days' time.

One of the boys lit a taper then threw the bottle into the jungle. There was an explosion, and white and orange smoke billowed up from the clearing. Amit and two more leaders came running over and remonstrated with the boy. After the commotion had died down, Amit explained to Shelley in English what had happened. The boy's main infraction was that he had soaked the wick in petrol and not kerosene. Kerosene burns slowly and gives you time to run away, Amit said.

Amit told Shelley they'd be leaving soon. 'Darkness falls quickly here,' he said, 'and we have quite a descent.'

By the time Shelley woke up after three, (or was it four?), days in Calcutta, she felt like a different person. She hadn't discovered the source of the bones – but she'd learned about a whole new world.

Amit didn't seem too passionate about her cause and Shelley was worried that he may be just humouring her. He was more interested in using her as his special observer and envoy. He didn't seem to think that the body-snatchers and bone merchants were committing any great crime. As he had said, he was more concerned with live people than dead ones.

And he demonstrated that by everything he did for the polio home – or was it for Kavita? Mixed motivations maybe.

She had to admit that the bones issue had diminished in emotional pull, compared with the Naxals and their struggle. Here was real oppression – of peasant by landlord, of low caste by high born, of

Muslims by Hindus and Hindus by Muslims. She had seen for herself those beautiful young people. She had seen the idealism in their eyes.

Tuesday's Jail breakout was not going to be your regular everyday demo. No, this was real protest, Maoist style. The camp she had visited was one of hundreds. Amit was responsible for five camps, and all five were going. Many other camps also were going to be involved in Dum Dum Central, and there'd be maybe five hundred Naxals fighting at the Dum Dum breakout. There would be deaths, that was certain.

Amit's driver was waiting for her in the foyer later that morning. 'Sorry to keep you waiting,' she said to him, knowing that he spoke no English, but having no alternative. He smiled and opened the door.

The girls' polio home had the same sign out the front as the boys' hostel, except it was a little girl in a long dress. Same red tears. Bare feet, one twisted in, and a crutch. Shelley felt that lurch in her chest.

They had driven through some huge metal doors into a courtyard of buildings, three or four storeys high, red brick and cream masonry. There were galleries facing onto the courtyard, and she could hear singing all round. Young girls' voices, and an almost familiar song. An older nun in the same blue habit as the nuns at the boys' home but with a white headscarf spoke to someone behind her, and shooshed with her hands. Shelley stood and waited until the old nun shuffled over to her and gave her a kiss on each cheek.

'You came. I'm so pleased.' Shelley turned around and there was Kavita, in a long blue sari and a white headscarf. 'This is Sister Kaur,' she said. Shelley bowed her head. 'Now we shall take some tea.'

They passed though into a smaller courtyard billowing with creepers and red trumpet flowers. A young nun brought them sweet spicy tea. Terracotta beakers again. Delicious, but Shelley declined the second cup.

Kavita told her about the home and her role. 'You might like to help me this morning – I will be doing range of movements, active and passive, on everyone, and then strengthening exercises for those who can manage, not always the same as those who most need it. We simply haven't got time. We've had a new little one overnight, but I don't think she will survive. She's worse this morning.'

'Oh.'

'They're all girls here, of course. But the families don't bring them. Or bring them late. That's why there are more children at the boys' hostel.'

'Oh.'

'But once they have respiratory problems, well, we rarely save them, boy or girl.'

'Oh.'

'We don't have iron lungs here, like you do.'

'Do we?' thought Shelley. She really had no idea. What a terrible thing to admit. She may as well be honest. 'Do we? Have iron lungs? I really don't know anything about polio in Australia.'

'You have many adults in iron lungs – I think some have been in them for twenty years.'

They walked through another courtyard, slipped off their shoes, then up more stairs. Shelley heard children's voices, and some adults laughing and sounds of metal scraping metal. They were on a tiled landing outside a pair of large wooden doors, with a sign, not in English.

'That says "Cripples Ward", said Kavita, 'in Hindi and Bangla.'

'Oh.'

Kavita pulled open the doors and the general chatter grew louder. There was a cool breeze coming through multiple tall doors which opened onto wide balconies. Shelley saw, firstly, the beds lined up on the balconies – small white metal cots, sides down. The room itself was large and around the edge there was a fringe of white beds. But the patients were on the floor in the middle of the room. They were children from babies up to maybe three years old, in blue cotton dresses. Beautiful long plaits of hair. They all looked up at Kavita and started to laugh and wave.

Only then did Shelley notice that the girls couldn't move from their spots. They were lying in all sorts of contorted and twisted poses. One lay on her back with her legs splayed out like a frog. Others were curled up with legs tucked under them. The only girl who could was moving around was up on all fours with bony buttocks sticking up, dragging herself along on the backs of her wrists.

'These are our little girls,' said Kavita. 'In this room we have our babies.' She said something to the group. The girls smiled up at Shelley and started up a song. 'It's by Tagore,' said Kavita, 'our great poet.'

'Thank you,' said Shelley at the end, and then her version of *dhan'yabada*, which she hoped was 'thank you' in Bangla.

Kavita took Shelley down to a cot at the other end of the room. Lying on it was a baby about twelve months old. She had fine black hair parted on one side. She was lying on her back, eyes closed, gasping like a fish in a bucket after the hook's been taken out. Her lips and ears were blue. Her eyes were racing from side to side. She couldn't breathe, she couldn't move – she was suffocating.

'All her effort is going into her breathing,' said Kavita, 'She's exhausted. Not long to go.'

'You mean she might die?'

'She definitely will die,' said Kavita. 'We don't have oxygen and we don't have any respiratory support. She's hypoxic now, in respiratory failure. Poor little darling.' Kavita stroked each of the child's arms and cheeks in turn. 'See the colour of her tongue?'

Her tongue was purple.

'We do have some iron lungs but they're all broken, and we don't know how to fix them. Or we don't have the parts. See over there?'

Shelley saw a gaggle of about ten bulky white metal coffins on wheels on the balcony.

'They've been donated, of course. That's the problem with donations – usually the equipment doesn't work. And one of the worst things is if we start them off in an iron lung, it may work for a while, but then it will eventually break down. By then we've come to love our girls, and it's very hard.'

'Oh.'

'Or power blackouts. Very common. And then our little ones die. Just like that. We don't have a back-up generator. So better not to start them off, really.'

'I see.'

'I know in Australia you used to have wards and wards of children in iron lungs. But you wouldn't have that now, would you? Now you've had the vaccine for, what? Over fifteen years?'

'I don't know, I'm sorry.' How ashamed she felt.

'Just one moment please Shelley.' Kavita walked over to one of the nuns standing near the balcony and pointed out the baby. The young nun came down, and picked up the little girl gently, and took her to a wicker chair. She placed her on her lap, head cradled to her chest. She started to rock the baby and sing, pressing her cheeks to the baby's head. Shelley could see tears.

'It's hard on the young nuns,' said Kavita. 'Most of them have brothers or sisters at home the same age.'

Shelley's eyes now filled with tears. The poor little thing.

'Shelley, I'm sorry. It helps if you do something, so why don't we start some chest physio on these little ones. We'll start with postural drainage, deep breathing and coughing. Then if you're able to keep helping, we'll do some resistance exercises for their heads and necks. Then we put them through passive ranges. The dreaded contractures – terrible in this ward. We have to ratchet some of them. Plus we've got some home-made contraptions. But we just don't have enough staff, and we don't have any surgery, as I told you yesterday.'

Shelley noticed that the young nun had moved onto the balcony with her little patient. She had the baby over her shoulder and was still singing and rocking. The writing was on the wall, but Shelley couldn't bear the thought of the little mite dying.

'All right.'

'It's so good of you to help me, and the girls will like it.'

Two younger nuns were waiting near two cots pushed together with their sides down. Kavita set Shelley up with some oil and a towel and a pile of cotton squares for their faces.

'These first two like to come together.'

A little girl was lifted on to the bed.

'Rubina,' said Kavita. 'And this is Lani.'

Rubina's legs were twisted like skeins of wool. It was hard to see where any joints might have been. The nun lay Lani next to Rubina, and the two girls held hands. Shelley patted Rubina's head.

'Excuse me, Shelley, but don't do that. We never touch anyone's head.'

'Oh?'

'It's disrespectful.'

'Oh, I'm sorry.'

'That's okay. You weren't to know. You can't do much for Rubina, her contractures are too advanced. But we'll do a bit of chest physio and then some passive, then some light massage. That feels nice for her, and I think the human touch is very important.'

'Yes,' said Shelley.

'These two love each other very much. If one of them goes – well, it doesn't bear thinking about.' Kavita smiled through a few tears.

Tears came so easily here, Shelley thought.

Kavita showed her how to hang Rubina's head over the edge of the bed, on the left side then the right, how to encourage deep breaths, and how to percuss to achieve productive coughing. Nine times each set, three repetitions.

'Go easy with the percussion,' said Kavita. 'She's very thin, and we don't want to fracture her ribs. Try with just a gentle tapping with the side of your hand.' Kavita cupped her hands and showed Shelley how to drum lightly up and down the chest.

So Shelley did that, nine times a set, and three repetitions. Lani stroked Rubina's shoulders when she could.

By the end of that Rubina looked like a floppy toy.

'Maybe we've done a bit much,' Shelley said. Kavita smiled at Rubina and patted her hand.

'Yes, you're right, maybe. We'll just give a nice gentle massage now.' She said something to Rubina who gave a wan smile. Shelley massaged some scented oil into Rubina's shrunken legs, while Kavita continued treating little Lani.

The two girls held hands again and were taken back to the floor.

Next was Pradeep.

'Much more important to do Pradeep.'

'Yes?'

'Yes, she has very rapidly progressing contractures. She's old enough to do active movements – she can obey instructions, but you won't get much range initially. You need to really stretch the joints. I'll show you. After the stretches you should notice an improvement. Unfortunately, you will have to cause her a little pain to get the result. But too much and you will tear the tendons and make the contractures worse. And then we put her on a cross for a couple of hours.'

'Cross?'

'Yes.' Kavita pointed at a wooden machine with bandages and wires, in the shape of a cross. Medieval torture, looked like.

'Okay, I'll try.' And then, 'Do they have families, Kavita?'

'Yes.'

'Yes?'

'We are their families.'

Slow footsteps. Sister Kaur was shuffling up the stairs. Now she held onto the door frame and said something to Kavita.

One minute later Amit came in, looked around for Kavita and then strode up to her. There followed a kiss on the lips.

Not much doubt about that, thought Shelley.

Kavita washed her hands in the tin pail on the bench and walked with Amit towards the stairs.

'Do you mind carrying on, Shelley? Three sets of nine repetitions, with a rest in between. Thank you so much. I'll be back in a few minutes.'

Shelley did her best with little Pradeep. She asked her to show what she could do with knees first, then ankles, toes and hips. Pradeep tried hard, but movement was minimal. Then Shelley put her through a passive range of movement, wincing herself as the joints refused, like rusted old garden tools. How much pressure should she exert? And how much pain should she inflict? She didn't know. She couldn't bear to cause pain anyway. They tried active movements again. The girl made valiant efforts but nothing seemed to have changed much. Shelley wiped her face gently and wished she had a sweet. She didn't even have a shell.

She ransacked the recesses of her memory for a finger game and remembered, 'Five little ducks.' Pradeep giggled as fewer and fewer ducks came back. Lucky there was a happy ending when they all came back to kind mother duck. But what would Pradeep know of happy endings? Or kind mother ducks?

Pradeep pointed to the cross and shook her head vigorously. The nun laughed and took her back to the others. Shelley washed her hands with yellow soap in the washing up dish.

She walked around waving her hands in the air to dry them and ended up near the window. She could see Kavita and Amit, down in a dark alcove off the courtyard. They were up against the wall, and Amit was kissing Kavita's face and neck in gestures of urgency. Kavita was crying.

Shelley ricocheted from the window and walked rapidly to the other end of the room. Her heart was racing. Ridiculous, she thought. Calm down. They're allowed to be lovers. Or whatever.

She looked around for something to do. The Sister had gone, the girls were quiet and Kavita had gone. Should she go find someone?

She heard steps and Kavita was back. She came over and placed a hand on Shelley's arm. There was a reddening of her eyes and some tiny jewel-like tears on her lashes, but most people would never have noticed, Shelley thought, especially as Kavita gave Shelley a bright smile.

'Thank you, Shelley. Sorry I was longer than I thought. Amit had some business to discuss.'

'Fine,' said Shelley. 'Of course.'

They left the ward and walked along a veranda until they came to a small doorway which concealed a series of stairs running up to a tower with a view over Calcutta. Kavita showed Shelley the river, the park, the Dalhousie district and Howrah. There was a detectable breeze – faint, but wonderful. The traffic noise was muffled, and all in all it was very pleasant. They sat on a stone bench at the centre of the tower, with the circular parapet running around them. Shelley could see the river of muddy silver, with the dark red chimneys of Howrah beyond. There was a haze over everything, and only the taller towers and factories poked their horns through the mist, so that the scene looked like a historic watercolour.

Kavita pointed to an area of forest in a valley. 'That's where Dum Dum Jail is. You see the big stone walls? And over there is our look-out post.' Shelley recognised the ancient wedding cake.

'Yes.'

'So that's where our event will take place next week. You understand what's happening now?'

'Yes, I think I do. But Kavita, how do you feel about all those young people in danger? The prisoners in danger too?'

Kavita was silent a moment. 'Frankly, Shelley, not too good. I don't feel too good about it.'

She turned away. Tears were welling, Shelley knew.

'You're right to be concerned. There is grave danger for all of them. Even Amit.'

'But I thought Amit wasn't going to be in the front line.'

'That's what he says. But you never know with him.'

She was wiping the back of her hands over her cheeks. Excuse me, I'm sorry.'

'So, you and Amit are—are—'

'Oh, it's not like that at all.' Kavita's voice had become quite soft. Breathy. 'No. We are different castes and cannot marry. It is impossible.

He is Brahmin and I am Vaishya. Besides Amit is betrothed to another woman, someone he has not met yet. But it's all settled. They will be married in three months.'

Now the tears were coming.

Shelley must have looked shocked.

'Don't be so surprised, Shelley. It is the way things are done here. Amit says he doesn't want to meet her beforehand because it will just bring despair. He says if he can't marry me then he doesn't care who it is.' Kavita laughed a bitter laugh.

'And you? What will happen?'

'Oh, I'm in the same position,' said Kavita. 'My family has negotiated a perfect match for me too. And I shall stop all work, voluntary or otherwise. It's all arranged.'

'And who will do your work here?'

'We have no-one.'

'And have you met him? Your husband-to-be?'

'Yes.'

'And?'

Kavita said nothing.

'You don't like him?'

'He's been married before.'

'What happened to the first wife? He is not going to have two wives, is he?'

'No, no. She died.'

'Of?'

'Injuries.'

The ancestral home of Rabindranath Tagore was remarkable for its size, its colour and its cleanliness. The stone colonnades were the deep red of ripe tamarillos, and the green shutters and delicate white fretwork made an entrancing contrast.

Imposing yet exquisite. And clean – not a trace of the black grime that decorated everything in Calcutta. And even in good repair. No sheets of corrugated iron nailed up to cover a hole in the wall, no crumbling landslides of plaster. Shelley concluded that Tagore must be a god. The theory was strengthened when she saw a portrait of the great man – tall, with flowing white beard and hair, he definitely could pass for God.

Amit had suggested they go there 'as a break'. Shelley hoped he wasn't forgetting about her bones project. Amit led her around the verandas, and they peered into cool rooms enhanced simply with just one painting, one carpet or one vase of orange blossom.

'It is beautiful, is it not?' remarked Amit. 'I love it almost as much as I love Tagore.'

She decided to have a go at a Tagore quote. '*We live in the world when we love it*. I believe that's from Tagore.'

'You are quoting Tagore to me. That's very impressive. But what does that line mean?'

'I have no idea,' said Shelley.

'And neither do I,' said Amit, and they both laughed.

Amit stopped laughing and looked at her as if he had seen something different, and Shelley felt a little frisson. What was this? He was charming and handsome, for sure, but she should not be experiencing frissons. Must be jet-lagged. Judgment not quite right.

'I can recite Tagore to you for three hours, if you like,' he said.

Shelley laughed. 'That would be lovely, but two might be enough.'

The garden was an orderly square of lawn bordered with clipped trees, and Amit pointed out a low wall which would do for a seat. What luxury, in the middle of Calcutta. The traffic noise was subdued, and the honking horns sounded quite harmonious – a Calcutta symphony.

Amit started to make good his offer to recite volumes of Tagore, which he seemed to have learned by heart. He also interwove his own expressions of praise. 'India's champion of humanity,' he said.

'Right,' said Shelley.

'Shelley, I have a confession.' Amit looked shy.

'Yes?' said Shelley.

'I love Rabindranath Tagore. So, through Rabi, you have found the way to my heart.'

'Oh. Well, thank you.' She wasn't quite sure what Amit meant, but it was an opportunity. She should seize the moment. She reached into her bag. 'Amit, I wonder if you would look at my Tagore book – the one that I found with the bones. I just thought you might be able to find some clues.'

'You're worried I've forgotten about the bones, aren't you?'

'No. Well, possibly, just slightly.'

Amit laughed, and took the book, and leafed through it slowly.

They were the only people in the courtyard, apart from a young man with a wheelbarrow and a coconut whisk. No pan or shovel. He was picking up every seed pod and leaf with his hands. She watched him as Amit recited.

Amit followed her gaze, and said, *'Come out of thy meditations and leave aside thy flowers and incense! What harm is there if thy clothes become tattered and stained? Meet him and stand by him in toil and in sweat of thy brow.'*

He handed back the book.

Now she looked and saw the young man's legs were very thin, and he had a limp. His clothes weren't clothes, not of a recognisable sort, no – they were rags. Dirty grey rags. Something that might once have been a T-shirt, now full of holes. She wondered what Bob would say. Bob. That could be Bob. Same size, and now she looked, the young man had bowing of the tibia and fibula too. Polio. It was Bob.

She felt an axe chop into her heart. Was this how Bob used to be? Sweeping leaves meticulously for bugger-all money until – until what? Did he get sick and just lie down and die? Or something worse? Was there a mother back in the slum and little brothers and sisters relying on him, and one night Bob didn't come home? And now he was in a box under her bed. And his mother never knew. Never saw him again.

A few tears started to run down her face and drip onto her dress. Her so-called Indian dress, the green one. She had some toilet paper in her bag, and she scrabbled for it.

Amit sat up. He looked alarmed. This had come out of nowhere, in the middle of his poetry recitation.

Shelley tried to pull herself together. She wiped her eyes properly, then blew her nose. Everything that came out onto the tissue was black.

'It's just that—' She gave a little wave with her hands to indicate the boy. 'Just thinking of my bones and where they came from.'

'I see, yes. It's quite possible.' Amit laid a hand gently on her forearm. *'You must accept the simple truth, once you discover it, and then work to change things.'*

Amit made it sound like all she needed to do was wave a wand. She had no clue as to what the simple truth was.

'Now let's walk a little, and I will continue to bore you with Rabindranath Tagore.'

'Sure,' said Shelley. Be brave, she told herself. Trust Amit. He's a good person.

They walked slowly around the square of lawn, and the sweeper stood back to let them pass. Shelley smiled, but he just looked at her. She would have liked to have given him some money, but Amit was in full flight, and she didn't know if giving something would be seen as patronising, or asking for trouble, or both.

Amit picked up on her indecisiveness, interrupted his recital and said, without changing his tone of voice, 'Don't open your bag and don't give him money, that solves nothing. There will be plenty of needy people later on. Much more needy.'

Amit nodded at the young man, then continued. 'When Tagore died there were more than fifty thousand mourners. A huge crush of people around the bier. People were grabbing strands of his hair and beard so by the time his body got to the ghat there was no hair left. And then before the flames had died down people rushed the pyre to pick up mementoes. Bones, ash, anything. There were hardly any of his remains left for the *Ganga.*'

'Oh, how awful.'

'Just the navel. At least they left that.'

'Oh.'

'It's the most important part.'

'Oh?'

'The only part that doesn't burn. And it must be returned to the holy river.'

They were well past the sweeper now, and Amit stopped. 'But, Shelley, I must ask you – why are you so interested in our great poet?'

Shelley didn't know how to answer this. What would Amit think if he heard she'd been learning from a skeleton? Decide she was a nut case? Probably. Better leave that out of the conversation. They started walking again.

'Well, because I found the book with Bob, I mean the bones. I've read it many times – so lovely – to tell the truth I've become a bit obsessed with Sir Rabindranath Tagore.'

Amit stopped again. 'Never call him "Sir".'

'Sorry? Didn't he get a knighthood?'

'He renounced it four years later.'

'Why?'

'The Amritsar massacre. One of our darkest days. So Tagore gave his knighthood back.' Amit's eyes were glistening.

'I'm sorry. I didn't mean to offend you.'

Amit shrugged.

Shelley felt terrible. The happy atmosphere had disappeared completely. She was remiss in not knowing that Tagore had renounced his English knighthood, in not knowing about that massacre. She should have known about it, especially as she'd big-noted herself as a Tagore fan. Why did she always put her foot in it? But it showed how easy it was to hear only one side of history – the white side.

Perhaps she could mention the book again, show respect for Amit's opinion. He hadn't made any comment about it. Such an important piece of information, she thought.

'I don't know if you had any ideas about the book. I can show you another time. In case you'd like to review it, the underlining and writing and so on.'

Amit had been gazing at the path, but then looked at Shelley for a moment; his voice was kind. 'I'm going to need a little time to think about it, look at it again,' he said.

Perhaps she'd been forgiven. At least he hadn't rejected her mission completely.

They'd done a complete circuit and were approaching the sweeper again. Shelley felt she had to make some sort of connection with him.

'Amit, I really want to give him a little bit of money.' Amit didn't respond. 'Please.'

Amit was looking severe.

'Could you maybe just ask him if he knows of Trivedi Bros? Maybe where the new Trivedi Bros is, if there is a new shop? Then I can give him some money for his trouble. I just feel like he might know.'

Shelley wasn't quite sure if she meant this, but she definitely wanted to bring Amit's attention back to her mission, which seemed to have got pushed down the list yet again, and time was running out.

'Wait here then.' Shelley couldn't read Amit's face anymore.

He approached the boy, who looked terrified. Amit must have managed to reassure him because the boy started explaining something and gesturing over the walls.

'You are a genius, Shelley. He says they are at an address near M.G. Road, that's Mahatma Gandhi Road, which is this side of the river. Near the hospitals. I suppose it's true – but you never can tell.'

'Amit, that's wonderful. Can you give him this?'

'All of it?'

'All of it.'

'This is where he said they are,' said Amit, slowing down opposite a strip of shops that looked like it should be instantly condemned, just like the rest of Calcutta. 'Now to find somewhere to park.'

Shelley took her cotton bag and looked at the ground ahead before she got out of the car. Stepped carefully across a puddle full of rubbish.

In front of them were signs almost larger than the shop fronts, with English letters larger than the Hindi: 'Banerjee Medical Supplies', 'Bhogilai Pvt Best Medical Supplies' and 'New Medical Supply Agency'. Each had the usual peeling paint and black soot, grimy windows and security gates in various degrees of closure. Shelley could just see that behind the dirt and dust which coated the exterior of each shop was a colourful display of commodes, urine bottles, vomit dishes and tubing. Everything was in white and red, with plenty of red crosses.

Amit led the way past these establishments and then dived into a small alley, more of a drain really, which in turn opened onto a back lane lined by tall brick fences.

They surveyed the closest building. High fence with coils of barbed wire along the top of the walls. Promising. Locked gate further down. Large sign above the portico: 'TRIVEDI & SONS, SCI & ANAT SUPPLIES'. Very promising.

'Amit, maybe we should work out a strategy before we go in? Like who's going to speak and what we are going to say?'

'Very good idea, Shelley. I bow to your suggestion.' Amit made a tiny bow.

They moved away from the front entrance and stood in an alcove. It took a moment for Shelley to realise that the alcove was also occupied by three goats.

'Well, what I'm looking for is proof that they procure human bones and export them to the University of Australia. And even better if we can find out where the bodies come from.'

'And do you think they will tell you that?'

'They might tell you.'

'I doubt it.' Amit pulled her back against the wall as a donkey cart laden with white woven sacks was coming down the narrow lane. She tried to avoid touching the wall or the goats or the donkey. As it plodded past, she saw its hip bones sticking out and fleas all over its back.

'Yes, we must get our story right.' Amit stopped there. He didn't seem to have anything to suggest.

'Well, how about this? I am from the University of Australia, and I want to buy some bones and you are helping me?'

'They'll be suspicious.'

'Oh. Well, how about – we have some second-hand bones, and wondering if they'd like to buy them?'

'Second hand? They might think you mean your bones and that you're offering them.'

They both laughed – but Shelley thought it wasn't so funny.

'How's this?' Shelley said. 'You ring ahead. We say we're calling about the University of Australia account, and that I'm the Purchasing Officer or something and we want to increase our order. They should love that. But University policy now is that all large suppliers must be visited.'

'Sounding good,' said Amit, 'but what happens when we get there?'

'We make it up,' said Shelley.

They had gone back to Amit's factory to make the phone call and were in the office. The sales staff were milling about in the showroom, trying to find excuses to walk across the line of sight of the doorway and peek in. After all, this was the second time she'd visited. She could smell the slightly scorched air left by bolts of fabric. Maybe someone would bring her some water. No, a bottled drink.

Amit was speaking in Hindi, but Shelley knew what he was saying, as they had rehearsed.

'Hello, is this Trivedi's Anatomical and Scientific Supplies? Good. My name's Mr Mukherjee and I'm calling to confirm my appointment today.'

Reply, male voice.

'With someone from Sales, I believe.'

Reply.

'It is regarding one of your regular customers, University of Australia. I am the Australian Trade Consul for Bengal.'

Shelley smiled.

Reply.

'Hello, yes, it is Mr Mukherjee here. I'm calling to confirm our meeting today. I'm the Australian Trade Consul and I have the representative of University of Australia with me. You have received our correspondence I presume?'

Reply.

'Yes, the mail has been very bad. But the University of Australia is your long-term customer. Could you confirm that for me, so I can be sure I am speaking with the correct business? They purchase approximately one hundred items per year from you I believe. Yes, I'll wait.' Amit gave Shelley a smile. He was clearly enjoying himself. Fancied himself as an actor.

'Sorry, you did say one hundred per month? Are you sure? Just one moment please.'

Amit looked at Shelley and spoke in English. 'He says they purchase one hundred boxes per month? Seems unlikely?'

'Yes, impossible,' she said, 'Must be confused.'

Amit was speaking in Hindi again, as rehearsed. 'Good. Well the University Procurement Officer is in Calcutta today and she would like to discuss increasing the order. No, increasing. She wishes to come and meet you, check on stock and availability, and obtain a quote.'

Reply.

'Yes, this is a very good opportunity for your business.'

Reply – a question.

'Her name? It is—' Flash of panic on Amit's face.

Shelley realised what the question must be, grabbed Tagore and showed Amit a random page. *Poem 38*: '*... the joy that sweeps in with the tempest ...*'

'Miss Joy Tempest. That's correct. What time? Two pm? We'll be there then. Oh yes, may I just check the address?'

Amit had hung up. 'One hundred boxes of bones a month?'

'Clearly a mistake,' said Shelley.

Amit and Shelley didn't have long to wait at the front gate. Approximately one second after they pushed the doorbell a young man in white kurta and trousers opened the door, bowed and made a namaste, showed them past a small pond alive with fish, and then up some steps and though an open front door. The room was dark, and lined with pigeonholes and small drawers, and there were five men sitting around, some on stools and a couple on the counter. They were all dressed in similar white tunics and stood straight up when they saw Shelley and Amit.

Amit greeted them in Hindi and namastes were made and then he introduced Miss Joy Tempest. All the men made further namastes as did Miss Tempest in return. She had the feeling that she might have been the first European and the first woman in this shop – ever.

She'd done her best with business attire appropriate for the Procurement Officer for the University of Australia. Her blue-patterned dress from the Indian shop was finally earning its keep; and a white scarf would help quell the curls if she tied it around her head; a pair of reading glasses she hardly ever wore and a notebook and pen should lend a professional air. She was attempting to stand tall and look as if she had a budget of half a million dollars. Not easy.

She was offered a chair, chai, a cold drink, whisky, local rum, a snack. They couldn't do enough for her. Shelley was enjoying all the attention. A cold drink in a bottle would be great.

Amit did the talking. Brought out some business cards and handed them out. Indicated Miss Tempest a number of times.

Shelley wondered what the pigeonholes would have been for, as now they were all empty. Thank God they didn't have pigeons in them. There was no hint of the type of business conducted on the premises. In prime position on the desk was an old-fashioned typewriter – the sort that went ping when you started a new line – with a single piece of paper in it. Next to it, in perfect alignment, were two small wooden boxes – one containing a single pencil, and the other a stack of business cards. At the end of the desk was a small brass statue of Ganesh, the elephant god. Apart from these items and the numerous staff, the office was empty.

A young man had been instructed to present Shelley with a business card. She took it in both hands, after glancing at Amit to see if she was observing correct protocol. He seemed to nod. She couldn't help but notice how rough the cardboard was and how frayed the edges.

But more important than that, she wished she had a business card, for she knew they were of great importance in the commercial world here. Amit was chatting to one of the older-looking men, no doubt coming up with a credible explanation for the lack of reciprocal cards from Shelley.

The most senior man, judging by his beard and the height of his stool, bent down under the wooden counter and lifted up a large grey ring-bound folder. Licked a finger on a knobbly hand and started at the beginning. Everyone in the shop watched. Page after page. Sunlight in slats. Purchase order after purchase order. The dust specks suspended. Invoice after invoice.

There it was, a payment advice slip on a University of Australia letterhead. Shelley's eyes were bursting as she tried to read the small handwriting upside down. She couldn't. But she could see a figure '100' and a large number – possibly '5,000 R'. That would be about five hundred dollars for the order, or five dollars a box. How she would like a copy of that document.

Then there was another, and another, and then the next and the next. Dozens of payment advice forms. The old man appeared satisfied. He asked Amit a question. Amit gave him some information and indicated Shelley once or twice.

'He said the University of Australia must be very large, to require so many bone sets. They are very grateful for your custom, and he says your University must take Anatomy teaching very seriously.'

Shelley smiled and made a vague gesture involving her heart which was supposed to say thank you.

'Amit, can you say thank you for providing such excellent service?'

Amit delivered the message.

And then, 'Could you ask him whether this is a standing order – like one hundred sets per year?'

Amit spoke to the gentleman again. He looked puzzled and pointed to a number of invoices in his book, turning the pages and reading out dates.

Amit moved around to look over his shoulder and nodded several times.

'Yes, it's a standing order – correct. You've been buying one hundred sets a month for the last two years.'

Shelley had by now adopted a fixed smile, but at this moment she felt she could quite easily swallow the smile. She was stunned.

'Of course,' she said, 'my mistake.'

Amit continued chatting in a respectful voice, making almost imperceptible bows from time to time, and showing no surprise. A few folded five-hundred-rupee notes changed hands. Shelley followed Amit's lead and made many smiles and tried to look as though one thousand and two hundred bone sets a year would be a normal purchase for a university.

'Amit, can you ask him whether any other Australian universities purchase their bone sets here? He doesn't have to say which ones. Maybe the University of Australia onsells to some of the others?'

'I already asked him that – he says the other universities don't buy bones – they use commercial firms like Ramsay's Medical Supplies – and he says his company here is the main supplier to them. And he said each Ramsay's branch might buy one hundred sets a year maximum. That is why they are so impressed with your University. In fact, they love Australia University.'

'There must be something wrong. Can you ask him if we are up to date with payments?'

'Yes, he's told me that already. Says University of Australia is a very prompt payer.'

Astonishing.

The older man beckoned to one of the juniors.

'He's going to take us into their showroom, and they're going to make hand copies of the last twelve invoices for us,' he said.

'Amit, you're a gem. But what's been going on?' She was concentrating on looking professional and relaxed.

'They are very happy that you want to double the standing order.'

Shelley just about choked. 'I bet they are. Don't make me laugh.' She had a thought. 'Amit, can you see if they have copies of the shipping documents? You can say it's standard procedure now to review all documentation.'

'I'll ask,' he said. 'Lucky you're such a good client. I have the impression that you're their best customer. They'll give you anything you want.'

'And you're helping. With money – thank you.'

'Oh, that's just a few rupees. Never goes astray in India. What do you mean "gem"?'

'I'll tell you later. It's a compliment.'

The young man had been waiting. He opened a wooden door situated between two of the cases of pigeonholes, then reached an arm in, and turned on a distant light. The doorway was small and even Shelley had to bend over a little, as she followed the assistant into a narrow passageway. The walls were lined with old Hindi newspapers, and the floor sloped down, as if they were heading to a basement of some sort. She was aware of Amit behind her, and someone who was probably the manager behind Amit. There was a smell of something sharp, familiar – formalin, that was it.

Miss Joy Tempest and Mr Amit Mukherjee might never be seen again, she thought, except as body parts. But they couldn't back out now.

They followed the assistant through another door and entered a low-ceilinged showroom. The walls looked like they were made of crumbling dry stone, but the floor was a more modern white linoleum. There were no windows, and Shelley concluded that they must be underground. And in some danger of being buried alive.

The assistant was now switching on various fluorescent lights, and some dark dangling plants turned out to be articulated skeletons. They were in a hanging garden of skeletons in fact. She could also make out several long glass cases, and various charts and posters hanging on the walls, with titles like 'Nutrition', 'Functions of the Liver', 'Reproduction'.

The assistant was scurrying around, and glass cases were flickering into life. A friendly looking blonde called *Resusi-Anna* was on the top shelf, and underneath her, looking a little dusty, was *Cardio-Jo*.

In the case closest to Shelley was a hand-lettered sign: 'Models on Forensic Medicine (Art)'. The artist had been given free reign. He/she had had a field day with: 'Defensive Wounds Model (Art Model)', 'Decomposed Body Model (Art Model)', and 'Sulphuric Acid Vitriolage Model (Art Model)'. And, my God – 'Maggot Action Model (Art Model)'. A glass case of horrors.

In another case were specially prepared bones. An articulated foot. A female pelvis and baby's skull being sold as a pair.

The young man spoke good English and was pointing out the features. Genuine human bones, neat and clean, dried and bleached. The full skeleton comprised the skull with twenty-two bones, articulated mandible, cervical and lumbar spine with physiological lordosis, thoracic and sacral spine with physiological kyphosis, seven cervical vertebrae, twelve thoracic, five lumbar, and the sacrum. The clavicles and scapulae. Twenty-four pairs of ribs, sternum with manubrium and xiphoid, eight carpal bones, five metacarpals, fourteen phalanges, seven tarsal bones, five metatarsals, between eight and fourteen phalanges. They could be varnished if requested and, if articulated as a full skeleton, came with a stand and dust cover free of charge.

Miss Tempest wondered about the half-sets in boxes? Oh yes, plenty of those. And the young man took her to a side room and demonstrated that there were indeed hundreds of half-sets in boxes ready to go. In fact, that group there was the next University of Australia shipment, one hundred boxes addressed to Mr H. Jones. Did Miss Tempest know Mr Jones? Ah, good. Well, the arrival date for this shipment was September twenty-first, if she cared to watch out for it.

Oh, and had he mentioned that the bones could be varnished at a small extra cost?

Miss Tempest asked whether she could perhaps look inside one of the bones boxes just to remind herself what those bones looked like. Thank you. Could he please spread the contents of the box out – on the cabinet there? She had no issues – just part of the University's new audit procedure.

Thank you. She had decided not to increase the order today. She needed to check with University staff their forecasted enrolments for the next two years. The University will let Trivedi know as soon as possible whether there will be any change, but it's very good to know Trivedi can increase supply if necessary.

Miss Tempest wondered, naturally, where the bones came from? Were they Indian people and how did the bones get to Trivedi?

Well, he was not at liberty to disclose this information, but he could assure Miss Tempest of an uninterrupted supply.

'Oh good,' she said.

A few more five-hundred-rupee notes were finding their way from Amit to the hand of their host.

'And where do you prepare so many bones so beautifully? Here?'

'Oh no, Miss Tempest. The smells would be too strong for Dalhousie. No, we have a modern facility in Howrah.'

'Oh?'

'Near the bridge?' asked Amit.

'No, further out. We have patented processes – commercial-in-confidence, you understand, so we do not allow our clients to visit there.'

Could Miss Tempest ask one final question? What was the weight of the boxes of bones? Gross, for one set. Four kilograms? Thank you. It was getting a little warm, wasn't it?

Now was your next order to be varnished or unvarnished?'

'Madame? Varnished or unvarnished?'

Shelley felt elated and depressed all at once. Elated because they were hot on the trail. Depressed because even in India no-one cared. No-one seemed to think of the humanity behind all this tragedy. Besides, her leg was hurting. Too much standing.

They were back in the car, and Amit had just asked her what she wanted to do now.

'How far is Howrah?'

'Maybe five miles only but it's a very big place. Full of factories, all red brick, and lots of chimneys. Dark Satanic mills. From the Raj.'

'Oh.'

'I have no idea how to find a bone factory. It's like a pebble in a haystack.'

'Oh.' But she'd found out so much, she didn't want to be thwarted now.

'Let's have chai,' said Amit. 'When in doubt, *adda* and chai.'

'Great idea,' said Shelley. '*Adda* and chai.'

They drove for about twenty minutes but covered only a mile or so. Amit stopped behind a line of rickshaws who were presumably parked, as the drivers were all asleep on their front seats. He jumped out to open the door for Shelley. She took a hobbling leap over the puddle and didn't end up in the mud, which was good as she had her useless sandals on.

Amit took Shelley to a tiny establishment which sold excellent chai, he said. They had to walk down a set of stairs under the shops and sit on old wooden stools at tables made of ancient beams. Around the walls were posters to do with politics and theatre performances from the 1930s. The customers were all in earnest conversation and Shelley felt that history was being created right here.

She looked up at the street and all the legs hurrying, ambling, shuffling, hobbling, dragging past. Millions of people struggling to survive.

Why didn't they value human life here? Did anyone other than Shelley Conway care that young people might be grabbed off the streets with nobody knowing and turned into a box of bones? Did that history matter?

And why on earth did the University of Australia need one thousand and two hundred boxes of bones per year?

'Amit, I want to show you something. I've shown you it before, but I feel we haven't extracted all the information. It's the Tagore from my box of bones with words underlined. May I show you again? I'd really like you to think about it.'

Amit took the book and regarded the passages seriously. 'There are numbers with circles around,' he said, 'and all these words that sound so, so – gloomy somehow. Gloomy and outdoorsy. Mist and dew and shadow. Mountains, stream, wild, black. They're all Tagore's words but sound pretty bleak. Doesn't sound like India – sounds like a Scottish moor.'

'Yes,' said Shelley. 'That's what I want you to have a think about. Could it all mean something? Apart from the address, which we already know about.'

'I doubt it,' said Amit. 'But let me write them down.' He took a small notebook from his pocket and wrote down a list of numbers and words.

'Now I'll write them down in a different order.'

'Well,' he said after studying the words and numbers for a while, 'it could possibly mean something. That might be an address in Howrah. I'm going to show my friends here.' He indicated a group of men in deep conversation further back in the room.

'I'll just look at the documents they gave you, if you don't mind, Amit,' said Shelley. Amit retrieved the envelope from somewhere under his kurta, gave it to her and went to talk with his mates.

It really was true – one hundred sets a month. Yes, there they were on the Bill of Lading. One hundred sets x six kilograms = six hundred kilograms per shipment. That was one month. Shipping would be expensive.

Amit was chatting with the café patrons, and there ensued a discussion with much referral to the notebook. Soon the whole place was offering suggestions.

'We've come up with a few possibilities. This is going to take a tour of Howrah, something I have never done myself.' He thought for a moment. 'I think it might be best if I get my driver. That way we won't be worrying. Have you finished your chai?'

Amit proposed taking Shelley back to the hotel so she could have a rest while he fetched his driver. Great idea, Shelley couldn't believe how hot and dusty she was, and how tired she felt.

Shelley was waiting for Amit in the lobby, feeling Lilliputian as usual. She was resting her left foot up on the struts of the huge coffee table – her leg was horizontal but still nowhere near the glass top. She wondered if her leg was getting shorter. Maybe if she tried elevating the right. Tried to keep them even.

It was hot, even under the fan, and she was completely exhausted. So much to think about she couldn't think. Her leg was sore.

She remembered people pulling her legs when she was young. Hurting her so much she couldn't help screaming. Screaming for her mum and dad. Of course, they never came. They couldn't, could they? But she didn't know that. She just knew there was no-one there who cared for her.

It was in that blue room in the Children's Hospital, where the walls were the colour of pigeon's eggs, and she could hear the pigeons with their little pigeon engines idling outside the window, and she could see them swaggering along and observing her agony with interest, using their shiny black eyes. Doing nothing to help her. She'd never liked pigeons, with their non-stop noise and their strutting and their awful colours – grey like wolves and green like aliens and red like blood. And when they were killed by a hawk there was such a mess of feathers and usually a beak or an eye. Messy in death, they were. She hated pigeons.

And just lately that pain was coming back. Must be the stress of the trip and seeing all those cripples.

'Shelley, Shelley.' She jumped. Oh, the pain. Her leg.

It was Amit, come to fetch her.

'Amit, I'm sorry. I must have gone to sleep.'

He looked fresh and clear – his eyes were shining, his teeth white, his lips full.

'Shelley, I've had a look at the three potential addresses that my chai-wallah friend suggested, and there's really only one that makes any sense. One of the three doesn't actually exist as far as I can tell and one of them is in the middle of a huge jute factory. We'll have a look there, but I think it's unlikely. Which leaves 104 – 106 Kalu Ram Road.'

Shelley's face would have shown her despair. 'That's the old Trivedi. Where we were a few days ago.'

'Yes, the address we have already visited. But,' continued Amit, 'I just wonder if we were too hasty in our conclusions. I feel we should go again and look around the back of the building. There's a lot of slum space there I wasn't aware of. This time we must go right around the building.'

They were at Good Old Trivedi again.

'We'll go round the back,' said Amit. He had some words with the driver, and they parked a bit further up the road. Trishaws and rickshaws and afternoon trade flowed past.

Amit's driver opened the boot and took out a small three-rung ladder.

'We might need this,' said Amit, pointing to the ladder. 'Many businesses in Calcutta have high walls, especially ones with something to hide.'

Young boys had started to gather. The driver spoke to one and gave him a couple of coins. The little bloke looked about seven or eight. He was dressed in rags and consisted of bones with skin on top. He stared at Shelley.

'He's probably never seen a western woman before,' said Amit. He spoke to the boy, then laughed. 'He's asking me if you're Hanuman, the monkey god,' he said. 'It's the hair, they've never seen anything like it.'

Their young guide led the three of them plus ladder into a tiny passageway, really a culvert with a filthy stream at the bottom. There was no space for bikes or rickshaws, but there were plenty of people – people who stopped and stared at the European woman with bare arms who was walking gingerly along the culvert. Shelley was wearing her ridiculous 'Indian' sandals, and was keeping her feet astride the stream, trying to avoid what looked like sewage. Up on the sides of the culvert was red splodge after red splodge – betel nut, Amit said. Shelley tried to avoid these too, but as people pushed past, she was forced to capitulate and just walk through the splodges. She'd always found it hard to walk on a slope. She'd slung her cotton bag with her camera diagonally across her chest. The little fellow, in bare feet, and Amit, in proper sturdy sandals, strode on through everything. The driver was somewhat encumbered by the ladder, but put it on top of his head, and managed to manoeuvre it through the twists and turns. Nobody gave him a second glance – perhaps they thought he was carrying a tray of *naan*, Shelley thought, or maybe people always walked about with ladders.

They threaded their way around the plywood and hessian and tin. Shelley had glimpses of cooking pots and coals and faces in the dark. People were on their haunches, grinding things between stones. Children peered out through cracks, and young women slid into the shadows. Shelley felt some splashes of water and moved away from a man who was giving himself a dousing using a tin bucket and a rusty pump. A toddler was squatting down nearby. He stood up and moved to a second spot to do more. Shelley saw the result – something that looked like it had been squeezed out of a yellow mustard bottle.

Their little procession made turn after turn; the driver having increasing trouble with the ladder. Amit looked around frequently to make sure Shelley hadn't been left behind.

No way would she let that happen.

The footpath eventually emptied into something more like a creek. The water looked even filthier, and the banks were a tangled mass of vines and rubbish. Shelley thought she could see a hole scooped out from under the bank on the opposite side of the creek, underneath a collection of pieces of basket, coconut fronds, and scraps of corrugated iron. A dwelling. A woman was washing a baby in the creek, and a little boy was lifting water up to his mouth. Their young guide pointed upstream to a cyclone wire fence running across the creek, and then he retreated to the shade of some large trees.

Shelley could now pick out the rear of Trivedi Bros, with its high walls reaching right down to the creek, and beginning again on the other side. The gap in the brick fence was covered by a cyclone wire fence as high as the walls. Amit's gaze was fixed on a point beyond the cyclone wire, in the creek, and then Shelley saw. Well, first she smelt, then she saw. Initially she thought it was rubbish trapped against the cyclone wire. But then she realised that she was looking at a neat row of cigar-shaped bundles bound with rope and nets, and with rocks placed around to weigh them down. Corpses. Corpses with flesh eaten away to various degrees. About thirty of them. At the upstream end an intact body, at the downstream end a perfect skeleton, still articulated.

'This is their cleaning facility,' said Amit. 'All natural, no chemicals utilised. Fish and beetles do the work.'

Shelley stared in horror at the eaten flesh which was alive with crawling things – maggots, worms, beetles. The smell was revolting and was making her gag. She had never smelt anything like it, not even in dissection.

The driver had backed away downstream, next to the little boy. He had manipulated the ladder through all those narrow laneways, but he now put it down on the ground, in front of Amit, covered his mouth and nose with one hand and waved the other, to show he couldn't go further.

Amit pointed to the bodies. 'Let's hurry up and get out of here. But don't forget they could be my comrades.'

Amit's comrades? Had she heard right?

Amit used the ladder as a sort of scythe to clear a path through the mass of vines which surrounded the ramparts of Trivedi Bros. Shelley was trying to drape the front of her dress across her mouth without being immodest. Anything to block out that smell.

Amit waded through the jungle and managed to reach a wall where he tried to prop the ladder. He pulled away handfuls of vine and creeper to create a path, so the ladder could lean against the wall and not topple back. The driver and the boy stood watching.

Amit was tall, and only had to go up one step. Silence. Then he came down without saying a word and held the ladder for Shelley.

Even though she had prepared herself for something like this, Shelley was still shocked by what she saw over the wall. There right in front of her was a low corrugated iron roof. And all over that, bleaching in the sun, were bones. Bones and more bones. Bones in order – arranged anatomically. Hundreds of skulls neatly piled, femurs and tibias lined up like firewood. Small bones in wicker baskets, carefully sorted, as if they were off to the market. A basket of cuboids here, a basket of naviculas there. Bigger bones, like ribs, all placed neatly on bits of cloth. The skulls balanced carefully, like coconuts. It was the dreadful evidence she had both feared and desired. So orderly, like a regular business. India's finest export-quality bones.

Below the drying roof was a courtyard strung with wire clothes lines. There were dozens of vertebral columns, hanging like Christmas decorations, and a few skeletons, twisting and turning like mobiles, proudly intact and fully articulated.

The smell came in waves, and Shelley was feeling not only nauseated but a bit faint on the ladder. She remembered the camera in her bag. Sweat was pouring down her face and the viewfinder in the Instamatic was so steamed up she couldn't see. She was scared they would be spotted soon by the Trivedi Bros, or some local vigilantes, and her hands were trembling. She pointed the camera in the general direction and took about a dozen photos, over a third of her film supply, and hoped the photos would come out.

As she came down, Shelley couldn't help but feel vindicated. 'It is true,' she said to Amit.

'I never disbelieved you, Shelley.'

She wasn't sure whether she disbelieved him. But she had to remember it was her quest, not Amit's. He had enough causes.

'I should stake out this place,' said Shelley, 'and see who brings the bones in and where they come from.' A bit of false bravado. Taking the lead.

'If you really want to know,' said Amit, 'you will have to go to the burial ground. But it's not a very good place, and I really think you should go back to your hotel to recover from all this. Then you can decide what you want to do. But if you want to go, I will take you.'

Perhaps he was feeling ever so slightly guilty.

Amit was right – the burial ground wasn't a good place. Not for her, not for anyone. For a start, the smell. The evening driver had parked the car under a large tree, and they'd wound down the windows to get a bit of air, but it hadn't helped. To be fair, Amit had warned her. There were so many deaths right now, the burial grounds couldn't cope, he'd said. At least the Hindus burnt their dead, much more sensible.

Here the smell could kill you, she was certain. Corpses, plus rotting jackfruit and durian. It was nauseating. It was vile. There would be a moment when you thought it might be better, and then another pulse would come. Shelley felt her stomach heaving and clapped her hand to her mouth. She was salivating profusely and could feel cold sweat on her forehead. She was trying to swallow the saliva, but the gagging forced it up her nose.

They were sitting in the back seat. There were quite a few other cars and trishaws parked around, but all appeared to be empty. In fact, there were no people here at all. If Shelley hadn't felt so sick, she might have laughed. Two back-seat lovers outside the burial ground. How romantic.

The burial ground was tucked in and around huge trees. 'Mangoes,' Amit had whispered when she'd heard the soft plops and looked questioningly at him. The moon was out already, and Shelley could see soft glimpses of light reflected from one of the taller white statues. It was just like cemeteries at home, a little ghostly city.

She took some deep breaths and tried to quell the nausea. Vomiting would make a terrible noise.

It seemed remarkable that there were so few people here, in the middle of Calcutta. Not only remarkable but worrying. She and Amit had been hemmed in by humanity for most of the last twelve hours – thousands of people wherever they went – busy women in saris, bare-chested workers in dhotis, children throwing stones, and beggars. Beggars everywhere. Beggars without arms, without legs, without arms or legs, beggars with ulcers, blind beggars, limping beggars, beggars with babies. A panoply of afflictions. So sad, especially the little children. It had taken all her strength not to give up, not to tell Amit she wanted to go back to the hotel, back to Australia.

The quiet was unnerving, and her revulsion at the smell was tinged with fear. Amit had told her that even body-snatchers were scared of consecrated ground – they wouldn't enter some Christian burial grounds because of the ghosts. On the other hand, it was probably a good time to find grave robbers, he had said, because there were many, many deaths right now, and families were too scared to send their sons and grandsons to watch over the graves. Normally, teenage boys were sent to guard the graves at night, but now the living were as at much risk as the dead.

Shelley thought she could see lights flickering from the depths of the burial ground, and tapped Amit on the shoulder, but Amit just shrugged and made a hand signal that seemed to indicate 'relax'. As if.

Could it be a fraction cooler here under the mango trees? Shelley was starting to feel a bit drowsy. Long day. Jet lag. Emotion. Heat. Trivedi. Bones. What a place Calcutta was.

She woke with a jump. Someone was shaking her shoulder. Where was she? And then she remembered and followed Amit's outstretched arm. Lights, a parade of fairy lights wending its way through the trees in the burial ground.

Amit opened his car door slowly and quietly and beckoned to Shelley. He had a large flashlight in one hand. They didn't close the doors, just pulled them to, and walked to a tree beside the gates. The lights were coming closer, and Shelley could make out a few human shapes and some flickering lanterns. They appeared to be carrying two long bundles. Shelley caught glimpses of the blue of tarpaulins. They were moving slowly, lanterns up and down, presumably negotiating an uneven path, broken up by rocks and tree roots. Shelley's heart was racing. She was terrified they would be discovered, and she had no idea what Amit's plan was, or whether he even had one. She was starting to realise that this was his way of doing things. Minimum fuss, maximum surprise; minimum preparation, maximum effect. The little team of porters and their bodies were just coming out of the burial ground when Amit stepped out from the shadow of the trees, flashlight on.

The shadows dropped their two bundles which thumped onto the ground. One of the bundles started to roll down the slope. A limb sprang out. Or half a limb. The party scattered, several running back into the burial ground, others dodging to left or right. Amit yelled something to his driver, and the two of them grabbed one of the runners as he attempted to sprint past. They had one arm each. Amit shone the flashlight in his face, and revealed a terrified young man, perhaps only fourteen years old, gabbling and wailing. He spotted Shelley in the torchlight and began to scream. Amit's driver spoke to him in a stern voice, and he dropped to his knees, pleading. Amit then spoke in a gentler voice, calming him.

They dragged him over to some rocks and then all three squatted down. Amit asked the questions. If the answers were not satisfactory, he raised his voice a little, but mostly his manner was kind. After about ten minutes of conversation, he drew a banknote out of his pocket and gave it to the young man. He pointed to the bodies, then gave him an extra note. The boy tore down the path and onto the street.

Amit spoke to his driver, then turned to Shelley. 'I am sorry, Shelley, that you did not get to speak to our young grave robber. He thought we were ghosts, especially when he saw you.'

'That's understandable,' said Shelley, 'but what did he say?'

Amit's hair was not perfectly arranged, and his kurta was sweaty. 'I think we'll go to my home and then talk,' he said.

'But what about those?' said Shelley, pointing in the direction of the two bodies. She had lost track of the rolling one but thought it had fetched up in vines or against a rock. The only light came from Amit's flashlight, now balanced against a stone. The driver had switched off his torch and was squatting on the ground having a smoke. The tobacco smell was a relief.

'Ah yes.'

'Shouldn't we notify someone?'

Amit smiled wearily. 'Who?'

'The police?'

'They're not going to be interested, Shelley. What's dead is dead.'

'What will we do, then? With the bodies I mean. Their poor families.'

'We've got some choices,' said Amit. 'The first thing we could do is go and pick up those two bodies, re-wrap them and then re-bury them. We've only got two flashlights. We'd have to walk around slowly for hours to have any hope of finding the right graves, though I think they'll probably be over in the Eastern corner.' Amit indicated the general direction with the torch. 'But it's a very large burial ground, and the batteries will almost certainly run out before dawn.'

The thought of being in that cemetery at night with no torch made Shelley feel panicky. She could hardly imagine wandering around those passageways between graves and monuments, tripping over creepers, vines catching you in the face – maybe even stepping into a grave.

'There must be something else we can do,' she said. 'Can't we get the Government to deal with it? And that would be proof of what's happening. So they can put a stop to it—'

'Shelley, the Government of India is corrupt. There will be bribes and pay-offs all up the line, starting with the police. That's why they use a blind eye. We will probably end up in Dum Dum Central ourselves if we make any complaint. And of course, I am not anxious to be labelled as a troublemaker.'

'But we can't just leave those bodies here,' said Shelley, 'for the dogs and the jackals and the—the rats and whatever else—' She didn't know if they had jackals in India but was sure there would be rats.

'The best thing, Doctor Shelley from Australia, would be to call those boys back and let them continue with their dastardly deed.'

It was so dark she could scarcely see Amit's face. She could see the driver's cigarette, but goodness knows who else was lurking in the shadows, or behind the gravestones. The stench of death was suddenly trumped by a draft of something sweet, like lilies. My God, please, someone, get me out of here.

'Okay.'

Amit spoke quietly to the driver, who nodded, as if he had been expecting this all along. He calmly stubbed his cigarette out on a rock, then leapt up, sprang behind a headstone, and dragged one of the exhumation team boys out of nowhere. It was just like catching a rabbit. Amit was shining his torch in their direction. Shelley couldn't be sure if it was the same boy as before, but he seemed equally terrified. Again, there was a bit of a talk, and another banknote changed hands. The boy vanished.

Amit flashed the torch around. It made Shelley nervous when the light left their little patch. The corpses lay obediently in their spots. Amit seemed satisfied. The scene was surreal.

The teenage boy was back, and behind him the little team with its lanterns. The boys each grinned at Amit and proceeded to re-wrap their bodies. Shelley gathered courage, grabbed Amit's torch and walked over to one of the tarpaulins. White sheets and ropes had been cut crudely and a body was just visible. It looked like a young woman. Her arms had been pulled out of the wrappings, what was left of them, both arms had been severed at the elbows. Shelley could see a splintered stump of humerus.

'The knife must have been blunt,' Amit whispered. 'Or they used an axe. She's a Muslim. And she must have been married because she had bracelets. That's what the grave robbers mostly want – the gold bracelets. It was – interference with pregnancy—'

'Abortion?'

'That's it, abortion. Maybe the husband is not the father. She died two days later – the family would have nothing to do with her. Of course, she didn't get a proper Muslim burial, and the boy said she had no jewels apart from the bracelets, but someone got to her first and cut the arms off, so this is all that is left for them – her bones – not worth much – especially without arms—'

'Oh.'

'She's really an impure person in their culture,' said Amit. 'In Hindu culture too, the same – she was lucky to get a burial at all, she should have been thrown in with the untouchables.'

Amit took Shelley by the arm and stood her beside a huge fig tree away from the young men, who were tidying up their corpses.

'Shelley, our young friend told us some other things, which I must convey to you. These boys don't have homes. Or families. They live under bridges. Every so often bad men come with sticks and knives, and grab one or two of them and take them away. Terrible things happen to these stolen ones, and the boys know that sometimes one will end up at Trivedi. They've seen it, and that's who they thought we were tonight, snatchers.'

'Oh, no.'

'Sometimes the poor boys are buried alive, and someone comes back later for their bones.'

'No, Amit, no.'

Shelley was sensing the floating feeling, and Amit's voice was deep and growling like a slow record.

'I am sorry to tell you this, but this is what we heard tonight. You might have noticed I gave them some money, and that is why.'

Shelley started to shiver. A rigor took hold, and she couldn't stop it. Shiver, shake, shudder. She sat down on a rock.

'You must have suspected some of this, Shelley.'

Amit took a handkerchief from his pocket. He bent down and wiped sweat from her forehead and shone the torch in her face. 'You look very drawn. I am sorry. I don't think it was wise to come here after all. We will go back to my house once you feel strong.'

'Strong? She felt like she could just die. Her Bob, one of those poor boys? All those boxes in the storeroom at the med school – were they boys who were snatched? Bodies dug up?'

'I'm going to look for my driver. Just stay there Shelley, until I find him. Don't move.'

'Amit, please don't be too long.'

Shelley thought she might never be able to stand up again. Her knees were wobbly, she was sweaty and cold, and she felt feeble. It was dark, and all she could see was the ethereal glimmer of monuments in the graveyard. On top of that she was having hallucinations – hearing noises, people shouting in the distance.

But now a light was coming, bouncing up and down. It was Amit running back to her, his voice behind the flashlight shouting. 'Shelley get up, we have to run. Hurry! Hurry! I can't find my driver. Hurry, or they'll kill us.'

'What? Who?'

Amit was lifting her up under her shoulders. He was shouting. 'Get up, Shelley, you have to run fast. They think we've dug up the bodies. We have to hide quickly. Stay close and watch the light all the time – stay right behind me. I know it's hard for you, but you must.'

Shelley was up and all faintness was gone. She was right behind Amit, and they were scrambling over some rocks to get up onto a path through the cemetery.

Shelley saw monuments looming like ghosts. Creepers everywhere, so easy to trip. Be careful – watch your feet, jump when you have to. Watch that foot, watch that leg. Torchlight sweeping, shadows moving. Rocks to trip on. Vines on the ground. Dark all around. Pairs of eyes. Headstones, graves. Massive mausoleums. A city of mausoleums. Weaving. Ducking. A startled rat. Another one. Fucking dozens of them.

Voices behind – a mob, angry. My God. Keep up. Amit was puffing and so was she, the path uphill now and it was much harder.

'We're not going to make it to the other side – we'll have to find somewhere to hide.'

The yelling was definitely coming their way. Angry shouts, getting closer. More and more people shouting, getting closer again, all around them. They can see the torch – they know where we are.

Amit was shining the torch into a partly open mausoleum. It seemed to be a double one. Part of the wall had collapsed, and a skull was visible in the moonlight. Another skull, and bones on a shelf, lots of them.

'Get in there. Shelley, you have to, no argument, I'm coming too. It's big enough. I have to turn the torch off. Now.'

Shelley sat on the ledge of the mausoleum and put her feet in. She could fit through the opening in the concrete. She had no idea how far down it went or what she'd land on. Would it be coffins, or bones, or mud? My God.

Amit pushed her and said, 'Get in.'

She worked her way through the crack and stepped into the unknown. Her feet landed on softness, maybe leaves. But rocks underneath. God, were there bodies? At least it wasn't wet. But earth was tumbling around her, she could sense it. Maybe they would be buried alive.

There was a dry rot smell, like mice and decaying forest and dust in the rain and compost – it was overwhelming. She put her finger hard up against her nose. Mustn't sneeze – push hard, Shelley.

Amit was next to her. He spoke very quietly. 'Lie down Shelley. Crawl that way as far as you can, away from the hole. Hurry. Make yourself as small as you can. Quick. I'll cover us with leaves. Then you have to be completely silent and still. They'll be looking around for us, and they'll kill us if they find us.'

My God. Could this be true? It must be some sort of dream, surely. Amit was piling leaves and soil and sticks on top of her. She hoped it was sticks, not bones. She wondered where the skeletons were. Was it so old the coffins had rotted? But it must be a crypt and be lined by concrete, surely, to have this space in it? Please God make it an old crypt and someone's removed the coffins. Please God, no rats. Amit pressed up close, pushing her into the far side of the grave where torchlight wouldn't reach.

Shelley spoke to herself without making a sound. 'C'mon Shelley, pull yourself together. Remember what you're here for, not to be a baby.'

The voices were coming. They sounded as if they were overhead. Yelling, shouting. Please don't let them have dogs. Lantern light visible through the crack above them. This was far worse than any movie. Worse than *Sound of Music* in the graveyard. Amit holding her. Keeping her close. She was shaking and her heart was thrashing. Please don't let her teeth clatter. Please don't let her sneeze. Push on your nose Shelley, hard. Please God if they find us let them have guns so they can shoot us quickly. Please God let the concrete collapse and kill us before they do. Please God.

Voices off to one side now, getting a bit softer. But don't trust anything. Oh, the sweat. She was drenched. Don't let go of me, Amit.

And what if they couldn't get out?

Shelley decided she'd probably been asleep, but she wasn't sure. It was hard to know what was real and what was nightmare. The crowd had raced through the cemetery and into the streets beyond. The shouting and explosions had gone on for ages, but eventually the noise must have died down.

Once things had been silent for a very long time, they climbed out of the grave. Shelley realised how sore she was. Sore and stiff, felt like she'd been run over by three trucks and a bulldozer.

The moon was now high in the sky – a sharp disc that was bathing the cemetery in clear light. The monuments and gravestones stood stolid, and cobwebs were draped, shroud-like, from one to the next.

What a night.

'I think we're safe now,' said Amit in a low voice, which still sounded very loud.

They crept down the paths towards the entrance. Shelley held onto Amit's warm arm, all the while checking over both shoulders. Her leg was throbbing, and she couldn't stop limping. She jumped at a scuffling sound, and actually felt glad to see a rat.

They both saw the glow of the cigarette. Shelley froze.

'It's my driver,' said Amit. The driver was leaning back on the fence, legs outstretched and smoking, as if this was a perfectly normal place to be at four am.

'He knows a lot but says nothing.' Amit pulled some notes out of his now-filthy clothing.

They got into the back seat and Amit put his hand on Shelley's knee. 'I don't know how to apologise.' His hand moved up and down a few centimetres, and then he removed it.

'It's okay,' said Shelley. She was too tired to speak.

'They killed a tourist in Kashmir burial ground a few years ago for the same thing. He was Australian too. Stoned him to death, I think. I didn't want to tell you this last night—'

'It's okay.'

'But at least you know where the bones come from now.'

'Yep.'

'India is full of things that are not right. Revolution is the only thing that will change India.'

'Ye-e-ss.' Shelley was dirty – filthy in fact – sweaty and tired. That was really the only thing she could think about.

'Now you need to go back to your hotel for a shower and a sleep.'

She couldn't even reply.

Shelley slept for the whole day. She woke up at around three pm, and, after some thought, decided she felt half-human. She lay in bed looking at the shreds of the curtains blowing back and forth in a little breeze and listening to the street sounds below. It was almost comforting, this world-in-a-street. The whole of life playing out on an unsealed road right under your nose. She rolled over for a stretch and noticed something white under the door – an envelope. Her heart romped along for a second or two and she felt as though she couldn't catch her breath – a flashback to those envelopes under the door at home. But then she calmed down – those people, whoever they were, couldn't reach her here. She got up and retrieved the note.

Dear Miss Shelley Conway,

I would like to take you to see Rabindra Setu at six pm.

Yours truly,

A. Mukherjee.

Shelley had no idea who or what *Rabindra Setu* was, but she'd be ready at six pm. But first she was starving, and she needed to wash some clothes.

She dressed quickly and went down to reception and ordered what she hoped would be a lot of food. She knew 'dhal' and 'roti' and said 'curry two' – and held up two fingers, hoping this might mean something. The result was excellent – they brought it to her room, and she ate the lot. She had a very long shower and washed as many clothes as she could in the process and strung them all over the bathroom. Now she looked like a genuine Calcutta resident.

She wished she'd brought more dresses and had not wasted space on the jeans. And since the jeans were no use, the T-shirts were useless as well. She'd been cycling the two Indian shop dresses – the green one and the blue-patterned one – and the white harem pants – and had been saving the longer red cotton paisley dress for good. But there was now no choice – she deemed *Rabindra Setu* at sunset 'good', even though she had no idea what they would be doing. Could be mountain-climbing, knowing Amit.

'You look very attractive in that colour,' said Amit, when he arrived. 'Your hair does not look so red.'

Right.

'Oh, I hope I did not offend you. Your hair is beautiful. Like garnets in fact.' He put his hand out and shaped the outline of her hair as if it he was fashioning a precious sculpture, and then rewarded her with an entrancing smile. Her heart gave two skips.

'Thank you.'

'Shelley, you are so brave.'

She would rather he'd kept on with the beautiful theme.

'Now I want to show you *Rabindra Setu* at sunset, because it is one of the great sights of the world.'

'And what is it?'

'Oh, you don't know? Then we shall keep it a surprise.'

They drove for about fifteen minutes, and Shelley was again mesmerised by the intimate life of India on public display. Amit stopped in a small street where there was a line-up of stalls selling everything from slippers to chai.

He opened the door for Shelley and then turned and spread his arms to frame the view. Down from the road was a body of water of palest blue, and in the distance a bridge that looked like it was pegged to the sky.

'This is *Rabindra Setu*,' said Amit.

'The water?'

'No, Shelley, the water is the *Ganja*. The bridge is *Rabindra Setu*. "Setu" means bridge, and "Rabindra" is of course your Rabi.'

'My Rabi?'

'Yes, your Rabi. That's why I thought you'd like to see it. And it is even more beautiful at night. Like you.' He smiled at her.

'Oh,' said Shelley. She was unsure whether being compared to a bridge at night was a compliment. 'And the *Ganja* – that is the Ganges? The actual Ganges?'

'Oh Shelley, yes,' said Amit, looking at her intently, 'that's the *Ganja*. Our mother. That is our way to our next life.'

He turned back to the river. 'It is technically called the Hooghly here, but it is the *Ganja*.'

Shelley looked over the river. A watercolour wash of blue – a gradation from azure through cerulean into a milky sheen, and then eventually an orange mist. Opposites on the colour wheel. Blue into orange.

She'd learned about the river at school – important, long, sacred, defining. It was peaceful and yet mighty. It had a beginning and an end and yet was endless – circulating from the Himalayas to the ocean and back. Sacred for birth and death. And now she was standing on its banks. Tears came to her eyes.

Amit put his arm around her shoulder and then turned her to face him and kissed her forehead. 'Here you are at the beginning and end of everything.'

'Now, follow me closely.' He was carrying a torch, although it was not yet dark.

After a hundred or so metres Amit turned and said, 'We're just in time for sunset, Shelley. Not that we see the sunset because the sun is behind us, but we see the last rays of the sun on the bridge and the water.'

They picked their way down a small gravel path in between little dwellings and stalls. A lady with a scarred face and a red head covering held her hands out towards Shelley as if she was blessing her, a group of children stared, a young woman with a gold bindi on her forehead held out a tray of balls of what looked like rice.

'Rice balls,' explained Amit over a shoulder, 'for your ancestors.'

He stopped and spoke to a man sitting cross-legged on an upturned metal pail. The man called to a little girl who fetched a beaker and a brown plastic bottle with a screw-top lid. Amit passed over some notes, well above the value of the two items, Shelley thought.

They were now just above the level of the river and there were concrete steps leading down into the water, under a canopy of branches and leaves. Shelley couldn't tell what sort of trees. The leaves made black heart-shaped silhouettes against the iridescent light from the river.

'Pipil trees,' said Amit. 'Sacred. People build their houses around them. I will show you later.'

'These are the ghats,' said Amit. 'Steps. Be careful. They are slippery.'

He took Shelley's hand and helped her down to the bottom step, then asked her to cup her hands. He gathered some water from the river in the beaker and poured it into her hands.

'Now you must pour some water over the stones, and then into the river.' He showed her. 'Good.'

Amit poured some water over his face and into his mouth. He pushed his hands back through his wet hair.

He looked at Shelley with the water drops on his forehead and said, 'I come as an orphan to you, moist with love.'

'Amit?'

'Moist with love, Shelley. I come moist with love.'

'What?'

He put a hand under Shelley's chin, turned her face a little, and kissed her on the mouth. Then he said, 'Oh Shelley,' put a hand on the centre of her back, pressed her hard to him and gave her another kiss. A deeper one.

He released her. 'Sorry, Shelley, but there is a poem which is affecting me.'

Amit put his hand over his heart. 'Jagannatha was a famous poet.'

'Oh?'

'Yes, long before Rabi. He fell in love with a Muslim woman, and they went to the *Ganja* together to ask for redemption. Just like you and me.'

Shelley hadn't realised they were asking for redemption.

'Yes, and they sat on the ghat at Varanasi – a very holy place.'

Amit had put an arm around her, and they were both looking at the river as he spoke.

'And he wrote this poem. I will recite it for you, but first you must look closely at the *Ganja*, Shelley, and remember which step. That one? We agree. Good.

'Now I will recite Jagannatha's poem:

'I come to you moist with love,
I come without refuge to you, giver of sacred rest.
I come a fallen man to you, uplifter of all.
I come undone by disease to you, the perfect physician.
I come, my heart dry with thirst, to you, ocean of sweet wine.
Do with me whatever you will.
Do with me whatever you will.'

Amit was looking at Shelley now.

'Jagannatha said that to the *Ganja*, Shelley, but I am saying it to you. Do with me whatever you will.'

Shelley was moist all over now.

Amit kissed her again and this time pulled her very close.

After a few minutes, Amit held her away from him and smiled in an impish manner.

'But I haven't told you everything yet, Shelley, no.'

He shook his head melodramatically and his voice changed to a mournful tone.

'No, as they sat on the steps together, Jagannatha and his lover, the river rose, one step per line of his poem, and by the end they were washed away.' Amit looked mournful, as if he might cry, but then turned to her and laughed.

Shelley laughed too. But Shelley's laugh had traces of genuine sadness.

Amit turned back to the river. 'Is it at the same step?' he asked.

'Yes,' said Shelley. 'It is.'

'Then we are safe, but only to a point,' said Amit. 'You are having an effect on me, Shelley. I must purify myself.'

He smiled at her and began stripping off his clothes. His tunic, and a gauze singlet, and the cotton trousers and lastly some white boxer shorts. He passed all the garments to Shelley, saying, 'Do you mind, Shelley?'

He kept smiling. His black eyes were soft and deep.

The trees would be concealing them from public view, surely.

The clothes were warm.

He stood in front of her, arms up, displaying his front, and then his back, then the front again.

'What do you think of the Indian man, Shelley?'

'Oh, he's okay,' she said.

He looked concerned.

'No. I take that back.'

More concerned.

'He's the most desirable man I've ever seen. He's a gem.'

He threw his head back and laughed, and tiny water drops scattered around his naked body like a snow globe.

Then he turned around and walked down the steps into the river.

She saw his buttocks ever so slightly paler than the rest of him. Strong, confident. Muscles in his back. Striding into the water without hesitation. Diving in – then reappearing and flicking his hair back off his forehead. Crescents of scintillating drops. Looking up at her. Showing off like a boy.

When Amit wasn't looking she held his clothes up to her face and smelt them. Amit's smell.

He was out after a few minutes, putting the dry clothes onto his wet body.

'Now I'll just fill this bottle. He squatted down carefully and leaned out over the ghats. 'I should step out into the faster water but I'll settle for this.'

He screwed the top on and then finished dressing, and they made their way back up the ghats to the path. Amit gave the beaker back to the man on the pail and thanked him.

It was now dark, and Amit went first with a torch and his water, and Shelley followed along, on a small path lined by one-room dwellings. People were sitting cross-legged on the ground or squatting at small fires. No electric light bulbs down here near the river. The dogs were now awake too and drifting in and out of the light of the fires. Rats were taking the opportunity to dash across the path.

Amit's flashlight was panning back and forth to left and right. Shelley was conscious that behind the little stalls to the left there was a blackness which was the river. She could hear the occasional slow beaching of a wave.

The torch lit up an enormous octopus with a hundred tentacles – in fact a pile of flowers on the riverbank.

'Left over from the flower market,' said Amit. 'Yes, we are near Nimtali Burning Ghats here. Look.' He shone his torch at a wall which led down to the river. A painting of a skeleton. 'That's the Burning Ghats right there. The ashes can be raked into the river there or be taken out in a boat.'

'Oh.'

'That's why the flower market is here – so the flowers are ready for the cremations. Only certain flowers though – there are rules for the flowers.'

'Rules?'

'Well, they mustn't be perfumed.'

'Oh?'

'No, because we should not smell perfume before the gods do.'

'Right.'

'So that's why the marigolds – they have no smell. And there must be one hundred and eight flowers per necklace. That is a special number.'

The reflections in the black water were so bright and so vertical and so orange, it looked like the bridge above must be alight with fireworks.

Some boats were tied up to the bank downstream, and cooking fires were glowing on the sterns.

Shelley thought these were the only people around, and that everything was deserted at the base of the bridge. However, as she looked closer, she saw moving silhouettes and shadows and a fire and realised that there were people there after all.

'Apparently there are a lot of boys there at the moment, because of the fighting. The boys like to be right under the bridge in the middle of the pack because the snatchers take the fringe dwellers. The boys are like penguins. They circulate around during the night so everybody gets a chance to be in the safest position. We'll just sit here for a few minutes, and then we'll go home.'

Amit had found a little clearing in the mangroves where there were some concrete blocks.

'We can sit here,' he said. He pointed up high. 'The most astonishing thing about *Rabindra Setu* is the number of people crossing by foot, day or night.'

Shelley had to agree. Pedestrians crossed one level under the cars, and it looked like an ant trail from where Shelley and Amit were. Hundreds and hundreds of tiny people.

'Half a million a day,' said Amit.

Calcutta was humanity, Shelley thought.

She was having trouble staying awake. Night and day had become one, and all these experiences were becoming one long dream. She sat closer to Amit. He laid her head on his shoulder and she fell asleep.

It seemed like a minute, but it was apparently an hour later when Amit shook her, saying, 'Wake up, wake up.' It took a few seconds for Shelley to realise where she was and what was happening. Amit had his arm around her and was pointing to the base of the bridge.

The bridge was alive with reflections from the water, and the little blazes underneath, and the steel girders almost looked as if they were alight. Shelley could see the shadows of the crowd of people, mixed in with the fires, but it was hard to tell which shadows were people and which were flickering flames. But there were definitely larger shapes now – men were casting towering black shadows against the bridge. They looked like boogeymen from old European fairy stories. They were grabbing boys willy-nilly like chickens. There seemed to be two men, and each had a boy under an arm. The captives were struggling, and the other boys were racing at the men, kicking and punching them – but their attack was inconsequential. The men were brushing them off as if they were mice.

'We must do something,' said Shelley, standing up. 'We must save those boys.'

'They'll kill us,' said Amit. 'They'll have machetes and we'll be hacked to death.'

He swished a hand back and forth to demonstrate.

'But look at what's happening,' said Shelley. She was shouting now, pointing to the bridge. 'Just look!'

'We can do much more by staying alive.'

'No, that's wrong. I'm going to do something. I don't care if I get killed.'

Shelley was running to the bridge. She dodged mangroves, and pieces of concrete and oceans of rubbish. She splashed through puddles in her sandals and jumped what she judged to be deeper bits of water. It was hard without a torch. The bridge was about a hundred metres away – not far – but in the dark she couldn't sprint. She had to jump over one dog, and then swerve around another one. They could so easily turn on her. She was screaming as she ran.

'Stop. Stop it. Stop.'

She didn't know if Amit had come with her or not.

She could see still the men with a boy each. They were now about fifty metres away. They didn't seem to have heard her screams and were heading downstream as if they were coming home from the market with a live crab. Maybe they had a boat.

She did not even have a weapon. What was she going to do? People were coming out. They'd heard a bit of commotion, but the men still didn't know she was following. They hadn't heard her screams.

She could see a machete dangling. The other was sure to have one too. She stopped yelling. Surprise would be a better weapon.

She was gaining, leg and all, and knew all she would have to do was surprise them. She looked over her shoulder and thank God, Amit had come along. She had caught up to the one on the left. The boy was slowing him down by screaming and wriggling and kicking.

Shelley used every ounce of muscle to jump and land a big blow at the base of the man's skull, pushing him forward as hard as she possibly could. Rabbit punch. She forced him to trip and fall on his face. He gave a prolonged groan that sounded as if a tree was being felled. The boy wriggled away like a fish off the hook.

Amit had tackled the second man, and now people were coming from everywhere. The first man tried to grab his machete but someone in the crowd had a cudgel and got to him first. The machete skidded over the ground. Ferocious whacks and thwacks to his head, back, legs. More and more. His skin had split and blood was pouring out of his scalp. Shelley heard a crack which she knew was a skull shattering. He was going to end up a forensic model.

The second man was not faring any better. The crowd was screaming at him. They knew exactly what he'd been up to. He was standing with his knife threatening anyone who came near. But a man with a very long pole took his legs out from under him, and he too flailed on the ground. He was at the mercy of a mob that had no mercy.

Both boys had vanished.

Amit had a cut on his face which was bleeding, and spattered blood on his shirt, and was panting. He pulled Shelley back from the melee. 'Come on,' he said, 'we have to get out of here.'

He steered Shelley into the darkness and said, 'Now run, right behind me, don't delay.' For the second time in twenty-four hours, they were running for their lives.

Shelley was still trembling for some time after they'd arrived back at Amit's villa. Even though she was warm enough, and fresh and dry from a shower, she could not stop shaking.

Amit had given her long robe. 'From my father's business,' he'd said. 'And I've just remembered I left our water container at the river. I wanted to make sure you had some *Ganja* water to drink.'

There is a God, thought Shelley.

What a day and a night they had had. Was it a day and a night? She was losing track of time. She and Amit seemed to be still alive – that was the thing.

'Shelley, you were incredible. It looked like you know karate.'

'One of my many skills. We call it self-defence.'

'Interesting. But it is most improper for you to be here, now, in the home of a single man, without a chaperone, most improper.' He laughed. 'Don't worry, Miss Agatha Christie, no-one will know, and I am a very well-behaved man. But it's good that you know self-defence.' More laughter.

They sat in a courtyard garden, Amit on a wicker chair and Shelley on a daybed covered in an embroidered fabric. There was a delicious perfume of orange blossom. Amit had made a cold tea drink. Shelley was weak and shaky, and the tea was perfect.

Amit stood up and said he would bring pakoras. Shelley wondered if these might be slippers or something to eat. She hoped something to eat. She didn't know whether it was jet lag making her so hungry, or maybe she'd had nothing to eat for quite a while. But she did wonder why there was no housekeeper.

When Amit came back, he set a plate of little pastries down and then made a statement. 'I never have women in my home, Shelley,' said Amit, 'but you are different. There is so much I want to tell you and we have so little time. We've had adventures – adventures I never want to experience again, even with you.' His eyes were shining. 'But I have important things to tell you, and I mustn't delay.' His lips looked soft. Shelley was waiting to hear what Amit wanted to tell her. She hoped it wasn't about the bones.

'The bones—' began Amit, and Shelley's heart sank.

'—are not what I want to talk to you about at this moment,' he said. 'We've had enough of bones for the time being, I think you'll agree. No, what I want to tell you is how beautiful you are. First, before I tell you anything else.'

'Oh.'

Amit moved closer and curved his hand around the edge of her hair, barely touching it, as if it might spring back at any moment. 'Such hair.'

'Pretty wild, I'm afraid.'

'Wild child,' laughed Amit.

He had on a fresh white top and trousers. He moved closer. She could smell mint, and aniseed, and velvet soap.

Then some thoughts occurred to Shelley. Unpleasant thoughts.

'Amit.'

'Yes.'

'I can't help thinking about that poor young woman in the burial ground.'

'Yes, of course,' said Amit, and moved back. He got up and fetched a small, carpeted stool and placed it under Shelley's left foot.

'You are exhausted, I know, and I do apologise for not taking better care of you. Especially as your leg must give pain.'

Shelley waved her hand.

'I should not have taken you to the bone enterprise or the burial ground at this time of fear and violence. I should not have taken you to the bridge at night. I felt you were robust in spirit, though obviously not in body. I had no idea what would happen. And I realise I should have been treating you as a delicate gift. But I do believe now you have the proof you wanted.'

'Yes.'

'To be quite honest, I did not think we would see all the things we have seen,' said Amit.

'No.'

Amit offered her a pastry. At last.

'Now we both should get some sleep,' said Amit. 'You in particular. You must be completely exhausted. You've placed the last piece into the puzzle. But we have another big day tomorrow. A very big day.'

Shelley couldn't help feeling there was still a piece of the puzzle missing. But she was too tired to think.

Tuesday. The day. Even though she'd been completely knackered, Shelley had not slept well. Once Amit had taken her back to the Anup Hotel she seemed to have got a second wind. She was definitely feeling anxious, there was no doubt about that.

All night she'd listened to the Indian orchestra outside – cars honking, people yelling, dogs yelping, bats clicking, crickets thrumming, roosters crowing, frogs burping, nightjars creaking. For the young Naxalites, knowing this night could be their last, these noises would be glorious music.

Amit collected her before dawn. If anyone enquired, they were simply going to visit the Little Sisters polio mission, on one of Amit's regular charity visits. Generous, like his father. 'Anyone' needn't know that Amit would leave Shelley at the hostel and continue his way to join the freedom fighters.

Amit didn't speak until just before they arrived at the hostel. 'Shelley, today you are an observer. Not completely independent I acknowledge, but not partisan either. Do you think you can manage? Because we are going to need the truth. The world needs to hear the truth, not Government propaganda.'

'Yes, Amit, I can manage.'

They turned off the main road into the park and the little driveway which led to the mission. The gatekeeper appeared immediately, even though it was well before dawn. He gave a namaste. Amit leaned out of the window and said something, and the old man performed a deeper namaste.

'He's wishing us well.'

Amit switched the engine off. A neon light was flashing so that his face was alternately red and blue. He turned to her and smiled, his white teeth reflecting the lamps outside. His eyes were moist. He put an arm around Shelley and brought her head onto his shoulder. His breath smelt of aniseed.

Shelley loved aniseed.

'My Shelley, brave girl, I won't be in the front line today, but I do need to lead our people, you understand that?'

Shelley felt a mixture of anxiety and fear. She couldn't bear to think of him being hurt, wounded, tortured. She wouldn't even know.

And they hadn't even had a chance to talk about the astonishing number of bone sets ordered. She didn't even know if he cared.

'I'm worried, Amit. I'm worried something will happen to you.'

'Comrade Shelley. You are brave and selfless. Not as selfless as Kavita, but you've proved yourself. Not many western girls would do what you have done. I know you are a true Maoist and we can trust you to tell the truth to the world.'

He cupped his hand under her chin and turned her face to his. 'So now I must kiss you. Maybe for the last time.'

He said this as if he were reading from a rule book.

Amit kissed her softly and deeply. It was not a rule book kiss.

They both became aware of a light through the windscreen, getting steadily larger.

Amit pulled back and quickly ran his fingers through his hair.

Kavita's face was an apricot colour in the light of the lamp. She peered into the car as Amit wound his window down.

'Good morning, both of you.'

She leant in and kissed Amit on the lips, the confident kiss of a lover. Shelley opened her door.

'Come and have some tea, Shelley.'

By seven am Kavita and Shelley were at their post in the tower. Shelley prayed the building would last a few more hours before collapsing completely. The roof had fallen in, so the floor was covered in terracotta tiles and roof beams, as well as large pieces of wall.

They lifted some beams onto larger piles of rubble and made a bench to sit on. Kavita had brought a notebook and Shelley had brought her Instamatic. She hoped there'd be a few pictures left on the roll, but the indicator wasn't too reliable.

They could look down into apartments on either side, but all seemed to be ready for demolition. No sign of life. It was unnerving. Amit had told them that the demonstrators were starting at about eight am, before the heat. Right now, the street looked its presumably usual self – a broad avenue lined with fig trees. Kavita said that its proximity to some of Calcutta's historic buildings spared it from heavy traffic. But there were plenty of people below hurrying to work or the market or the school, oblivious to what was about to happen. Shelley felt the building swaying sideways, or were they moving up and down? It was a bit like being in a gum tree back home, trying to rescue a small animal or child.

The Jail could have been a colonial mansion. Salmon pink walls. Jade green shutters. Even the prison gates in bright blue were quite attractive. This could have been the comfortable domicile of a prosperous merchant. It was only when you looked to left and right and into the distance, and you saw the high stone wall extending around the hillside with all the look-out towers, that you realised its true purpose.

Sure enough, at eight am, Shelley heard the first demo noises. Demos must sound the same the world over. She could hear the cheering and yelling and the leaders with their chants in Hindi.

'*Halla bol, halla bol.*'

'Raise your voice,' translated Kavita.

Shelley saw two things. Firstly, a man in a western-style suit who'd been standing waiting for a bus, reading the paper, looked toward the demonstrators, and then up at the Jail. Shelley realised at that moment that it was Amit.

Secondly, soldiers with upright spiked sticks were appearing at the Jail. That was the front row. Soldiers in baggy white shorts, white pith helmets and long pointed staves. Behind them, falling in at an incredible rate, were hundreds of additional troops with automatic weapons. How did they know to be there? Someone must have tipped them off. Amit clearly saw them at the same time as Shelley. He stood for a moment as if thunderstruck, then turned around and examined his own troops, who were now just coming from the corner. Lots of rabble noise. All young, some in jungle greens. A lot in white shirts and long pants. Holding banners, and red and white hammer and sickle flags.

'Students,' said Kavita, 'students have come too.'

They were shouting. They were angry. Marching down the boulevard. They didn't know what was ahead.

Pedestrians had scattered. Traffic had miraculously disappeared. Just the demonstrators in their hundreds. And the soldiers in their thousands.

Kavita clutched Shelley's arm. 'Someone's betrayed them,' Kavita said, in a dull voice. And then, with a cry of alarm, 'Amit.'

Amit was running. He was running towards the soldiers. A man in a suit with a newspaper in his hand running for his life towards the soldiers. The demonstrators slowed down, and the chanting stopped. Did they know it was Amit? What was he trying to do?

The sticks were raised. The guns were at the ready. A single shot rang out into the air, a warning shot. Amit was waving his arms. Was he saying, 'Don't shoot' or 'Shoot me'?

Another shot sounded. Amit stumbled. He fell on his front, then tried to get up. The demonstrators hurled themselves after Amit and the soldiers charged at the demonstrators. Amit was staggering, clutching his belly and waving an arm until he fell onto the dirt. Even then he was trying to crawl towards the Jail but was instantly stamped on by black boots running over him.

From within the Jail came the sounds of enormous explosions. Black smoke rose from behind the walls.

Kavita and Shelley were watching the tableau as if it was a movie, but it wasn't a movie. Shelley could hear screams as people were speared, dismembered, beheaded. She could smell the blood and shit and dust and fear. Amit's body was trampled by scores of boots, like a sack of rubbish. She saw boot after boot on his head. She saw the students and Naxalites being mowed down in dozens, and the remainder being picked off, one by one. She saw the soldiers chasing and beating. She saw the street covered in blood.

It was all over by eight thirty am. She had been a witness: no-one had escaped from Dum Dum.

Shelley watched as the street cleaners came with handcarts and brooms and shovels. They must have been waiting in the side streets. It was a surreal horror. The workers casually flipped bodies into the wooden cart, soldiers and protesters together. They didn't even check for signs of life. Just raked up the limbs and heads, and unidentifiable lumps of flesh, whether soldier or protester, and threw them into the barrows together. And the heaps of gore – smashed organs, blood mixed with clay – that was all scraped up with shovels and thrown into the mix. Just a normal Tuesday rubbish collection.

Mangled heaps of humanity. And the pile that was Amit was still down there,

Kavita looked terrible – grey and sweaty.

'We cannot go to him. We cannot.' She was sobbing, and the words were coming out in chunks. 'And I don't have any status anyway. I cannot touch his body.' She gave a cry of utter despair.

'What will happen?'

'Amit's brother will find out about it and come for him.' She was now whispering, and Shelley could hardly hear the next bit. 'He doesn't even know I exist. I am nothing. I was nothing when he was alive, and I am nothing now he is dead.'

Amit's body, what was left of it, had been passed over by the carts. Shelley was watching it all the time – a heap of trampled muck and gravel. The workers hadn't touched it.

'It's because he's in western dress,' said Kavita. 'And the authorities will know he's a Mukherjee. They'll bring a special cart.' She was correct. A small handcart trundled down the street and an old man tried to drag the mangled heap that was Amit into it. Blood and entrails dribbled along the road. He called for help from a younger man, and together they rolled Amit's body over the edge until it fell into the cart. Shelley watched as Amit flipped over. Half his chest had been blown off and she could see the palisade of severed ribs and a big cavity. His head lolled precariously – his neck was almost completely severed. It looked as though his face was blasted off too.

'Don't look Kavita, don't.' But Kavita did, and then crumpled like a piece of tissue into the rubble on the floor.

Amit, all akimbo, was taken off stage. For that's what it seemed like – a play.

The stagehands were very efficient and the cleaning up was done within an hour.

'They're used to it,' said Kavita. 'They've done it dozens of times, and they want to finish before the heat. They have to get the road ready for the day.'

Shelley and Kavita went back to the girls' hostel. At least that's what Shelley thought happened, in retrospect. She could not remember much once Amit's body was taken away.

The Sisters looked after them, she could recall that.

Strange memories came to her during that afternoon and evening. She was lying on a cot, not sure where. People were shouting at her and moving her leg, hurting her. Someone seemed to have a hammer and was trying to bang her leg straight. She heard electric saws. There were no windows that she could see out of – just light coming from a high window. The tiles on the wall were pale pigeon-egg blue. Pigeons outside were making endless canoodling noises. They couldn't care less.

There was no-one she knew. There were parents somewhere in the world but not with her.

Her leg felt like it was in a furnace. She was screaming for them to stop. But they wouldn't and just kept shouting – angry voices. She began to float away from her body. Someone said, 'We're losing her,' and then there was shouting in loud deep voices, and clashes and lights and pain. It went on for a long time and she spun higher and higher towards the ceiling.

She woke in a saturating sweat. There was a fiery pain in her leg. Where was she? What had happened? Who did she know? It felt like she knew no-one.

Amit's body was burned by the river the next day, under the sign saying 'NIMTALA BURNING GHAT'. Shelley had been able to smell the fires from miles away. It was a smell of cooking flesh and burning cow urine and dung. The smell of death.

The river was the same moving waterway. Now, in the morning, its forget-me-not blue was daubed with dark red, as the Howrah reflections were dragged into the water, reflections of brick chimneys, factories, and warehouses. Shelley recalled something Amit had told her once: 'Wherever you see red brick, that's the East India Company.'

On their side the bank was marked by regular plumes of smoke, with little figures milling about each fire. Shelley could see that each column of grey was a scaffold with a body smouldering away. Bells were being beaten in mournful regular rhythm, and monkeys darted from pyre to pyre.

Kavita was standing close to Shelley, explaining things. She said the fires had been burning for two thousand years.

On the ghats nearby, where Shelley and Amit had stood just a day or so ago, life seemed to be continuing as usual. People disappeared into the water and re-emerged like mirages. They were soaping up, rinsing off, washing clothes and collecting water. Workaday life, workaday death.

The river was heaving along. 'Full moon tonight,' said Kavita, 'that's why the river is so fast.' It seemed to be taking with it a lot of north India – basket-loads of leaves, coconut fronds, water hyacinths torn from their beds, and dead dogs.

Other people were greeting each other but no-one spoke to Kavita. She's an outcast, thought Shelley – she might even be pleased I'm here.

Everything was being arranged by Amit's brother. They had been allowed to proceed early, Kavita said, because of the family's caste and because it was no problem for them to purchase wood. 'Some families can't afford even five pounds of wood, and then the cremation is in doubt. They have to wait all day, with the body in the sun, and then use any left-over wood they can find.'

Shelley must have looked shocked. 'Don't worry, Amit's brother will make a donation to those families, so they don't have to wait so long,' said Kavita. 'That's why it's good for Amit to be first.'

There must have been a hundred people here already, and more walking down the paths. Most of the men were in white kurtas but the women wore brilliant gold-embroidered saris in orange, red and yellow. People were chatting quietly, and nobody was crying. Shelley could see some of them patronising the stalls at the top of the riverbank – garlands of brilliant yellow marigolds, beakers of chai. A barber was doing good business, with a steady stream of men to shave.

Shelley commented on the crowd.

'That's because of Amit. And the family's standing in the community. And the circumstances.'

'Oh. You mean—'

'Many people here will be Naxal sympathisers.'

'Oh.' That was a surprise.

'And intellectuals. You might even see Satyajit Ray.'

'Oh?'

'We'll stand with the women. Though they might not want me to be near them because of everything. But you should stand with them. I'll show you.' Kavita was speaking as if she was in a trance.

Shelley stood back to look at her and noticed how pale she was – like a wraith – in her white sari, carrying a white silk bag of yellow marigolds.

Kavita became aware of Shelley's inspection and said in a more definite voice, 'Don't worry, and don't be sad. And make sure you find Amit's driver at the end – he will take you back to your hotel.'

'Yes, thank you, Kavita.'

'Amit will have a very good afterlife. He was a good man. See the respect.'

'Yes.'

'At the end his ashes will go to the *Ganja*. Amit's brother will do that from a boat, once the tide goes down. And the most important part, the part that must go to the river is the navel. Everything will be burnt except the navel.'

Amit's pyre was still empty. A flat iron frame with firewood underneath. There were men in white standing around, ready with cans of oil. Shelley approached one of these men – a man whom Kavita had suggested – one with long grey hair in ropes. She held out a periwinkle shell, made a namaste and then some gestures, then another namaste. The man took the little shell and made a slight bow back.

A young woman in a yellow sari was standing further up the ghat and was receiving attention from other women. Shelley asked Kavita who she was, thinking a sister maybe.

Kavita turned away. 'I don't know,' she said, in a very flat voice. 'But that is his mother.' She indicated an upright lady of about fifty years, with a few grey strands in her otherwise black hair. 'Mr Mukherjee cannot be here, of course, because of the fighting. But there is Amit.'

Amit was coming, on a cot borne on the shoulders of several men, all in white. '*Bolo Hori, Hori Bol*,' they were saying.

'The men in the family must give a shoulder,' said Kavita.

At the sight of Amit, Shelley could not prevent a gasp. She tried to quash it, but the result was a half-swallowed yelp. A woman in front of Shelley turned around and said to her in English, 'He will have a good afterlife, don't worry.'

Amit was lying on a layer of branches. He was dressed in gold and purple silk. Garlands of golden-yellow flowers were wound around his head – one hundred and eight flowers per garland, Kavita said – but half of Amit's face wasn't there – it was just a sticky dark hole. A basil leaf covered one eye socket. A second leaf was floating in the bottom of the hole. Shelley could also see something white, deep in the sticky crater.

The men in white poured water from the river into the hole, and where his mouth once was, and then over the remainder of his face.

Then they sprinkled rice and something else on his feet. His body was covered in a sheet and a great heap of orange and yellow marigolds. The oil would be sweet-smelling, Kavita said. She was giving Shelley a soft running commentary in a distant monotone, like a recitation, almost as if it was something for her to cling onto. She didn't look up or down, or even at Shelley, just at the pyre.

Shelley felt strangely distant as well. She felt like she was still watching that play. The fact that she'd seen Amit die, that she had witnessed all that horror, that no-one was attempting to hide his hideous injuries – did this explain her lack of tears? Was she in some form of shellshock? She was normally so tearful in sad situations, but right now she felt like a dried-up sponge.

The men piled sticks over Amit, and more garlands and flowers, and the man with the long grey hair placed her tiny periwinkle shell between Amit's feet. The men combed Amit's hair with their fingers, sprinkled ghee and perfumes on his face and body, and poured more scented oil over him.

Then, without delay, six different men came with burning bunches of grass. Amit's brother made a recitation, then lit the pyre at the head.

Kavita was speaking to her. 'Be brave, Shelley.'

Shelley was surrounded by silks of all flame-colours – orange, red, yellow – and oiled hair and perfumes – and everyone pushing to see. Glossy black hair. Skin. Oil. Perfume. Heat.

There was a fizzing as the grass caught and then the deep whoosh of oil igniting. Sudden gust of heat and eddying air. Amit was in flames. Shelley was forced to step back. Her face was burning – a furnace of orange and yellow flame burning her face. She had to move back. Everyone was pushing back, getting away from the fire.

Shelley became aware of a bright white figure to her left, glowing. Like a tumbleweed, a white ball danced into the fire. A tin clattered onto the ground, another whoosh, and the smell of petrol and a splitting, deadly scream. A scream of terror. A scream of agony.

Kavita, my God, Kavita. Help. Someone help. Shelley was screaming as well. She couldn't move because of the crush of people around her. Someone do something, get something, stop her.

Such a scream. The figure now incandescent. Screaming on and on. Shelley looked around frantically. People were falling onto each other. Someone get something. A bucket, or a towel. Anything to fill with water at the river.

But strong arms pinned her so she could not move and could hardly breathe. They were saying words in Hindi. She knew what they meant.

No, don't. Don't save her.

The flames roared around the dancer, and she became a black stick figure, a stick figure in a contortion of agony in the flames. And the scream stopped.

But the fire was burning bright. Amit and Kavita. The flames reached up high. All around her was burning, burning. The arms pulled Shelley back even further. She could see two black coils of smoke and maybe a tiny third plume joining them.

The fire burned until they were just bones, oily blackened bones together – and all their ideals were gone.

Melbourne

Mum, Dad, Rory and Skye were there to meet her at the airport. Shelley felt like she'd been away a year, not just a few weeks.

'Did you bring us anything?' That was Rory, of course.

'You mustn't say that, Rory,' said Mum.

'But did you?' asked Rory again. Shelley gave Rory a second kiss.

'I did,' said Shelley, 'but you'll have to wait 'til we get home.' The world was in fact unchanged.

As Shelley walked out of the terminal behind Dad, the glare hit her. She felt like a nocturnal animal caught in spotlights. The Australian sky was so bright and so bare – no buildings, no signs, no wires and no people.

At home she got out the silk dressing gowns for Mum and Dad and the carved elephants for Rory. She'd bought a Mother Theresa doll for Skye, and some gold necklaces. Just as well she bought the necklaces, for Mother Theresa was not a hit.

'Did you see Mother Theresa?' asked Mum.

'No, Mum, but I met some very, very good people, and I'm going to go back there as soon as I can to help.'

Shelley couldn't see her parents' faces at this very moment, but she could feel the instant crackle. The look from her mother to her father was like an electric fence.

But within a day of being home, back at Uni, back at College, Shelley felt like she'd fallen into a black hole much, much worse than any black hole of Calcutta.

It was Sunday morning. A bagpiper was practising somewhere in the College grounds. He must have gone to the exclusive Presbyterian school. Normally she liked bagpipes. They skirled in your blood and made your bones vibrate, but right now they sounded like death.

She was sitting on her bed looking at nothing. She couldn't muster up the energy to talk to Bob, or to stand on the desk and look out the window. She felt wired in position. What was the point of moving? There was nothing to look at, nothing to look forward to.

She should get the books out and do some study, she knew that. Find her lecture notes on lipoprotein lipase. But what was the point? She was probably going to get kicked, kicked, kicked out of med school anyway. And lipoprotein lipase was not going to help all those kids in the hostel who'd missed out on so much, so many things, and one thing that should be simple, a birthright in fact – polio vaccination. And whether or not they were crippled with polio, they were likely to end up in little black boxes. Boxes of bones.

She had been through Armageddon. No-one could possibly understand, even if they were interested, which they weren't.

She had some terrible secrets to keep or disclose, and she had to make some major decisions, but she had no-one to ask. Who could she confide in? Everyone had some sort of finger in the pie, or whatever the saying was. Something that stopped them from thinking clearly and speaking the truth.

She still couldn't believe Amit had died. That he'd gone. For that brief period while she knew him, her life had had a new force. It had felt like she was plugged into a new source of energy which was empowering a part of her she hadn't known existed. She'd felt electrified. A buzz under her skin.

Now the power was switched off.

She knew there would never have been any future for her and Amit. She knew and accepted that he really loved Kavita. But somehow that didn't matter. She loved Amit so much, she only wanted for him to be able to fly through life, changing the world. She, Shelley, loved Kavita too. Who wouldn't? She was a beautiful bird, a lovely and delicate thing. She and Amit were perfect for each other.

Amit would have been forced into marrying Yellow Sari. Would have had sex with her, when he didn't even love her. How repulsive. Children too. And Kavita would have been with a violent husband. He might have hit her, he might have been emotionally cruel, kept her inside, kept her poor, allowed the other women in the family to bully her, been cruel to their children. All of that. Shelley could hardly bear the thought of it. And perhaps Amit would have known that – yes of course he would – he would have had to live with that burden. That anxiety. And he would not have been able to do anything about it.

Yes, it was best that they had both died. But they had left Shelley behind.

She now realised what Amit had done. He had enchanted her. That was the only way to describe it – she'd been enchanted.

And now he was gone, and there was a wound in her chest like someone had swung an axe right into her heart. It was strange how the emotion – the loss, the hopelessness, the despair – the great lake of sadness – it was all there behind her sternum, in her heart. Just like all the songs said. Why didn't she feel it in her adrenal gland or her little toe? That was something medical research should look at.

All those young freedom fighters. Dead, wounded or being tortured right now.

Mao says there must be armed struggle, and there can never be revolution without blood – but how much blood?

And now she knew the provenance of the bones, but what could she do about it? The casual way one thousand and two hundred Indian lives were used. Criminal, but not breaking any law. So evil, she sometimes thought she must have got it wrong. She had to do something about it. But what could she do? The change had to come from India, just as Amit said.

The bagpipes had moved onto 'Amazing Grace' – the dreariest dirge ever written. That piper probably knew nothing of death. She did.

Shelley gave Tomas the Indian spices – the turmeric, the ginger and the saffron – and told him about the purple and gold. Tomas looked as if he didn't believe her. It did seem a bit far-fetched – the story about crocuses in the foothills of the Himalayas. Tomas had lost weight while she was away and really looked anorexic now. He needed to eat more of his own food.

They'd finished the dinner shift early and *Trois Bouteilles* was empty. The stoves were turned off, the kitchen was clean, and the Dripolator was disconnected at the wall. Tomas asked her to come for a drink with him – said he knew a good place.

This was unusual – the first time ever, in fact.

Outside, the city was getting going. Lights were flickering on, and couples were laughing, arm-in-arm. Always made her feel lonely, those happy couples. They never thought of the effect they might have on single people.

Shelley was just checking the time and deciding what to do, when she realised that two men sitting at an outdoor café across the street had been there all evening.

'Tomas, don't look now, but see those two blokes over there?'

'Well, I can't see them if I'm not allowed to look. What about them?'

'They've been there all night, and only now are they getting up.'

'So?'

'Well, don't you think that's strange?'

'Suppose they have to go home sometime.'

'Tomas, you are so frustrating.'

One man was shorter and dressed in what appeared to be a light-weight baggy suit and a pale wide tie, though it was hard to be sure what colour, from a distance. The other bloke was heavy and tall and was wearing a lumberjack-type checked shirt and a baseball cap.

They really did look like your traditional boss and thug. The brains and the brawn. They got up as soon as she and Tomas made a move to go. While the boss paid the bill, the thug stood on the footpath keeping track of Shelley and Tomas. Or so it seemed.

'Well let's call a taxi, see what they do,' said Tomas.

Shelley and Tomas stood on the kerb hailing a taxi, and the two blokes did likewise.

Tomas told their driver to go round the block twice then take them to the Waiter's Club up the top of town – he was a member – those blokes wouldn't be able to get in there.

'Good idea.' Shelley was relieved.

'And they'll have to climb up all those stairs *before* they find out they're not allowed in.'

Shelley laughed. 'And the big bloke doesn't look too fit.'

'The fat one? No. And I'll get Mario to let us out the back way, so if they wait out the front for us, they'll be waiting quite a while.'

They had a good laugh in the back of the taxi.

It was only when Mario had got them a table and a glass of red that Shelley said, 'Tomas, who were they following – you or me? That's question number one. And question number two is why?'

'I doubt they're following you,' said Tomas. 'What possible reason would they have?'

Shelley had already decided it was most definitely her they were following, and it was to do with her India trip. 'I could ask the same thing, Tomas – what possible reason would they have to follow you?'

'You might be surprised,' said Tomas. 'But they're bad types, no matter what. Stay away from them.'

Shelley looked at dear Tomas – so like a reed in the wind, tall and breakable. No roots to speak of. She could just imagine the thug swatting him away with the hairy back of one hand.

They had a second glass and a plate of antipasto, and then proceeded through the kitchen and down the back stairs, thanks to Mario. All seemed clear.

'I'll come with you to the taxi rank,' said Tomas.

They were walking down the lane and were just near the taxi rank at the corner of Maxwell Street when they heard organ music cascading down the steps of the Anglican cathedral.

'Too late for church,' Tomas said. 'Must be an organist practising. Though it's very late. After eleven.'

'Let's have a listen.' Shelley loved pipe organs.

They walked up a few steps to the foyer and found a pew hidden from general view by a set of bookshelves, still in the entrance, but exposed to the music. They slid in. Not only was the pew hidden from the street, it also had a soft cushion.

And the music was wonderful.

'Happy to sit for a bit?' she asked Tomas.

'Yes. Stay out of sight though.'

Through the glass doors to the church, they could see the organist, ginger hair and blue jumper, who was tiny in comparison to the hundreds of pipes above him. He wouldn't know if he had an audience or not and wouldn't care – he was in another world of pedals and diapason stops.

'The Bach D minor,' said Tomas.

Shelley knew the music, though could not have named it just like that. Tomas was always surprising her.

They listened in silence, and Shelley felt the reverberations in her bones. That was when music got to you, when you could feel it in your bones. And nothing was better than organ music for getting into your bones. Even Bob would be able to feel this music. When you thought about it, the middle ear was just bones too, tiny bones.

Shivering bones made her think of Bob, and then Amit and Kavita. All her sadnesses flooded into her mind.

The Bach Toccata and Fugue ended in a final formal chord that stayed in your bones.

'Everyone should have this opportunity,' said Shelley. 'To feel music in their bones.' She had tears in her eyes – couldn't help it.

Tomas spotted the tears and then pointed out a bench in the church garden. 'Why don't we talk out here,' he said. 'There's something you should be telling me about.'

The dark masonry of the church was lit by a bank of spotlights. The lawn was neat and brilliant emerald-green, and there were shiny hedges growing in the black wrought iron fence. Everything well kept. In order. Above them the majesty of the bluestone cathedral.

And behind them, coming out of a laneway, were their new friends.

'Bugger them,' said Tomas. 'What the hell are they up to?'

'Well, why don't we just sit and have a chat and make them wait,' said Shelley. She was surprising herself with her new-found courage.

'I don't like you to be in this situation, Shelley,' Tomas said. 'Being dragged into something you know nothing about.' He'd clearly decided it was him they were after.

Tomas knew about the bones, but he didn't know anything about extra complications. Or the huge numbers of bone sets. So she told him about it. And about how she didn't know what to do. And how bringing skeletons into Australia wasn't illegal. An actual crime would have to be committed, in order for the police to be interested. And she had so little evidence. So much was at stake – her place in med school, her life even, her family's safety. But if she called in the police, and she was wrong – or the med school found out, which they would – or these bully boys found out, which they would—

Tomas was quiet after that. Quiet for a long time.

'Tomas?'

'Yes,' he said.

'You okay?'

It was only when she thought about it later that she realised Tomas hadn't actually replied to that question. She'd just rattled on in her self-absorbed way.

'I can only think of small changes that will take a long time,' she'd said. 'I'm going to write to the Attorney General to see if they can ban importation of human bones. I'd like to get India to ban exportation of human remains, of course, but that's the last thing they'll be worried about right now.

'And something else has occurred to me. Hindus are generally cremated – even the lowest castes. So, the people being dug up or killed might be Muslim, and the Indian Government might not care all that much.'

Prattle, prattle. That's what she'd done.

'Problem is, Tomas, if I go to the police the Dean will kick me out of the med school. That's what he wants to do. He'll use some ancient by-law saying that a student who brings the University into disrepute or interferes with the learning of other students should be instantly sent down. They won't want any scandal, that's for sure. And I have no proof whatsoever about anything. Even if there is something going on. And if nothing can be proven I might have really stuffed up. No second chances with this sort of thing, you know.'

'I'm worried about you, Shelley,' said Tomas. 'I don't think you should be drawing attention to yourself.'

'I agree with you, Tomas. But it applies to both of us. I'm wondering if I'm being followed, and you think it's you they're following. That's weird.'

Tomas' face was paler than ever. 'When the Soviets came in and took over my country, we had secret police everywhere. I know all about being watched, Shelley.'

When Shelley got back to Pluto she triple-checked the door and put both her bed and her desk chair against it.

Swot vac and exams meant there were no lectures, no pracs, and no dissection. That meant no opportunity to see Jeffrey. Shelley was desperate to express some of her grief to someone who'd understand.

At last she saw him in a corner of the med school foyer.

'Jeffrey! Jeffrey!'

'Oh, Shelley, what a terrible thing. I am so sorry you were there for this awful tragedy.'

'Jeffrey, I'm devastated for you and your family. Amit is a—a— wonderful man. I mean was.' Tears were threatening.

'Yes, my family's in shock. My father's flying home next week. I should never have let you go to Calcutta—'

'No, that's fine Jeffrey. I'm so glad I went. I've discovered all about where the bones come from – it's worse than we imagined. I'll tell you all about it. And Amit was so kind to me, and—'

'You know he was supposed to be married in only three months' time?' said Jeffrey. 'To a girl from a very good, very suitable family from Chennai. Yes, a good, well-matched girl. He should have been focusing on the preparations, especially as he hadn't met her yet.'

'Jeffrey?' said Shelley through tears.

'Yes?'

'Please don't tell anyone I've been to India, okay?'

Shelley thought she should pay a social visit to Horrie, without giving anything away.

'Horrie, how are you?'

Horrie was reading the form guide, or was he? He threw something into his desk drawer and closed it quickly.

'Lassie, I've not seen you for a while. Come here and let Uncle Horrie touch that hair.'

She could smell alcohol; she was sure of it.

'It's okay, Horrie, I'm only checking if you need my help in the next week or two.'

'I can always do with your help, my dear.' And his eye went round and round.

'Okay – how 'bout I come Monday? I could tidy up the storeroom for you.'

'No, no.' The second 'no' was quite emphatic. 'That's not necessary. But you could help me with embalming. We're going to have a few new bods next week, I think.'

How Horrie knew who was going to die, and when, was a mystery. Anyway, she'd cooked her own goose she had. She hated embalming.

'Okay. But I can't stay too long. Exams.'

Shelley fronted up for the exams and discovered for the first time since commencing med school that she knew something. No passion present, but she knew something.

The Anatomy oral was interesting. Smiling Death was on the bones table of course. Horrie was hovering, ostensibly making sure all the required bones were there, but Shelley knew that he was hoping to see some fun.

Smiling Death had a co-examiner this time – a young woman, a trainee surgeon Shelley had seen in the dissection room a few times. Apparently, she was the first female surgical trainee ever. Well, so people said. She had a friendly face, and old-fashioned brown wavy hair. She seemed nice, and she nodded encouragingly as Smiling Death pointed his knitting needle at Shelley and then at a tibia.

Shelley wondered if Smiler remembered her from last time, or did he use that cold stare on everybody?

'Tell me what this is and show me all attachments.' Delivered in his stentorian style. Not so much as a 'good morning' or a 'please' or a 'would you'. Just a command.

'Yes, Sir. And Ma'am. This is the left tibia, most probably from a young person, possibly a girl or boy from Calcutta. She or he was probably lower caste, for example the Dom caste, or a Sikh or a Muslim.' There were no shimmering lights this time, no growling voices, no tears.

The young surgeon was listening. Smiler was narrowing his eyes.

Shelley continued. 'Someone who was persecuted. She or he was probably eventually murdered. The grave was desecrated, and the body was taken to a human bone preparation facility. It was weighted down with rocks in a filthy creek and beetles and fish ate the flesh. The bones were boiled, and then soaked in hydrochloric acid. Finally, they were left to dry in the sun, so they would be a pleasing white for the overseas purchaser – who was, in this case, the University of Australia Medical School.'

Shelley took a quick breath, then continued before Smiling Death could get a word in. She was speaking very fast. 'In answer to your second question, I can point out that the insertion of the patellar tendon, which is the continuation of the quadriceps femoris muscle is here in the tibial tuberosity; the tensor fasciae latae muscle, which is continuous with the iliotibial tract, inserts here into the lateral tibial tubercle, also known as Gerdy's tubercle; and the conjoined muscles of semimembranosus, gracilis and sartorius all insert into the antero-medial aspect of the tibia here; and the—'

'Enough!'

'Is there anything else you would like to know, Sir?'

Smiling Death's eyes had become almost platinum. His face had changed from white to puce, and there were engorged silvery-blue veins on his forehead. Shelley hoped he wouldn't drop dead. Not just now. Because she wanted to pass her exam, not do CPR on this wanker.

Smiling Wanker stared at Shelley with pure hatred. 'Goodbye, Miss Conway,' he said curtly, and flicked his fingers at her as if she was a piece of rubbish.

'Goodbye, Professor,' she said, and waggled her wrist, very slowly.

'Well, well, here's my little lassie. Come and sit on my knee, lassie.'

Today she could definitely smell the alcohol from the doorway. Saw the medical article that Horrie was reading. The surface anatomy of a big-breasted female with no clothes on.

'Just came to say hello, Horrie. See whether you need any help.'

'No, no, think I'm okay. Apart from being poor, that is.'

'Maybe it's the gee-gees, Horrie?'

'Ah, no-o-o. It's not that. I only invest ten quid a day.'

'Wouldn't that add up?'

'No, it doesn't.'

'Oh.' She couldn't work out the maths on that one.

Shelley had been worrying about Tomas. He seemed convinced that the boss and the thug were following him, not her. Tomas was strange at times. Obviously re-living the past. Why would they be wanting to follow Tomas?

The next Friday morning she rode round to *Trois Bouteilles*, even though she wasn't rostered for a shift. Must have had a premonition.

As she walked up to the restaurant, she noticed it was dimmer than usual. In fact, the lights weren't on at all. And there was a typed sign on the door. And she could see a few people inside. What was this?

TROIS BOUTEILLES RESTAURANT CLOSED TODAY

DUE TO A BEREAVEMENT.

Shelley pushed the door and saw a cluster of people at a table. Bottle of scotch and ashtrays. One of the other waitresses came over and squeezed Shelley around the shoulders.

'Oh Shelley, Shelley – you were his favourite.'

'No suspicious circumstances.'
Bullshit.

Code for 'couldn't care less'. Shelley knew who Tomas was hanging out with on the night he died. Single shot to the head, pistol beside him. How hard was it to ask a few questions?

She and Bob were sitting in her little bedroom on Pluto. She hadn't had a letter in a while, but still felt anxious whenever she looked at the door.

'You see, Bob? Now I have three deaths to feel sad about – Amit, Kavita and Tomas. Actually, four – there's Puffing Billy too.

'I'm a total mess, Bob. I cannot get over Tomas. I feel so dreadful.

'And I've got a bad case of do-gooder syndrome. I keep thinking of those children with polio. They need help. I'm longing to be able to go back there and help. I'm achieving nothing here. But I also know the truth: that it would really be them helping me.'

Bob was looking at the leaves of the Virginia creeper which now covered her window completely. Shelley turned him around so he could look at her. She opened the book.

I slept and dreamt that life was joy. I awoke and saw that life was service. I acted and, behold, service was joy.

'Service is joy,' she said to Bob. 'That's what I needed to read. Thank you. Well, I should pull myself together and sort out what I'm going to do about the bones. Next shipment comes September twenty-first. I can ignore it or I can do something. Obviously, I am going to do something. When in doubt, review the paperwork. I made that up, by the way.'

She got out the various pieces of paper that Trivedi had given them. There were all the invoices and payment advice forms from the University of Australia – about one hundred boxes a month or one thousand and two hundred a year. Staggering. Now she must look at that Bill of Lading again.

Fawkner cemetery was bright and cold, a far cry from South Park Cemetery or the Ganges River. She'd been to three cemeteries, or near enough, in as many weeks. Didn't seem right.

It was a long walk from the train station to Tomas' grave. She had to go past all the other sections where the memorials were packed in like miniature ancient cities.

Undenom A, on the other hand, was just a paddock in the back corner with a few new heaps of dirt, each with a jam jar or two of plastic flowers. A backhoe waited.

Shelley saw a small group of people and knew that this must be the place. She had on her red coat, and her red beret with Eva Novotny's gold brooch – Tomas would have liked that. She had a shell in one pocket and a book in the other. The sunshine was useless, and it was cold, bloody cold. Didn't feel like September.

The coffin had black straps under it and was lying next to a deep hole shored up with thin wooden struts. Shelley noted how long the coffin was, and that's when her chest suddenly gave way. Made-to-measure coffin. It really was Tomas. She blinked hard – no-one else was crying – tried not to think about what it all meant.

What was Tomas wearing in there? She'd never seen him in anything other than his white jacket, checked pants and socks and sandals. She hoped they had something to cover up the damage to his head. 'No suspicious circumstances.' How can they say that? How can they just accept it was a suicide? She knew it wasn't. She would get the facts together and tell them. If only she'd put the facts together when Tomas was alive. That he was an addict. Explained everything.

At least his body hadn't gone to the Anatomy department. Or so she hoped.

Only a few people showed up. Tomas had no family as far as she knew. A man in a dark suit spoke, and then Tomas' friend Arno – his mate from his Snowy River hydro days.

Arno talked about Tomas' life in Czechoslovakia. He described how the family was persecuted firstly by the Russians and then by the Germans, and then the Russians again. At least, that's what she thought he said. Tomas' father shot himself after all their property was confiscated. His mother died of the pneumonia she contracted because the family had to hide in a wet barn. His two sisters were raped and murdered by soldiers.

Arno said Tomas loved Kafka, and Dvorak, especially the 'New World Symphony'. Shelley was not surprised. 'Song of Home' would have meant the free world to Tomas – everything he strived for – democracy, freedom for his homeland. Everything but socialism and fascism.

They lowered the coffin into the ground on the straps. The man in charge said a bit more. People were throwing in handfuls of clay. Ordinary lumpy old clay. Shelley took deep breaths and told herself to regain control. She thought of Tomas, cold and alone in that box. How desperate he must have been at the end. And she thought of Amit. She didn't know which was worse, being buried or burnt.

She could see the dry dirt on the polished casket. Her shell hit the shiny top and rolled off into the earth. *The Trial*, Penguin Modern Classics, landed on its spine, open, revealing her handwriting.

More dirt was thrown in, covering up some of the words.

I have nt all my life res ing
the des e to end it.

-F nz Kafka.

Yes, somehow, she did know about Tomas but hadn't admitted it. Was that because she couldn't face her own demons? Normal people don't have assassins following them, and yet she and Tomas had both claimed them.

And then out of the corner of her eye, she saw them, standing under a tree with bare black branches and a last few spinning golden leaves. Boss and Thug. Fuck off, you two.

The third moratorium came and went. Yes, Shelley was up the front with sixty thousand people behind her, but she could barely muster up a chant, let alone anger. She had so many other things on her mind.

Then one day Mum appeared. Just like that, out of the blue. A little figure in a tan coat and beige beret. Walked into *Trois Bouteilles* and said they needed to have a chat.

'I'm nearly finished, Mum. I'll meet you out the front, at the end of my shift. Half an hour, okay?'

They went to the coffee lounge in Collins Street. Been there for ever and served tea on a tray with lots of little jugs, just as Mum liked.

The waitress had a frilly brown apron with 'Gay Paris' embroidered on the bib. She took Mum's coat. Gave them a round table facing the street, which was nice. They could see all the mothers in nylons and heels hurrying their Jennifers and Christophers along to the dentists.

Mum put her gloves in her bag.

Shelley was anxious. 'What's wrong, Mum? Not Granny or Pa?'

'No, it's just that I thought we needed to chat. Your father and I are worried about your career.'

'What do you mean?'

Mum turned up the two white cups on their saucers. 'Well, we don't know where you are or what you're doing half the time, but we think it's all too dangerous.'

'Mum, I'm an adult.'

Milk in first, just a bit. 'Yes, exactly. But you're not acting like one.'

'What?'

'Well, I may as well tell you—'

'Tell me what?'

The tea was made, so Mum only had to turn the pot. 'We're completely in the dark about this business in India, that's one thing. And we didn't ever tell you about your leg, that's another.'

'Yes, you did. It was polio. Because you didn't get me vaccinated.'

'It wasn't that.' Pouring the tea, using the strainer. 'What happened was you pulled away from your dad when you were waiting to cross the road. Walton Street, Saturday morning. You were little. Dad was taking you to get some special shoes. You know, cripple shoes. I don't suppose you remember.'

'No, I don't. You're not being very kind, Mum.' Shelley was starting to have trouble holding it together. Things were swirling.

She'd put two teaspoons of sugar into each cup. Shelley didn't like sugar, her Mum knew that.

'Well, that's what happened. You just pulled your hand right out of his and ran across the road. For no good reason. I think you were old enough to know better. Your father disagrees. But that's what you did.' Stirring. 'That's how you've always been.' Stirring. 'Headstrong.'

The tea still going around.

'You've caused us so much worry, Shelley. So many sleepless nights.'

There were brown patches on the back of Mum's hands. Might be tea leaking out. Mum's version of *café au lait spots. Thé au lait.*

'Not to mention expense.'

Teaspoon tapped.

'So the car swerved to avoid you and got your father. You ended up with your leg, but Dad – well he ended up with his broken back – all his vertebrae snapped – the doctor said his bones were rattling like dice in a box.

'Dice in a box. So that's when he went into the wheelchair and that's where he's stayed.'

Mum's voice was getting slower and slower. Shelley was floating, getting further and further away. Mum was tiny, way down there. But her voice was huge. Echoing. 'But that's what you did.' So slow and deep. 'That's how you've always been.' Growling. 'No good reason, Shelley, that's what you did.'

'I'm only telling you, so you understand how he is. He's never forgiven himself, even though there was nothing he could have done. You mean everything to him. And he never complains about his own lot, you know that. So if anything else happened to you—'

Tears were splashing into the cups.

'This life you're leading – never thinking of us.'

Mum had her good handbag, and she took out a white hanky with a fancy blue embroidered *E*. Always gave Shelley a surprise to see the *E* – after all Mum was 'Peg', not 'Elizabeth'. Not really. Mum blotted each cheek with the hanky – twice, three times.

'Oh, dear, I was hoping I wouldn't get upset. Don't tell your father about this.' She passed a cup, now cold, to Shelley with a shaking hand.

'Shelley, there are some careers that are suitable for you, and some that simply aren't. You'll just have to accept that. And please stop making us worry.'

Shelley took the cup. She'd have sugar today.

Mum was on the 4:50 train. Shelley saw her off, then walked back to work to get her bike. She rode back to Pluto, very slowly.

Somehow normal things were still happening. The seasons were still changing, for example. Shelley was riding to *Trois Bouteilles* one morning when she felt an acute stab of memory. The sun was warm, and she'd just passed her favourite trio of terraces, and caught the startlingly sweet smell of jasmine. She remembered dreaming of living in one of those cottages, and then realised that the jasmine was in flower, so it must be one whole year since she'd decided to get a new job, a year since she'd bought her box of bones, a year since she'd been in heaps of shit over Redlich, a year since she was going to move out of College and do something about all the bad stuff. A whole year, and what had she achieved? Bugger all.

Billy dying, Tomas dying. No-one interested.

Amit dying, Kavita dying. What for?

Boys snatched from under bridges. Killed, taken to the bone factory. Eaten by beetles, boiled up, put in acid, dried in the sun. Put into boxes. Shipped to Australia, ending up in room 420.

And no-one gives a stuff.

There is only one history – the history of Man. All national histories are merely chapters in the larger one.

Maybe she should enrol in a history course, Shelley thought, just one subject, and see if Tagore was right.

First lecture. Main Arts Theatre packed. 'History of Revolutions'. Lecturer – Dr Reuben Ingelbaum.

Same squeaky desks as in the medical building. Same giant blackboard. Same whiteboard, same whiteboard markers not working. University of Australia was at the forefront of technology.

But the difference was that everyone shut up when the lecture started. They wanted to listen. No paper planes. Big difference.

Reuben Ingelbaum was a man of significant build and hair. Looked like a bushy plant. He rambled but was knowledgeable. He was going to cover the great revolutions – American, French, Russian. 'And we're going to cover the Chinese,' he said, or rather trumpeted. 'What we now know to be the Chinese Cultural Revolution.'

Shelley sat up.

'This is a revolution we are only just beginning to appreciate, and it will be recorded as one of this century's greatest tragedies.'

A tragedy? Mao?

At the end Ingelbaum recommended a few textbooks but said there were none available on China. 'Not written yet. But they will be. Watch this space.'

End of triumphant solo. He even got a clap.

As she was leaving, a man in a denim jacket allowed her to proceed down the steps before him. Shelley thanked him, then noticed the short hair and the boots. The shiny boots. Yes, it was one of the spooks she used to spot at the demos, scrubbed up a bit. 'You can always tell the spooks by their clean shoes,' an old leftie had once told her. This one smiled in a frank manner. Not one bit embarrassed, it seemed.

'Haven't we met?'

'I doubt it.'

'I think we have, at the moratorium, the big one. And other demos. I feel sure we have. You're a woman of ideas. I've admired your opinions.'

What bullshit. How ridiculous was that?

'And I think I've seen you around the medical school. Doing good works. No, I mean it.'

Felt like she was blushing. What the fuck? Shelley Conway, stop it this instant.

'Did you enjoy the lecture?' He wasn't going away.

'Yes—no—yes, well—it was, well, it was interesting.' Why was she being so ditzy? She shouldn't show any further enthusiasm for this conversation, whatever she did.

'What did you think about what he said about China? I mean, aren't you a Maoist?'

'Well—'

'I don't mean to put you on the spot.'

'You do. Mean to, I mean. You are, in fact.'

They had reached the bottom of the stairs and were now walking into the foyer outside the lecture theatre. Shiny boots made a suggestion. 'Why don't we see if we can get a cappuccino round here?'

Probably thought cappuccinos were a trendy thing.

'Sorry. I don't mean to be rude.' He held out his hand. 'I'm Simon, Simon Lenski.'

By the time they arrived at the Caf, Shelley had heard a story about Simon Lenski being a final year med student. A most unlikely story.

He was also against the war and had attended lots of rallies. A very unlikely story.

'Union Caf hasn't changed,' said Lenski, picking up several paper plates and serviettes to take to the bin. 'I'll go and ask them for something to wipe the table.'

Shelley could hear money being counted and saw chairs leaning up against tables. 'Looks like they might be closing. Wanna go upstairs to the bar?'

Lenski gave a thumbs up.

The Union Bar was dark, noisy and smoky, but it was better than having to hold your feet up in the air for a mop. And you couldn't tell if the tables were dirty or not. Lenski bought the beers, and they found a coffee table and two lounge chairs a bit out of the main area.

Joe Cocker was on.

Lenski put the beers on two coasters and lifted the ashtray onto the next table, looking at Shelley as he did so.

'Nope, given up,' she said. Stupid. She didn't have to say that.

'Well done – when d'you give up?'

'Ten seconds ago.' Shelley tried to laugh. Now she looked like a moron. Vapid, fickle and a likely smoker, when she didn't even smoke. But, more to the point, why did she even care?

Simon laughed. 'Well, even ten seconds is good. To be encouraged. Cheers.'

'Cheers.'

'Well, what's happened to you, Shelley Conway? You seem to have gone into hiding. I haven't seen you at a rally for ages. You've lost your bolshiness.'

'Maybe, maybe not. Had to get a job. But tell me more about yourself, Simon Lenski.' Due diligence required before they got too palsy-walsy.

'Final year. Busy. You know. Medicine, Surgery. And a barman job. That's all I've got time for. Last year I went to a few rallies. Not this year.'

'Did you go to the moratorium? The one last week?' Shelley asked.

'No time. So much study to do. Plus, the rallies are getting smaller. I don't sense the urgency anymore.'

Not convincing.

Lenski continued. 'But you, you're a genuine reformer. Look at those things you do. Blood drive, soup kitchen, all that.'

This was a ruse, for sure, thought Shelley. How to be a Spook 101: first, flatter your contact.

ASIO must be onto her. They think she's out of line with her India trip. This could be big trouble. They suspect her of being complicit.

'I have a couple of questions for you, Simon Lenski, but it's getting a bit noisy.' Shelley hated shouting.

'We could sit outside.'

They found a circular seat around the trunk of a magnolia tree in the Union courtyard and sat there with the beers. They were probably not supposed to have glasses outside, but too bad. Quiet, cool, out-of-the-way. Footsteps on flagstones coming and going. A security guard locking doors. Drifts of lemon magnolia scent.

'What about these questions? Fire away.'

'Well, for a start, what languages do you speak?'

'Oh. Just a bit of French. Why?'

'Okay. Who is the Attorney General?'

'What a question. Federal?'

'Aah, yes.'

'That's a strange question. I should know and I don't. Are you going to send me packing if I don't know? Neil Borland, something like that?'

Shelley realised that she didn't know herself. But bugger it, she wasn't the one undergoing a security check. 'Okay, what's the capital of China?'

'Peking. Or does it have a new name? What is this? An IQ test? An audition for a quiz show?'

Shelley did some rapid thinking. Doesn't know who the AG is and that would be his boss if he was in ASIO. Doesn't smoke. Hasn't even dropped to why I'm asking these questions. If he is in ASIO he's none too switched on. But if he is in ASIO everything is stuffed. She took a big breath.

'I have to ask you something else, Simon.'

'Fire away. Again.'

So Shelley asked him the million-dollar question. 'Are you or have you ever been, in ASIS or ASIO?'

'ASIO?' Lenski broke into a coughing fit – his mouthful of beer spraying everywhere. 'Sorry. I'm a total coward. Show me a popgun and I faint. They wouldn't have me in a hundred years.'

Shelley couldn't help but laugh.

'I don't even have a trench coat. Ah-hah. I know what it is.' He bent down, pulled off his left boot and held the sole up to his ear. 'Boss, I think I've been sprung. Yep, by our target. I'm with her now, Union Bar. But my cover's been blown.' He laughed, a huge laugh that sounded like a sheet of roofing iron was about to blow off in a gale.

'Well, that's a pretty cute performance, but the fact that you've cleaned your boots – that's very suspicious.'

'You're a funny girl, Shelley.'

'No, not funny, weird. That's what everyone says. Weird.'

Lenski was looking up at her as he edged into his boot again.

She could still hear Joe faintly.

'A Joe Cocker fan too? A weird Joe Cocker fan?' asked Lenski.

'That's me. Anything Woodstock,' she said.

'Yep, me too.'

He couldn't be in ASIO if he liked Woodstock, Shelley decided. 'Okay. Truce.'

'We've got something else in common, I think,' said Lenski.

'Oh?'

'I think we're both mature-entry students.'

'Oh? Possibly,' said Shelley. She didn't want to give away too much.

The cleaners had turned the lights off in the Arts building and it was getting dark.

Lenski moved a fraction closer to Shelley. 'Anyway, the boots, you're supposed to look respectable on the wards, otherwise the nurses won't let you see the patients. You'll find this out for yourself soon. Stockings and lipstick for you girls.'

'Lipstick? They can stick that up their arse.'

'Charming prospect,' said Lenski. 'I won't ask what shade.'

They both had a chuckle. Shelley looked at Lenski again.

'You do look like a spook.' He had neat straight hair, just at his collar. 'Look at that haircut – spook cut number one.'

'Well, I won't say what your hair looks like, Shelley Conway, uber-radical.'

It was only ten days now until the twenty-first of September. Horrie would be wanting to make space in his storeroom, surely. Time to pay him a visit.

Horrie's rash was worse. Anxiety, wondered Shelley, or alcohol? One probably led to the other.

'What are you doing for the weekend, Horrie? Anything?'

'Actually, I'm going fishing.'

Funny, but that's exactly what I thought you might be doing, Horrie, thought Shelley.

'Fishing? I didn't know you liked fishing. Where are you going?'

'Daltona.'

'Nice. You got a boat, Horrie?'

'Yep.'

'Oh. What are you going to catch?'

'Fish.'

'Oh, okay. Oh well, good luck Horrie.'

'Thanks, girlie.'

When Shelley arrived at the Daltona pier – by the first train, just after dawn – there was only one other person there – a bloke on a camping chair at the very end of the jetty. The boat harbour was dead quiet – no action detectable on land or water.

She'd been expiring on the train with her hundred layers of clothes on, but now she was in the wind on the foreshore, she didn't feel too warm at all.

Shelley walked down to the end of the pier with her bucket and rod. Rory, who had been desperately hoping for an invitation to accompany her, had lent her the gear. 'Next time,' she'd said. Now she thought about it, he could have been part of her disguise.

The lone fisherman was in a red nylon baseball jacket, and a red and black football beanie with a bobble. His two rods were flat on the jetty, their lines stretched out into the water. He was sitting on a camp stool with his hands in his pockets. He turned around to take a quick look at Shelley, but hunched his shoulders higher as she walked behind him.

'G'day.' She knew she looked like the Michelin man, and in fact was having a little trouble walking.

'G'day.' He didn't turn around again.

'Cold enough.'

'Yep.'

She needed to be on the end of the pier to have the best view of the boat harbour, and thought it might be a good strategy to place herself near the fisherman so any curious person would assume they were together.

She indicated a jetty post. 'Anyone sitting here?' The stupidest question, she knew that.

The fisherman spoke to the water. 'Isn't it amazin' how there's ten thousand miles of coastline to choose from, but someone always comes up and sits right next to you.'

'Oh, sorry.' She started to move.

'No, I'm just kiddin' ya. Stay there.' He looked at her and possibly smiled. Hard to be sure when there were so few teeth.

Shelley put down the bucket and laid out the rod, then squatted down to do her rigging. She unwound out some line from the reel and looked in Rory's little green tackle box with 'RORYS KEPP OUT!' written on it in Texta. There were no hooks and she also realised she had no bait. There were a few sinkers in the box, and some colourful floaty and feathery things which didn't look too useful. So, she chose the biggest sinker, threaded the line through, tied a few knots and dropped the line in. Hoped the bloke wasn't watching.

'Won't catch much that way,' he said. 'No hook.'

'Well—'

'Here – I got some fresh sandworm.'

He pulled out her line, cut the sinker off, put it back in the tackle box and started again. 'You just want a light sinker for bream – that one's heavy enough for a shark. And you just want a small hook – they only got small mouths.'

'Thanks.'

He tied the hook on, about a foot above the sinker.

'This way they can see the worm.'

Tatts on the back of his fingers: L-O-V-E. H-A-T-E. Looked home-done. A prison job perhaps.

'Oh, thank you.' She glanced over at the boat harbour to make sure there was no activity.

'Then you get your sandworm, well just a half, and thread it on the hook so it's wrigglin' but all on the hook. See? You don't want a lot of sandworm driftin', 'cos the fish'll nibble it off, for sure. Cunning little buggers.'

'So, the sandworm's still alive and cut in half with the hook through it?'

He looked at her. He'd clearly decided she was a fruit cake. But he cast the line in anyway.

'I'll leave you to it, then.'

Shelley was in a good spot because she could see all around the boat harbour, as well as any boat going out or coming in. Of course, she had no idea what sort of boat she was looking for, what time, who would be on it, or even if it would happen at all. But she was keeping her eyes peeled, so it was just as well that the other fisherman had given up on her.

It was quite pleasant, if cold. The water was clear, and there was no rotting seaweed smell. That was her main memory of Daltona's glory days – the decaying seaweed odour. But none of that today, just a fresh briny smell. She hadn't brought a newspaper or a rug, so she just sat on the bird poo on the jetty. No matter. Little waves were chopping against the jetty poles, and she could see the mussels clinging to the posts and disappearing into the depths. Further back down the jetty towards the shore, seagulls were scrapping over something, and ropes were dinging against the masts of the yachts. All very peaceful. She could get used to this.

Shelley hoped she didn't actually catch a fish.

Didn't seem to be any yachts out. Must be too windy for sailing. It should be okay for motorboats – the forecast didn't sound too bad. 'Gales' were mentioned on the news last night, but they always were, every single evening.

As the sky lightened a few people started striding up and down the jetty, carrying eskies, bags, life jackets. It was Saturday after all. One by one motors puttered into life, spewed out a bit of bilge water, and were put into reverse. Then after much churning around the stern, they'd be in forward and chugging out into the bay.

After about an hour or so of general boat activity something more interesting occurred. Horrie came walking down the jetty. He was wearing a royal blue parka and was pushing a supermarket trolley which had several small black boxes in the top compartment, and a red fuel can on the bottom. He came to an old wooden fishing boat with a cream and green striped awning, and left the trolley alone on the jetty while he opened up the boat. He unzipped the awning, and rolled it up, all the while checking on his trolley every few seconds.

Shelley watched Horrie load the boxes, stacking them carefully, while balancing the boat. He wasn't holding them by the handle but had his arms underneath. Very interesting, because Shelley knew how light these boxes usually were. The current weight, for whatever reason, must be too much for the plywood, Shelley thought, and he doesn't want the boxes to fall apart and disgorge their contents in full public view. He must have put rocks in the boxes to make sure they sink. That'd make sense. He wouldn't be wanting boxes of bones floating around the bay or getting washed up on shore.

He left the boat, but zipped up the canvas, and went back down the jetty with the trolley for another load. He was looking around as he pushed.

This was going to take a while.

After he'd done about five loads her new fisher friend came over for a chat.

'Any bites?'

'Nup.'

'Checked your bait?'

'Nup.'

'Here.' He reeled in her line until the sinker and the bait were out of the water, and then he swung them over the jetty.

'Well, you've still got your worm.' He pulled the seaweed off. 'Still wriggling too.' He watched Shelley as he said this.

She grimaced on cue.

'You vegetarian?'

'As a matter of fact, I am.'

'Thought so. How come you're fishin'?'

He had a point.

'I can throw the fish back, can't I?' she said.

He looked out to sea for a bit. Counting to ten, maybe. But he tidied up the worm on the hook, and then cast her line in again for her.

'You on the look-out for coppers?' he asked. Friendly-like.

'Nup.'

He stood near her for a bit with his hands in his pockets, then took a pack and lighter out of the inside of his jacket, cupped his hands around a cigarette and lit it.

'You?' she asked, after a while. Seemed only polite to ask.

'Maybe.'

He stood next to Shelley and they both watched Horrie on the jetty. Now that they'd exchanged personal details, the fisherman was up for a chat.

'Wonder what's in those boxes.'

'Yeah,' said Shelley. 'I wouldn't have a clue.'

'Enough of them.'

'Yeah.'

'Tell you what – you keep an eye on my rods and I'll go aks him, okay? If a snapper gets on don't let it take the rod though.'

'Okay.'

So, Mr Love-and-Hate strolled down the pier until he came to the finger jetties where the boats were tied up. Shelley could see him leaning against a post, smoking, and watching the trolley go by. Horrie stopped for a minute, and then the two of them stood with their backs to the wind, hands in their pockets. Shelley could see the bobble on the fisherman's beanie bouncing as he talked.

She reeled in her line, quickly slipped the half-sandworm off the hook, dropped the half-worm into the water, and then cast it in again. 'Maybe they regenerate,' she thought.

Shelley hunkered into her jacket, and pulled down her beanie, a new raw wool one.

She'd love to be a fly on the wall down near that old fishing boat.

The duo broke up. Mr Love-and-Hate sauntered up and down the rest of the jetty for a bit, inspecting the boats, then back to Shelley and his rods.

'Any bites?'

'Don't think so.'

'Well, that bloke's up to something. He tells me one thing, then he says another and then he says something else entirely. I aks him what's in the boxes and he goes "bait", and then later on he goes "beer" and then finally he tells me to fuck off.'

He laughed a laugh which went up and down like a rusty seesaw. Might even have carried down to Horrie, who had looked up for a moment.

'He's up to something I can tell – maybe abalone. Best stay out of his way. Think I'll shove off. Just in case coppers come sniffin', y'know.'

'Okay,' said Shelley.

He looked at her more closely. 'Maybe you're not the full shilling.'

'Yep.' Shelley was very happy to have a role as not the full shilling.

'I'm a slice short meself. Brain injury. Acquired or acute, I can never remember which.' He gave another laugh. 'Anyways my advice to you is don't hang round too long. You wouldn't want him thinking you're spyin'.'

'Okay,' said Shelley, 'thanks.'

'No worries. Plus the fish aren't biting are they? Just reel in and see if you got any bites.' Shelley did so and pulled in a sinker and an empty hook.

'Well, there you go – a bite. Tell you what, I'll give you the worm off of my hook, and I'll leave you the box.'

'Thanks a lot.'

'No worries.'

He took the sandworm off his hook, then re-impaled it on Shelley's.

'If you catch a fish, well tell it to call his mates to hang around until I come back.'

'For sure.'

She watched him walk off the jetty, with his chair, bucket and rods, and then she gave the sandworm its freedom again, and tipped the rest of the bait into the bay.

Horrie had loaded over twenty boxes and seemed about to get underway. Shelley decided to set up camp elsewhere, somewhere where she could observe Horrie's return from his excursion. But first she'd get some hot chips at the shops in case he was a while, and also to be less noticeable.

When she returned, Horrie's boat was gone, Shelley tried to work out a good place to wait. It needed to be different from her previous spot but still with a good view of the boats. She took off her top jacket and the brown beanie and tried to look different. Tricky. She put the scarf around her head – her hair was such a give-away – and decided to sit on a cluster of rocks on the breakwater near the shoreline.

Sure enough, Horrie came back about two hours later. There he was at the wheel, taking an occasional swig of something. There were no boxes on board. Proof positive.

On the next lecture day Lenski made a beeline for Shelley as soon as the session was finished, and they ended up in the Union Bar again. Grabbed a beer and sat in the lounge area. Too cold to sit outside. Chatted about the American War of Independence for a bit. Simon bought some beer nuts.

'All we talked about last week was me, Shelley. What about you? I get the feeling something's happened.'

'Just had a bit on, that's all.'

'Nothing bad I hope?'

'No. Just shit.'

'Okay.'

The couple at the next table were laughing and glancing at Shelley and Simon.

'Disgusting at their age,' said Shelley. 'Playing tootsies under the table. I'm not going to look at them anymore. You tell me what's happening.'

'Well, he's got a wedding ring, she hasn't,' said Simon. 'She's no spring chicken. Gold chain on the glasses. More tootsies. He's got a gold tooth.'

'Gold tooth? Oh, this is too much. I'll have to get a better look.'

She changed chairs and dropped her voice. 'Oh my God, it's bloody Hyphenated-Heartthrob out with Senior Secretary. What a hoot. I haven't told you about my run-in with him, have I?'

'Nope. But it'll be another Shelley shenanigan, no doubt about it.' Simon laughed and put his glass down. 'I know who he is of course, but I don't know the lady friend.'

'Then you'll know what he does to cats. I wonder if she's a cat lover,' said Shelley. 'She looks like someone who might be devoted to Princess. We'll have to tell her that Princess's life is at risk.'

Simon laughed.

'The dirty old bastard,' Shelley concluded. 'Perhaps he's going to put a hyphen in her hymen.'

'Shelley! That's not ni—' Simon was laughing too much to finish the sentence.

The luvey-duveys were a bit startled by the laughter and kept their gazes to themselves from then on.

'So, what've you been up to? Tell me one thing. I can only cope with one adventure at a time,' said Lenski.

'Did you hear about the Redlich business?'

'I heard about it, but I didn't put two and two together. Was that you?'

'Yep.'

'Should have known. He's a bit of a creep.'

'He's more than a creep. He's a slimy, lying, arrogant, conceited, sexist pervert.'

'You like him that much?'

'And then I was head-to-head with Professor Heartthrob over there about the decerebrate cat experiment.'

'Oh, that prac!' said Lenski. 'We did that a few years ago. That was the worst. I couldn't agree more.'

'Did you complain?'

'No, I have to admit I didn't. I'm not like you, Shelley. You're someone with courage – someone who acts on her principles. You're fearless. You ride into trouble. Headfirst.'

'You make me sound like Joan of Arc.'

'Well, you are a bit like her.'

Shelley laughed. 'No way, I'm just Shelley Conway. I'm an idiot really, most of the time.

'Now here's a question for you. If I gave you three wishes, what would you wish for, Simon Lenski?'

'Well, the first wish would be another beer.' He stood up. 'Another one for you? That shouldn't count as my second wish though.'

Shelley took a proper look at him while he was at the bar. Maybe he's been a farmer, she'd have to ask. That would explain the boots. And those fawn trousers. An outside-type complexion. Hair on the back of his hands. Almost looked like worker's hands. She liked that. She had a bet with herself as to what he'd wish for. He'd be trying to look good. So, probably – end to war, end to poverty, and—and—Tigers winning the Grand Final.

He was back with two slopping glasses. 'Cheers again.'

'Cheers.' She sipped carefully before putting her glass down. Somehow beer didn't taste as bad as it used to.

'I'm waiting,' she said.

'Okay, well, in order it would be – end to war, end to poverty, and Demons winning the Grand Final.'

'I don't know what's wrong with me,' she said to Bob that night. 'Something bad, Bob. I'm a total shit of a person. I've ruined my father's life. Ruined mine too. I'm neglecting everyone. Mum and Dad haven't got a clue about what I'm up to. I feel like one of those little jointed plastic elephants in the Weetbix box – the ones that can't stop plodding down the slope until they topple over. I'm a dead loss, Bob. A failure, a total failure.

'I've wasted all this time and energy and have no proof of anything. I should have asked for help, Bob.

'The twenty-first of September – what about that? Have I failed to see some issue?'

She opened Tagore.

It is very simple to be happy,
but it is very difficult to be simple.

'What's that supposed to mean, Bob? That's a pretty useless thing to say.'

It is very simple to be happy,
but it is very difficult to be simple.

Shelley kept thinking about it. Difficult to be simple. What was the difficult thing? The simple thing? She'd been impetuous – had run across the road and made her dad paraplegic. Simple. Of course, she could remember it. All too well. Simple again. Admitting it – difficult.

'Dad?'

Coins rattling down into the innards of the phone box.

'Shell. Yes, mate?'

'Dad, I need to talk to you.'

'Any time, Shell, any time.'

'I'm coming home tomorrow. On the morning train.'

'It must be important. Should I be worried?'

'Nope, I'll see you tomorrow. I'll get a taxi from the station.'

'You know your Mum won't be here – she'll be at her library course.'

'Yep, I know that.'

Dad was out the back hanging out the washing. He'd installed a rotary clothesline that wound right down, and he had special bags either side of the wheelchair for the washing, plus long-handled grabbers. She looked at his purple swollen feet with toenails almost completely gone, his catheter bag, his expanse of shoulders and upper arms.

And how bad was the lawn? She would mow it while she was here.

'Shell, mate. Good to see you. Cup of tea?'

'Dad, I'm sorry.' The tears came like a tropical rainstorm.

'What's this? Sorry? What about, for goodness' sake?' He found a wet handkerchief in the washing bag and handed it to her. 'Now pull that bench over here. Sit down. Take a few deep breaths.'

Shelley did as she was told.

'I'm sorry I ran across the road, and you broke your spine and you're a paraplegic and you can't work, and you can't kick the footy with Rory, and—'

'That's enough!' said Dad.

He hadn't noticed the large wet towel across his lap. She took it and hung it up, had to fold it in half as the clothesline was so low.

Then she sat next to Dad and leaned towards him, tears making watercourses down his arm.

'Shell, it was just an accident. You were too little to know better and I don't even believe that you did run away. I think you tripped. And you had something wrong with your leg that should have been looked into earlier. You had the polio starting, all because of your mother's stupid ideas.'

Shelley sat up. 'But I do remember, Dad. I remember doing it, just because I thought I was too big for handholding. I wanted to be in charge, and show I had nothing wrong with me. I didn't want to have a crook leg. And I did that to you. All these years I've pretended I don't remember – but I do.'

'Okay mate, that's enough now. You didn't need to say sorry, but you have, and that means a lot to me. Simple thing but difficult, eh? Now you might help me with this washing.'

'Hello, Horrie, how are you?'

Horrie had finished putting the bods away and was taking off his dust coat.

'Sorry I couldn't help tonight, but I'll come tomorrow.'

'Ah thank you lassie, that would be a help,' he said to her breasts.

'Hey Horrie, how was your fishing trip?'

'Uh, oh, yes – very good.'

His face looked terrible. Little white volcano cones in amongst the general purple mounds. Pustular. That was Horrie. One huge pustule.

'What did you catch?'

'Oh, yes well – flake, plenty of flake.'

'Oh great.'

She was tempted to ask if he caught chips too, but held her tongue.

Shelley and Simon Lenski had got into the habit of sitting next to each other in the Revolutions lectures, and then having a drink afterwards. They sat outside near the magnolia tree on warm nights, and inside when it was colder. It made Shelley feel happy to hear Simon laugh his big laughs, especially if he was laughing at one of her jokes. People might turn around, but his laugh usually made other people feel happy, not annoyed or envious. She hadn't laughed like this in a long time.

He called her Shell or sometimes Agent 99. That was okay too.

One evening, the seat around the magnolia tree was taken, and so they moved to the lawns next to the library and sat on the edge of the long pool. An avenue of sodium lights gave the sandstone buildings a peachy glow, and the resultant reflections were luminous. A tiny breeze was having the effect of a paintbrush being trailed through the water, so the tangerine colours were swirled with the mauve of the twilight sky.

'Simon?'

'Yep?'

'Look at the reflections. They're taking all those severe buildings and turning them into something soft and lovely.'

'So they are,' said Simon.

'Have you ever thought that reflections are always more beautiful than what they are reflecting?'

'No, can't say I have, but I suspect you're right.'

'Actually, that reminds me – we had a public health person speaking today,' Shelley said.

'Oh?'

'He was saying there's no point standing next to the river pulling bodies out, you've got to go upstream to stop whoever it is pushing them in.'

'Yep, I've heard that analogy.'

'But I've been there, Simon. Upstream. It's beyond help. Dictators carrying out genocide, communists becoming tyrants. What difference can one little medical person possibly make?'

'Shell.' Simon sat up straight. 'Shell, I've thought about that, and—'

'Whatever we do, it's pointless. Sorry, I interrupted.'

'That's okay. I just wanted to say this. Shelley—' He was looking way past the pool. 'It's not pointless. Every life saved is an achievement. Every single life is worth a million lives.' He looked at her. 'Every single life. You have to believe that, otherwise it would be pointless.' He spoke into the distance again. 'The crucial thing is that we care. That we've got humanity. Much more important than which part of the stream. Or how many lives. The world needs people with humanity all along the stream. Then the world might change.'

He stopped. 'Do you agree, Shell?'

Simon was reminding Shelley of Amit. That intensity. That earnestness. But Simon was a realist, whereas Amit – Amit was an idealist. And yet here was Simon asking for the impossible.

'Yes, I do agree, definitely. And that's what universities should be encouraging in med students. Humanity. Acknowledging that humanity is a thing, that it exists and must be nurtured. But they do the opposite. Students who come into the course with a little humanity get squashed; any tiny little flame of humanity gets extinguished immediately.'

'Yes, they stamp it out straight away,' said Simon. 'Toughen us up. Make us do dissection and decerebrate cat experiments – make us as hard as nails. So when we come across humans we've lost any feeling we might have had.'

'Yes,' said Shelley. 'Put role models in front of us who have no humanity left in them, not a skerrick.'

'Yes,' said Simon. 'Make us think money is the goal. Money and staying out of trouble.'

'Yes,' said Shelley. 'And we must never cry.'

'Cry? God forbid. Cry? Cry when a baby's born?' said Lenski.

'No way,' said Shelley.

'Or when a baby's in trouble?'

'Not on.'

'Or when a baby has just died.'

'Absolutely not. Real doctors don't cry. Real doctors don't care that much.'

'Stamp that little flame out for ever,' said Simon.

'Yep, straight away and for ever,' said Shelley.

'Fuck them,' they both said. And laughed.

The following week Simon cleared his throat in a formal manner. 'I have something to ask you, Shell.'

'I'm worried.'

'It's something you'll enjoy, I hope.'

'What is it?'

'May I have the pleasure of your company on a date?'

A date? She'd never been on a date. Sounded pre-historic.

Simon took her to the Impact Theatre Company. Shelley felt completely out of place amongst these old rich people. All scarves and patent leather handbags. Doctors and lawyers. Not a socialist among them.

And then, horror of horrors, who should they see? Professor and Mrs Heartthrob Dawson-Wanker.

No evidence of Senior Secretary on this occasion. The play? *Cat on a Hot Tin Roof.* Dawson-Wanker seemed to love it. Probably gave him a few new ideas.

Shelley didn't get much mail, but one day a letter arrived for Miss Shelley Conway, c/- *Trois Bouteilles* Restaurant. The sender was Zaluczny, Peck and Peck, Solicitors and Barristers-at-Law, and the envelope was the worst sort – long and white. She took it home to her room and threw it straight into the 'GF' tray while she decided what to do with it. Shelley's filing system consisted of three baskets: 'GF' (Get Fucked); 'JL' (Jail Likely); and 'JI' (Jail Imminent). The envelope got on her nerves, there was no doubt about it. It was the first thing she saw in the morning and the last thing at night. After a day she moved it to 'JL', and after another to 'JI'. By then she'd decided jail wouldn't be all that bad, and she opened it.

12 September 1971

Miss Shelley Conway

Dear Miss Conway,

We act for the estate of Tomas Novotny and advise that you are a beneficiary under his last Will and Testament. Mr Novotny has made a bequest in your name with specific conditions. The bequest is to be used for 'the betterment of humanity'.

The funds will be placed in a Trust Fund with yourself as Trustee.

The value of the bequest is $20,000.

Would you kindly contact our office at your earliest convenience.

Yours sincerely,

Zaluczny, Peck and Peck.

Shelley took Simon out for a meal.

'Simon, I'm wondering if you could help me. A surprising thing has happened.'

'A surprising thing?'

'Yes. It turns out that Tomas, dear Tomas, has left me, wait for it, some money in trust to set up a foundation for the betterment of humanity.'

'Well, blow me down. How much money?'

'Twenty thousand dollars.'

'Well, blow me down.'

'Yes, and I'm wondering if you will help me.'

'So what's this project going to be doing?'

'Well, I want to use the money to start up a foundation for polio victims and a proper vaccination program for polio in India – that won't surprise you – and I want to raise more money if I can.'

'Good. Count me in.'

'Then later on, something for Czechoslovakia, if we can get in there.'

'Again, good.'

'So, support for the polio orphanage and getting polio vaccination going, that would be the main goal initially, but what do you think?'

The spaghetti marinara was behaving like an octopus with tendrils whipping all over their cheeks and chins, leaving a film of oil, garlic and parsley. The wobbly table didn't help. I must never eat this in public again, Shelley thought.

'Well cheers,' said Simon. 'Here's to you and here's to Tomas. Tomas and the betterment of humanity.'

Before the trains started on Monday, Shelley put Bob's box on her bed and opened it up. She could hear the first magpies and smell the bakeries.

'Now Bob, I haven't been able to sleep too well, but I've come up with an idea. I am going to lay all of you out on the bed – skull, mandible, clavicle, scapula, humerus, radius, ulna, articulated hand, sternum, ribs – looks like you've lost a few – pelvis, vertebrae – cervical, thoracic, lumbar, sacrum – I'll try to put them in order, we're missing a few, not surprising – pelvis, femur, and of course your poor tibia, fibula and articulated foot. Bloody polio, I'm sorry you had it, Bob. You shouldn't have.'

A tram rumbling, first one.

'There. Don't you look smart? I wanted to make sure you were mostly there. Because I'm starting up a campaign, Bob, to right the wrong that was done to you and your family. Well, we can't right it, but we can acknowledge it and apologise, and try to make life better for those poor kids in Calcutta.'

She looked out of the window and saw the sky turning pink and the stars almost gone.

'So, I'm putting you back in the box, Bob, skull and all. But I am not forgetting you. No way, you're my best friend. I thank you, Bob, for everything you've taught me – you and Rabindranath.'

'Now let's see what he says.' She sat down at her desk and opened the little book.

> *Humanity, with all its confluent streams, big and small, flows on and on, just as does the river, from its source in birth to its sea in death.*

'Yes, humanity is everything. And that sounds like Mother Ganges.'

Shelley leaned back and listened to the magpies. Thought about the *Ganja*.

Seemed so long ago, so far away.

'Bob, I'm wondering whether you would like to go to the Pathology museum. With a proper label explaining that you had polio, a preventable disease. Explaining that the developed world plundered your bones for their purposes, and explaining the whole bone trade. And explaining the scandal that is polio vaccination. I'm going to ask Prof Lennard to put your book next to you. What would you think?'

She started to put the bones back in the box.

'I'd come and visit you. And I'd tell Prof Lennard he has to come and visit you too.'

All there, well almost – an almost-complete half-set.

'We've got somewhere, the two of us cripples – remember that, Bob.'

Shelley opened her exam results – a first (Anatomy) and two seconds – then threw the piece of paper into the 'GF' basket. She felt she'd done well enough to be able to call on her old mates, Bandicoot and Diprotodon. By strange coincidence, she'd received one of Bandicoot's letters that same day, inviting her for a chat.

On Monday September 21st Shelley was in position before five pm. She figured that the bones would arrive after business hours but not too late, as Horrie wouldn't want to encounter the night security guard. She'd decided to hide in room 412 which was an unused office with some furniture that she could hide behind if necessary. She had her bottle of whisky and a simple plan – to walk down the corridor innocently, on the pretext of delivering Horrie's whisky, and surprise him in the act of receiving and opening the boxes.

Shelley heard some comings and goings as University staff left for home at 4:55 pm. Then all was quiet in the offices. It was starting to get dark outside. The birds were making twilight noises and the traffic din had changed from a hum to a quiet roar.

This little adventure hadn't seemed scary when she had initially dreamt it up, but for some reason she now felt fearful, and her heart was beginning to race. Felt like it was in her throat. Calm down, Shelley.

She was sitting on the floor behind the door, so anyone coming in would not see her immediately. But she had to be ready to spring up.

Calm down, she told herself again. You don't want one of those panic attacks now. Just be patient. Control your breathing. Control your heart rate. Your heart's probably audible out in the corridor.

Thud. Thud. Thud.

Think about trees.

Thump. Thump. Thump.

Think about waves.

Bang. Bang. Bang.

Don't think about anything.

She heard the lifts activate. At least one was going down, four floors. Now it was coming up again, four floors.

There was activity in the foyer. She heard a trolley, some swearing, and a continuous high-pitched lift alarm – the door must have been held open for too long.

'What the fuck? Would you hurry up? We'll be here all night.' That didn't sound like Horrie, but it was a familiar voice. Someone powerful. Shit. Whose voice? She couldn't place it. Two people out there? Maybe more people downstairs? More people coming? Everything was starting to feel risky. Why hadn't she got someone to help her surprise Horrie? Maybe she should have gone to the police after all. At the very least she could have told Simon about it. But she'd had so little to go on.

All she'd been planning on doing was giving that carbuncle Horrie a fright. Plus discovering what he was actually up to, with all these bones.

'How many trips?'

That was Horrie, most definitely.

'Twelve,' said the unknown but possibly familiar voice. 'We can do ten boxes each trip – hundred and twenty boxes altogether. Same as always.'

'Just checking,' said Horrie.

Good. She knew exactly what was happening now. Thank you, boys. That proved she was right with the numbers. But what on earth were they up to?

She had a cramp in her calf. Agony. She had to change position and stretch it out or she'd die. But don't make a sound, Shelley.

'Okay. We'd better get bloody moving then.'

Horrie again.

'As soon as this lift arrives, we'll take both trolleys down together, and don't hold the doors open too long. We don't want that fucking alarm going again, and security coming to check.'

That was the other guy. Who is it, Shelley? You know that voice.

'No, we don't, but if he does, what then?' said Horrie, sounding slightly anxious.

'We get rid of him, of course.'

'You mean, *I* get rid of him.' Sounding pissed off.

'Of course.' A pause. 'That's your job. You can use him for dissection.' An icy laugh.

Now she knew who it was.

Shelley heard the larger trolley grunting over the gap between foyer and lift, and then the second lighter one. Going down. She'd have to keep track of them, so she'd know when to make her move.

Five minutes later they returned. This time the trundling noise of the wheels was different. Both trolleys were loaded up. Down the corridor to 420. That's one trip.

A few minutes later empty trolleys came rolling back, waited, then clanged back into the lift, the noise echoing up and down the lift well.

She sat completely still, completely quiet, and kept track of the lifts coming up, and the trundling of the trolley wheels outside her door. One, then ten minutes later, two, then three, then four, then five, six trips. She was sweating and her heart was racketing along, but thank God, no loud noises in her ear, no floating feeling. Not yet.

Then seven, eight, nine, don't lose count, ten.

She wouldn't mind a swig of Horrie's scotch. No, not a good idea.

Eleven. Almost time to make a move.

She heard the first, then the second, trolley on the twelfth despatch pass her door and continue on down to the storeroom. She gave them a full five minutes. Heart now in throat. Boom. Boom. Boom. This was it.

She opened the door of 412, the bottle of Glenfiddich in her left hand, and walked slowly down the corridor, trying not to shake. Just calm, in control. Not much further now. Get your big voice ready, Shelley. You are in charge.

As she got close to room 420, very close, she could hear voices. Two men.

She took three more steps and there, she was looking through the doorway into room 420.

'Horrie? Mr Jones?'

Sudden silence. The lights were all on. Horrie appeared to be wading through a sea of boxes and brown paper. His inflamed face was turned to the door, and he looked like a pathological specimen. Some boxes were open – whisky, expensive by the looks, lots of gold labels. On his right was Professor Smiling Death, only he wasn't smiling. In fact, he looked like a petroglyph from Pompeii. He was rooted to the ground in a little city of black bones' boxes, and there was dust and straw everywhere. And over near the window was separate pile of what looked like house bricks, wrapped in white paper and plastic.

'What the fuck?' said Horrie. 'What the fuck are you doing here?'

'I bought you some whisky, Horrie, Glenfiddich. Just as I promised. You told me to come and see you any time after work.'

Horrie was opening his mouth like a goldfish. For once he was looking at her face.

She decided to smile.

Smiling Death was about to say something, but she got in first. She gave a melodramatic gasp of surprise.

'Oh, but Horrie darling, you don't need whisky. There's so much whisky here. Much more expensive whisky than this rubbish Glenfiddich. And Prof's here too! We can have a party.'

The last sentence seemed to persuade Prof that everything was not okay.

Horrie was shaking and sweating. Pompeii man turned slowly to look at him. It is hard to move quickly when you are a fossil.

Shelley continued babbling on briskly and brightly. 'The Professor of Anatomy here! Fancy you risking your reputation like this, Professor? You must love good whisky. Maybe you're into the heavy stuff, too? The smack, are you into that? And the money. You must love money. But it's disgusting isn't it, what you've been doing? Look at this smorgasbord.'

She cast her eyes melodramatically around the room, at the same time checking for weapons. She noticed some thin cream books on the floor – Tagore – multiple copies. She'd have a look at them later.

Smiling Death's appearance wasn't improving. In fact he looked worse.

Shelley decided to risk a lie, rather a big one. She was on a roll.

'I think you should know there are some important people in this building at the moment. They're all waiting to see you. Vice-Chancellors and police and people like that. They'll be very interested to see your whisky collection. Not paying duty is a criminal offence, you know. Punishable by a jail term, did you know that? But that's the least of your worries. Smuggling drugs might attract a very long sentence. I hope so. I happen to know a lot about narcotics, and they ruin lives you know. And then tipping unknown bodies from India into the sea should be a criminal offence, shouldn't it? I think most people would agree with that. Even one body is disgusting. What does a thousand look like?'

'Shelley, lass, I think you've misinterpreted—"

'No, I have not. But maybe we could strike a deal – you follow my suggestions, and I'll go easy on certain things.

'Firstly, I reckon you could drop your bone imports down to nothing. Yes, zero. There are enough bone sets around this University to last for ever. And Port Philip Bay doesn't need any more bones. You certainly won't be doing any more smuggling I trust? And I think you could advocate for legislation to stop the importation of bones into Australia. What d'you reckon?

'Secondly, a substantial donation to my polio fund might assist me to feel kind, Professor. Might. What I mean is I could assist you with a plea bargain. Maybe. It depends.

'And thirdly, the Vice-Chancellor is expecting your resignations. And of course, if you don't provide them you will be dismissed.

'And now if you'll excuse me—'

'Oh, by the way there are closed circuit cameras on you at this very minute. Modern technology is amazing, isn't it? Professor, could you just move to the left a little? I'm taking a few snaps as well, just as a back-up, you know. I want to make sure you're in the frame.'

Shelley took ten photos with her Instamatic. Lucky she'd bought the expensive one with the flash. Modern technology.

On her way out of the University she rang the Vice-Chancellor's doorbell. It was fortunate that she'd had that chat with him on the way in. He would be extremely interested in her latest news.

YOUR CHANCE TO ACKNOWLEDGE

DO YOU HAVE A BOX OF BONES?

DO YOU KNOW WHERE YOUR BONES CAME FROM?

COME TO A SPECIAL ACKNOWLEDGMENT CEREMONY

MAIN LECTURE THEATRE

SEPTEMBER 28, 1971

'Good afternoon, everyone, I'm Shelley Conway and I'm a second-year. Excuse me referring to my notes. I'm nervous.

'I bought my box of bones last year from our Professor of Anatomy, with the help of the Anatomy Assistant. I started to wonder where they came from. I did some investigation and found out it was likely to be Calcutta. I visited Calcutta, and I saw graves being robbed. The poorest robbing the poorest. Sometimes children are buried alive. Sometimes they can't run away because they are crippled by polio.

'We have a new Foundation – the Novotny Foundation, in honour of Tomas Novotny and his mother Eva. I urge you to consider donating to this fund, as an acknowledgment of the use of the Indian bones. The money will be used to vaccinate the children of Calcutta and to help those children already disabled by polio.

'And if you feel bad about your box of bones may I suggest some things you can do now?

'One. Donate to the Novotny Foundation.

'Two. Refuse to buy bones.

'Three. Sign the petition.

'Four. Do anything you can to promote polio vaccination.

'I'm pleased to say that the former Professor of Anatomy has kicked off our appeal with a substantial donation. He also set up a lending system for bone sets just prior to his retirement.'

'Ah, Miss Conway, do sit down.'

No tissues, none at all.

'You know Mr Smith quite well by now, don't you? I think I can safely say that we're all friends, yes?'

Shelley's eyes widened. What the fuck? Friends?

'We're very surprised at the goings-on in the Anatomy department.'

The Bandicoot nodded. Always agree with those higher up the food chain.

Awkward pause, before Shelley broke out. 'I have only one thing to say, Dean Thompson.'

'Yes?'

'It's a suggestion for the Hippocratic Oath.'

'So you can improve on Hippocrates?'

'As a matter of fact, yes. The title of the oath anyway could be changed, made more accurate – for your medical school.'

'The title? Pray tell Miss Conway? I'd love to know.'

'The Oath of Hypocrites.'

The beers were going down nicely.

Shelley had her head on her backpack and was looking up at the sky. The city had its most luminous sunsets in autumn, and the botany school lawns at the Uni were the best place to view them from. Life was perfect, as long as her tinny didn't fall over. She reached out behind her until she could feel it. Seemed stable enough.

The kookaburras were making their nightly racket over in the park and the cockatoos were screeching as they wheeled over the Colleges. Everyone settling down for the night.

'Thank you for bringing the beer.'

Lenski leant back on his elbows. 'No worries. But in return, this week you have to tell me all about the bust. You promised.'

'Did I?'

'You know you did, Agent 99.' He looked at Shelley. 'I like your hair by the way. Suits you.'

'Oh thanks. My medical mates are pleased I'm taking an interest in my appearance. They're suspecting a new man.'

'And are their suspicions correct?'

'Nope.'

'Disappointing. All right, come on – you can't escape anymore.'

'Oh, don't tickle me. I'll answer I promise.' Laughter. 'I thought you were going to ask me for my three wishes.'

'That's next. So tell me – how did you work out they were smuggling whisky?'

'I didn't. I just knew something was wrong because the boxes were heavier than they should be. And they were bringing in more bone sets than med students would ever need.

'But I wasn't sure until I saw the Bill of Lading – the weights of the boxes. And I saw Horrie getting more and more anxious. And dumping boxes of bones into the Bay. Or maybe just boxes, but I think bones as well. I didn't know what to think. Was it going to be extra bones or drugs, or what.'

'And where and when and who put the whisky in the boxes?'

'That, Simon Lenski, is a mystery, a mystery we are unlikely to solve. I think someone in Calcutta, because that's where the Bill of Lading originated, but it could have been Delhi or Singapore. There are other things I don't have a definite explanation for.'

'Like?'

'Well, the poetry books in the boxes of bones. The thing that put me onto Calcutta in the first place. I thought my box was unique, but when I caught up with Horrie and Smiling Death in room 420 I discovered that all the boxes had had a poetry book in them – the same *Gitanjali* book of Tagore.'

'That's curious. I've never heard any students mention that.'

'Well, that's because Silverlocks and Smiling Death remove them. Or should I say Silverlocks does.'

'Oh?'

'Yes, and all the books have words underlined and different page numbers circled and are peculiar to that box alone. What do you make of that?'

'Hmm. Sounds like a code.'

'Yes, I agree. At first I thought it might have been something to do with Horrie's gambling – numbers of horses – who'd been hobbled or put on steroids – or clues to their names. I've been looking at form guides for names like 'Uncertain Winds' and 'Mindless Habit'. But that hasn't borne fruit, that theory.

'But I think I've solved it. It is a code, but not for horses. It's for whiskies – a key to which whisky was in which box of bones. Every whisky has a key word. For example, 'Last' is the 'The Last Drop', and 'Black' is 'Johnnie Walker Black Label' and then the circled numbers are the age of the whiskies, for example forty years. I think there are further refinements which I have not yet solved: number of bottles, single or double malt, whatever. But I'm not an expert on premium whisky – are you, Simon Lenski?'

'I'm happy to be trained.'

'I'm pretty sure Horrie was paid partly in whisky, so perhaps he'd got the person adding the whisky to indicate which box he should pick – I know some whiskies are more expensive than others.'

'That's a good thought.'

'And then there's the smack. I haven't worked it all out yet, but I know they've been doing a very good trade.'

Lenski was quiet for a moment, and then asked, 'Were you suspecting that?'

'Well, I have to say no, no I wasn't. And I know a bit about the heroin market. So I should have dropped to that, but I didn't.'

'And who put those threatening letters under your door?'

'Oh, I'm sure that would have been Horrie. He knows where my room is, and he was the one who stood to lose if my investigations brought the bone trade to an end. The worst thing about that is the thought that Horrie was so close to me when I was in bed.' Shelley gave a shiver. 'He is a perv.'

'And Shelley, I've been meaning to ask you, what did you do between school and med school?'

'That, Simon Shiny-boots Lenski, is another story.'

'Joe Cocker again? They really need to get a new tape,' said Simon.

Shelley and Simon had their beers and their usual table.

'How's the hospital?' asked Shelley.

'Okay. Now, if you want to avoid being tickled, you need to tell me these wishes.'

'Yep. So for the first wish there's India. Vaccinate every child in Calcutta for a start. Then every child in India. That's just a small wish, that one.'

They both laughed.

'And the second thing I really want to do – that mission for kids with polio, the one in Calcutta – well, they desperately need a surgeon to go over and do operations – and so I wish I can be that surgeon. A Top Surgeon.'

'Well,' said Simon, 'I'm thinking about surgery myself—"

'What a load of rubbish,' interrupted Shelley. 'Last week it was paediatrics, the week before obstetrics—"

'True,' laughed Lenski.

'Do you want to hear my last wishes or not? I've nearly finished.' Shelley was smiling. 'I want to eliminate the bone trade. I've written to the Federal Attorney-General. That's a start.'

'Well done.'

'Thank you. Here's an amazing fact: Horrie and the Prof were not breaking any law when they imported one thousand and twelve sets of bones and tipped a thousand of them into the sea. That is entirely lawful. Whereas importing whisky without paying duty – and importing narcotics of course – they are criminal offences. Isn't that astounding?'

'Yes. Yes, it is.'

'But I'm glad they did that – smuggle the whisky and drugs I mean – because it gave me some hold over them.'

'I can see that.'

'Yes, thank God. Oh, I forgot.' Shelley sat up and reached into the depths of her backpack. 'This is for you. One of my favourites, if not my absolute favourite.' She held out a spider shell.

Lenski rubbed a finger along the outside, and then turned the shell over and looked inside.

'I love the orange-pink,' she said, 'and how it gets more intense as you look deeper. But you can never see the centre. So you don't really know what's inside. It's a secret.'

'Thank you, Shelley. A beautiful mystery, like you,' he said and looked at her.

Shelley felt her cheeks warm.

'Forgive me, but I just wonder if you're avoiding something, Shell. I hate to bring it up.'

Shelley looked at her beer glass. 'Maybe you shouldn't then.'

'But I have to, Shell, so there's nothing between us.' He took a deep breath. 'What about using one of your wishes for your leg? Don't you wish you could make your leg better?'

Shelley felt a little dart pierce her heart, but she kept her eyes on the glass.

'I know you don't like talking about it,' said Simon, 'but I do think we should discuss it sometime. Doesn't have to be now.'

Shelley kept on looking at the mist on the glass.

'You're so brave, Shell. You never ever let on that you're struggling. Even though you've got that pain, post-polio syndrome or whatever it is—'

Shelley traced her finger in the condensation. 'It doesn't stop me, you know. I ignore the pain.'

Difficult to be simple. What did simple mean here? The truth. The truth was simpler than inventing excuses.

'But I should tell you the truth. When I was a little girl, little but old enough to know better, I slipped my dad's hand and ran across the road and got hit by a car. So did he. Chasing me. I got this leg. Bad fracture, operations, screws and plates, ended up fucked. And my dad became a paraplegic.

'Well that's what my mum's told me. But there is another version.' At least she wasn't floating away and there were no growling noises.

'Oh?'

'Yes – I had a weak leg already because I had polio, and then I tripped crossing the road. I didn't run away.'

'But didn't you have polio vaccinations?' asked Lenski.

'Mum was against it – don't know why. She's a bit strange.'

A silence.

'But I do have one more wish actually—'

'Yes?'

'There's a little boy in Calcutta—'

'Oh?'

'Yes – his name is Mandip – and I want to take him to see the sea.'

6 Jan 1972

Memorandum

To: Prof Dawson-Jones

From: Dean Thompson

As a result of community representation on this issue, I intend to conduct a review of Animal Experimentation by Medical Students. At this stage I envisage this to include: a detailed list of all animal preparations used by the students, the species and numbers of animal used, number euthanised and a justification to why a video demonstration would not suffice, as well as the relevant Animal Ethics Approvals, and reports.

I would appreciate your input at this early stage.

Yours sincerely,

P. Thompson

10 Oct 1982

Notice to all students

A reminder that Section 39 of the Health Tissue
Act, 1982, prohibits the purchase and/or sale of any
human tissue within Australia. This includes skeletons and bone sets.

F. Smith

Registrar

Calcutta

'Mandip? Mandip? Is that you?'

He'd arrived – perfect timing. Shelley had only just finished getting organised. She'd had a bit to do, and she was so slow these days. The seats for the dignitaries, the water jug and glasses, the flowers. But she'd done it and the little official area was looking quite good.

The children from the hostel were under the fig trees, practising the national anthem. Shelley loved the national anthem. Words by Tagore. The voices drifted across the lawn like angel song.

Mandip was walking up from the gates. Shelley's heart always gave a lurch when she saw him. It had been doing that for twenty years – ever since she'd met him when he was eight. He was now so striking, especially in his dark grey suit with the knee-length jacket. His limp was part of the charm. Hard to believe he was going to graduate soon – she was so proud of him.

'Namaste, Shelley. Sorry I'm late. You've got some foundations. It is truly remarkable.'

Shelley looked over towards the construction site. Yes, foundations and frames. It had been a marathon effort, but they'd done it.

Shelley put a hand on Mandip's forearm. 'I just want to stand here with you for one minute, Mandip, and think about today. It's twelve years since we started our polio work and look where we are. You were only sixteen then, and now you're almost a doctor, and we're opening this facility. And it's already made such a difference to how much polio there is. I can't believe it.'

'And you've stopped that bone trading.'

'I don't know about stopped, but reduced it, yes. With a lot of help.'

'But we haven't made much progress yet with humankind, Shelley.'

'Nope, that's disappointing. But that's our next goal.' Shelley pulled a handkerchief out of her pocket. 'I know I'll cry today, so I'll get it over and done with now.' She laughed, while dabbing her cheeks. 'You started all this, Mandip.'

'But it wasn't me,' said Mandip. 'It was you and poor Tomas and Simon and Amit Mukherjee, and the Little Sisters and—'

'Be that as it may,' said Shelley, 'it all started with you. And you made change possible as well. I would have been treated like another bloody do-gooder white saviour without you.'

'Yes, I have to admit that's probably true. We're a good team. Good that you had me – and that you'd had polio too.'

They put an arm around each other and started walking to the official area.

'Who would think we'd ever say there's a good side to having polio,' Shelley laughed. 'Anyway, please let me show you something. I'd like you to check for spelling mistakes. But you're not allowed to find any – in any language.'

They walked over through the building rubble to the red stone foundations, where a small cream silk curtain was fluttering.

'There. You can use that cord. That's right, just pull it. Can you read the engraving on the plaque aloud for me?'

Mandip read:

I SLEPT AND DREAMT THAT LIFE WAS JOY. I AWOKE AND SAW THAT LIFE WAS SERVICE.

I ACTED AND BEHOLD, SERVICE WAS JOY.

RABINDRANATH TAGORE

He paused, then continued.

'And those three lines say, "Humanity for humanity for humanity" in Hindi, Bengali and English.'

'Please could you read that part again?'

'Humanity for humanity for humanity,' said Mandip. 'And there are no spelling mistakes.'

মানবতা FOR লিপ্যিন্তর FOR HUMANITY.

Disclaimer for *The Bones*

This is a work of fiction. Names, characters, businesses, places, organisations, publications, events and incidents are either the products of the author's imagination or used in a fictitious manner.

Those who would like to know more about the global trade in body parts may wish to refer to *The Red Trade* by Scott Carney, (MJF Books, 2015). There is very little published material, but the author found this book to be a reliable source of information about matters in the modern day. It corroborates many of the findings of the author's own research.

Times have changed

T imes have changed since 1970.

Medical schools rely more heavily on plastinated specimens and computer programs for the teaching of Anatomy nowadays. Dissection is still taught in some medical schools but has a much smaller role in the curriculum. Some medical schools in Australia do not offer dissection at all. Those that do use donated cadavers only for the training of students and surgeons.

Australian medical schools have great sensitivity towards the people who donate their bodies – they express sincere gratitude to potential donors and are respectful of their families.

Many medical schools hold annual gratitude services, to which families and other interested parties are invited. Medical students are taught to respect cadavers, and the behaviours described in this novel are no longer tolerated.

Legislation which prohibited the use of the bodies of institutionalised people for dissection was enacted in Victoria in 1975. The buying and selling of human tissue, which includes bones, was banned in Australia in the 1982 Human Tissue Act (Section 39). The exportation of human remains from India was banned in 1986. However, the practice may still occur in India and other countries.

There are still hundreds, if not thousands, of boxes of bones of unknown people under beds in Australia.

Acknowledgements

Many people have helped me in various ways with the writing of this novel.

In no particular order; they include: M.J. Hyland; Trevor Doyle; Kate Cole-Adams; Robert Sessions AM; Susan Jacob and the Graduate Association of Christian Medical College, Vellore; Shane Maloney; Bruce Nichols; Lisa Gorton; Merrilyn Julian; Antoni Jach and his Jach-lings; Peter Kenneally; Kerry Munnery; Louise Bassett; Lawrie McMahon; Maggie Barron; Chris Ringrose; Margaret Aldous; Fiona Heard; Julie Osment; Anna Howson; Jocelyn Howson; Barbara Demediuk; Simon Madin; Salvina Dora Madin; Jane Wilson; Paul Strangio; Jacinta Halloran; Andrew Ramsay; Rita Benson; Sophie Cunningham; Lorette Broekstra; Emily Bitto; Carrie Tiffany; Michael Winkler; Jacinta Halloran; Rob Benson; Jackie Beckmann; Sunil Poddar (New Delhi, India) and Anup Kumar Saha (Kolkata, India).

Thanks to my friends in the Lazy Writers' Group; the Glenfern Writers; the Non-Arduous Book Club; and special appreciation to Michelle Ananda-Rajah MP, Federal Member for Higgins, for launching the book.

Thank you as well to Debbie Lee, Independent Publishing Consultant; and the wonderful team at Busybird Publishing (Kev Howlett – Head Honcho; Les Zigomanis – Production Wiz).

And thank you to Sophie Breeze for her expert editing and proofing.

Eradicating Polio

Proceeds from the sale of this book will be donated to Rotary International and the Polio Global Eradication Initiative campaign to eradicate polio from the face of the earth.

http://polioeradication.org

About the Author

Katrina is a retired doctor and a writer.

She was at university in the '70s and was a regular at all the demos.

Katrina became a gastroenterologist, with a little flame of social activism that wouldn't go out. She was awarded a Harkness Fellowship to Harvard University, and on returning to Melbourne two years later, was appointed to St Vincent's Hospital. She worked with marginalised groups in society, including those with Hepatitis C, and went to the Pacific Islands for a year as a volunteer doctor.

Her life changed in her early forties when she was diagnosed with Parkinson's disease. At that time, she was the breadwinner for a family of four children. They had to give up expensive bread, and she had to change her type of medical work.

Around that time Katrina realised she had a few stories she wanted to tell, starting with The Bones, which is her first novel.

Katrina was proud to receive the Medal of the Order of Australia (OAM) in 2018 for services to medicine.

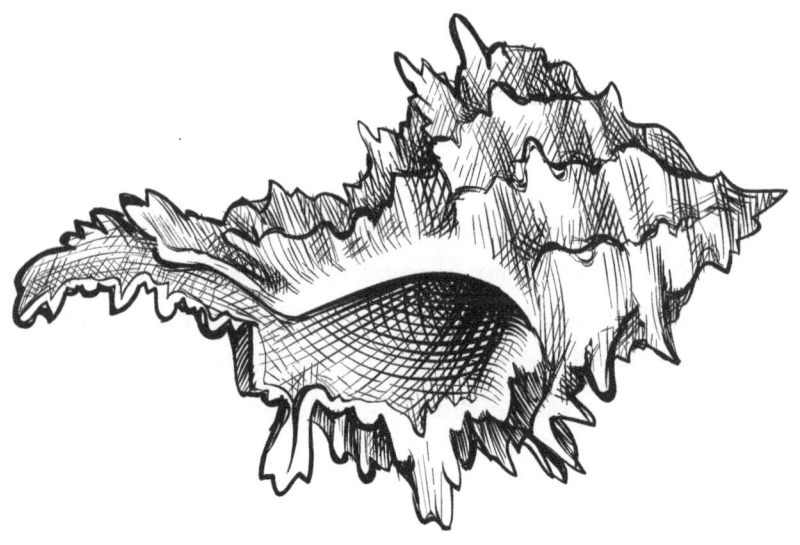

Ingram Content Group Australia Pty Ltd
Printed in Australia
AUHW020858180723
380984AU00004B/4

9 781922 954336